CHRISTINE HART

In Irina's Cards

The Variant Conspiracy, Book 1

This book was professionally typeset on Reedsy.
Find out more at reedsy.com

Chapter 1

I stepped off the bus behind Victoria's palatial Empress Hotel. A crisp cocktail of salt, diesel, and fresh flowers hit me in a gust of air. I caught my breath and looked around, every bit a tourist like half the other passengers on the bus. Even in March, British Columbia's capital already drew me in, but I'd made the trip for something more than scenery.

After eighteen grueling hours coming down from Prince George – affectionately called 'BC's northern capital' despite being smack in the middle of the province – I'd finally see the city from my dreams in person. For clarity, I wasn't chasing daydreams, or letting my imagination elaborate on Photoshopped landscapes I'd viewed on a website.

No, I mean visions. Unnerving and realistic scenes sparked by some dingy old Tarot cards I'd bought at a farmer's market. I knew the plan was ridiculous. Still, those cards told me a story, and I hungered to see it in person.

I picked up my backpack, stuffed with what I'd need for a few days in Victoria, and hefted it onto my back. In the distance, I heard the popping beats of hand drums, so I instinctively started walking towards the sound. My route took me through the flower gardens next to The Empress Hotel while the refined figure of the Provincial Legislature building loomed on my left. I emerged from the tree line and looked across the Inner Harbour. Twilight turned an unseasonably clear sky into a sapphire ceiling over old-world brick buildings and twinkling streetlights.

I crossed the waterfront street and followed the flow of pedestrians down a flight of stairs to a marina side market. The Harbour hopped with activity around performers and artists' booths. I joined in watching a man plunge a flame-tipped rod down his throat while pedaling precariously on a unicycle. Next to the fire swallower, a juggler flipped a handful of bowling pins up and around and up and around, while my gaze followed the loop. The juggler moved with the fluid grace of a ribbon in a light breeze. In the dim light, it almost looked like something behind him caught every other pin. In a blink, I thought I saw the swish of a tail.

I rubbed my tired eyes and surveyed the rest of the Harbour's lower level. The booths included a watercolor print display, a leather goods table, another lady with rough hand-fabricated silver jewelry, and a man doing live caricature drawings. A saxophone player opened his case and piped a soft jazz tune in front of the waterfront restaurant ahead. His horn wove into the tribal beats of the bongo player creating a unique soundtrack for the waterfront.

Light drained quickly from the sky and the crowd thinned accordingly. Chilly ocean air put an end to the party. I kept walking past the row of tables and wares, to reach the northern staircase at the edge of the Harbour. I had to find a place to spend the night.

I'd noticed a series of motels along the Greyhound's route into the downtown core. I needed to backtrack one block east and keep heading north to find a room. Urgency gripped me as I walked along the trendy boutique-lined Government Street. The light tourist traffic milling about disappeared quickly as though the darkness cast an unspoken curfew. I cursed myself for not printing off a Google map or booking a room before I left home. I pushed forward, practically marching into the wind that cut right through my fleece jacket.

I turned onto a street lined with gift boutiques and headed back toward the main drag, Douglas Street. I finally reached the cluster of cheap-looking motels I'd marked in my mind on the way to the bus depot. I veered into the parking lot of the odd copper-topped building that jumped out at me when I first passed. The Capital City Motel could be considered retro-kitsch or blatantly tacky. But I liked that sort of thing. I pushed open the glass door at the entrance. Relief washed over me as the wind finally stopped. A sixty-something silver-haired man at the counter looked up at me with an exhausted expression. I didn't feel welcome, but I had come in the door, so the decision was made. I rummaged in my backpack until I found my wallet and extracted it from the dense brick of clothing.

"Have you got a room available?" I asked hopefully and then added with a nervous laugh. "I hope you take debit cards."

"Yes for both, my dear," he said quietly.

He reached down with a wilted hand to pick up the debit machine. He lifted his other equally drained hand to find a sleeve for my key card. I looked away out of awkward guilt and noticed something odd on the counter. The polished wood surface had a blemish. Wait, no a bump. And it moved! A quarter-sized oval lump dislodged itself from the pattern and skittered across the desk. It paused on its way past me and looked up with a twitch of curiosity.

The creature's antennae flickered and it sped off along the countertop until it stopped and disappeared back into the wood grain. I felt my jaw hanging open as the clerk finally turned around with my room key in its sleeve. I stared at him, then over to where the chameleon-esque beetle vanished, and back at the clerk.

He smiled weakly. "That's one hundred and sixty-four dollars plus tax." He took my bank card. "Sign here please."

I punched in my code, signed the paper, and collected my key.

"Hey, you know you've got a disappearing beetle on your counter here," I said, partly in shock, partly disgusted. I realized what I sounded like when he gave me the same weak smile. "Never mind. I've been on the bus too long."

"Have a nice day, Miss Irina Proffer." His voice droned a joyless monotone. "And enjoy your stay in Victoria." I hoisted my backpack back over my shoulder and headed through the lobby towards the stairs.

Inside the stairwell, a damp chill amplified the musty smell. On the second floor, the scent changed to a combination of stale lard and carpet shampoo. I found room number 217 and jiggled my card in the door's reader until I convinced the handle to open. I flung my backpack and jacket onto the bargain shop floral bedspread and started the bath running. I had nowhere to be, so I figured the best way to spend my night was a relaxing soak. I was already lonely and bored – a lame traveler for sure.

I paused in front of the full-length mirror on the wall and cringed at my reflection. The funky punk haircut and bold electric blue color I treated myself to after I lost my job faded too quickly. I pulled small elastics off my two stringy braids and fluffed up the dull brown layers and not-so-blue streaks. I leaned forward and looked into my eyes. My green irises were brighter than usual against the bloodshot whites. I sized up the state of my charcoal hoodie and Union Jack shirt. No stains, but I looked like I'd been camping for a week covered in stray animal hair and lint. I'd been clean when I left my house. *Thanks Greyhound*, I thought. I peeled off it all and stepped into the bath.

Twenty minutes later, I finished detangling my hair from the cheap motel shampoo and conditioner. I flopped down on the bed, wrapped in one of the small, thin towels from the bathroom. I picked up my backpack and emptied it onto my bed. Getting organized always makes me feel better, so I donned my pajama T-shirt and sweatpants before proceeding to sort the contents of my bag. My now notorious Tarot deck earned a prime spot at the center of the room's tiny dining table.

As I refolded my clothes and arranged my belongings around the room, I thought about the week leading up to my long bus ride to Victoria. I had recently lost a shitty job that, for ten bucks an hour, involved wearing cheap rayon and itchy polyester business clothes, endlessly greeting jerks, and answering the phone all while herding salesmen at a greasy used car dealership. Greasy isn't a good enough word for Nechako Motors. It was a sleazy place run by a slimy man who ran afoul of the law. I hadn't been expecting much better since I'd skipped out on university even though I knew a high school diploma wouldn't get me very far.

The crowning moment of that terrible day had been losing my phone in a snowbank. My parents refused to replace it, hoping that my financial need would motivate my job search.

After a week of watching me mope around the house, my mom, Tabitha, and my stepfather, Darryl began each morning by circling jobs in the newspaper classifieds and printing off postings from job search websites. Prince George's unemployment hovered notoriously low, but I couldn't work up even the slightest interest in any of the jobs they found. My newly acquired free time highlighted the reality that my friends had all moved away for college and careers.

My best friend Bridget was backpacking through Europe with her boyfriend. My younger half-sister, Gemma didn't help matters with her disgusting overachieving. The apple of Darryl's eye with a preternatural aptitude in math and science, Gemma was already at the University of British Columbia on an academic scholarship, having passed on the year-off-plus-extension strategy I had chosen. Everybody had something important going on but me.

On a boring and lonely Monday afternoon at home alone, I picked up the tattered deck of Tarot cards I'd just bought. It was a strange purchase and totally out of character for me. Normally, I would have passed by the weird old man selling random junk at a local farmer's market. When I caught sight of the cards, I couldn't resist buying them.

I didn't know how to use Tarot cards. I needed some companion literature to understand what each picture symbolized. Yet, I could enjoy the artwork, even if I couldn't interpret the messages. I'd carefully shuffled the large soft cards, looking around and over my shoulder. The last thing I needed that day was for Darryl to walk in and catch me wasting time.

I divided them into three piles and flipped one off the top from left to right. I inspected them and let myself gap out.

As I stared at the images on the cards, their drawings overtook my field of vision as though I'd leaned forward and plunged my face into the pictures. Faded colors became vivid imagery, which melted away into real-life scenery. I recognized downtown Victoria and the Inner Harbour in front of the Parliament buildings. The oxidized green copper domes of the legislature gleamed in the cheerful sunlight.

I looked over at the vine-covered Empress Hotel with its valet attendants and well-dressed guests coming and going. The Harbour shone full of bright white sailboats with spindly masts. Daytime lapsed quickly as the sky darkened. The legislature disappeared beneath a cage of twinkling yellow-white lights. Street lamps bordering the waterfront and lights in the surrounding towers spilled into the water and reflected a shimmering second city.

The bustle of nightlife dwindled and my mind's eye left the Harbour. Daytime came again and I wandered through Chinatown. Steam rose from a grate in the gutter. I smelled barbecued meat and fried noodles. As I floated down the street, weaving through pedestrians at eye level, I looked into tightly packed shop windows and browsed carts on the street. Paper lanterns, trinkets, and bells surrounded pottery, produce, and woven baskets. I passed a narrow alley crowded with pedestrians just as the scene faded.

In a flash, I stood on a cedar-lined beach under the dull glow of an overcast sky. The ocean opened up and reached into the distance, merging into the muddled gray horizon as far as the eye could see. Windswept evergreens gave the landscape the distinctive look of the West Coast. My mind leaped forward along the beach.

My gaze zoomed in to rest on the face of a young man, vacant and lethargic, sitting cross-legged on a wood stump surrounded by driftwood. He wasn't bound or cuffed, but I felt certain he was trapped. And his features … he looked familiar. I'd never seen him before, let alone known him at any point. I'd also never seen a picture of my father who died before I was born. The boy could be a distant cousin. He had fine cinnamon hair like mine, but cut short, although long enough on top for a few curls. His narrow face framed a long nose. His skin had a warm ruddy hue, weathered as though he'd been in the sun. His bright amber eyes looked exactly like mine too.

I couldn't explain it, but after I saw that man, I couldn't think about anything else. I felt compelled to talk to him. He had answers for me. The fact that I didn't even know the questions burrowed into my brain, driving me to distraction in the days that followed.

A few days later I came up with a cover story for my parents. I would find work in Victoria. The quest for a job was easy to sell so I stuffed my backpack and got on a bus. I felt ridiculous at having spent a ton of time and money for nothing more than an image in my screwed-up head.

Having finally made it to Victoria, the question of 'What now?' occupied my mind in the dark motel room. Curled up under the bed covers, I stared at the bathroom door across from me. The electronic hum of a beer fridge and the faint sounds of a too-quiet city buzzed in my ears as I shifted and turned on the too-firm motel mattress. It took me almost an hour to finally fall asleep despite my utter exhaustion after the trip.

Chapter 2

The glow of an overcast sky woke me the next morning. I'd forgotten to close the blinds and my room happened to have an east-facing window. I was wiped out, but too alert to go back to sleep. Hunger tugged at my belly, so I forced myself to dress and go downstairs for food.

The motel diner had started serving breakfast. The aroma of fresh coffee, roasted potatoes, and buttery batter filled the air. I smiled to find the restaurant almost empty. I looked around the large bright room. Windows on the east side poured light into the space, highlighting the dated decor. The room, albeit clean, looked like it hadn't been re-decorated since the sixties. Mustard-yellow vinyl padding popped off smooth chocolate-brown plastic booths surrounding an open kitchen at the center of the room. Cream and sage checker-patterned carpet stretched from the lobby into the diner, faded in spots from foot traffic and sun. Family-sized tables, each with four vinyl-cushioned chrome chairs lined the windows bordering Douglas Street on the east.

A chrome-trimmed pedestal sign instructed guests to seat themselves, so I selected a booth and slid onto the cushioned bench. I picked up a laminated menu and flipped through the pages looking for the section on pancakes and waffles to make sure they also made crepes – which they did. A grandmotherly waitress with kind eyes took my order and I focused on watching the many passersby. Anonymity felt thrilling and suffocating.

After breakfast, I decided to go for a wander around downtown. I needed a phone, a computer, a map, a bus schedule, or any resource that could help me find the sites I promised myself I'd locate. Chinatown would stick out. I'd already caught a glimpse of it on my way to and from the Inner Harbour. My mystery beach proved the real problem, although my memory of it remained surprisingly vivid. I didn't know for sure that it was near Victoria, so I needed access to tourist literature, or preferably a public computer. I cursed myself for not doing more research in advance.

I started down Douglas Street planning to take a closer look at Chinatown before somehow finding the rugged beach from my vision. I only had to walk two blocks before I saw the ornate archway that unmistakably marked the entrance. As I passed underneath, the accuracy of what I'd seen started my stomach churning. Cluttered shop windows – check. Carts on the street – check. The scent of meat and noodles – also present.

I had brushed off my impression of the Inner Harbour and Parliament. I knew I'd seen them on television and probably in magazines. I'd lived in British Columbia all my life and the center of the Provincial capital was iconic. Victoria's Chinatown on the other hand, I felt fairly certain I had never seen.

My rushed introduction to downtown left me wanting to explore a bit more. I hadn't experienced the excitement of a city in years. So I walked briskly through the block of themed storefronts and veered back toward the Inner Harbour. I passed a trendy-looking street stretching up from an arched blue bridge. I caught sight of a gate for the 'Market Square' and those wrought iron words grabbed my attention like a glimpse of a long-lost friend in a crowd. Something important waited for me on the other side of that arch.

I closed the distance. A few meters inside, the structure opened up into a three-story open-air courtyard with very little signage on the top level, so it looked mostly like office space. The ground and basement levels held confections, clothing, toys, gifts, and more. If I had money, I'd waste a lot of it behind many of those doors. Instead, I slowly browsed.

I played my childhood game of *Things-I'll-Never-Own* as I peered inside each window. The game consisted of picturing an alternate version of my life in which I'd buy said item, and what I'd do with it if I did buy it. I usually preferred not to go inside any shops and risk snooty stares or overwhelming temptation. I did have *some* money, but to make it last a few more days at the motel and the trip home, I couldn't buy so much as an extra coffee or croissant.

Time to get back on track and do my door-to-door examination of Chinatown. I retraced my steps back through the gate and onto the street. The moment I stepped out from the protection of the building facade, cold air blowing in off the ocean assaulted me. Combined with the heat of the midday sun, the effect nauseated me, blending warm air and a chilly wind. Like the air and the earth couldn't agree on the temperature.

Halfway back to Chinatown, a fight broke out on the sidewalk ahead. I was instantly alert. I stopped, froze, and then took a step back. I couldn't remember the last time I saw a real, live, shoving and punching fist-fight in person. The two men started bouncing, almost like a dance. The blank, bored pedestrians on the street around them very suddenly woke. Eyes widened. Bodies recoiled. Faces frowned in disapproval or grimaced nervously, but everyone gave the pair a wide birth as they shuffled aggressively along the sidewalk.

The larger man with a crew cut had burly, deeply scarred arms under a tight white T-shirt. I watched him lunge repeatedly at an average-height, muscular skater boy in baggy pants. They looked like they were yelling, but I could only hear the odd syllable over the traffic. My first impulse was to backtrack, cross the street, and keep walking on the other side. Something about the fighters mesmerized me. I stood bolted to the ground, frantic to know what had generated such rage. More pedestrians kept walking around them, so I moved closer with a few cautious steps.

As they closed in on each other the big man shoved the smaller one again. The skater boy stood his ground fairly well, leaning back towards the aggressor with a challenging glare. The large one yelled, "Oh, you think *I'm* starting shit!" and punched the boy in the face.

The blow had little impact. The skater returned fire with a small jab into the larger man's torso – which had a stunningly devastating effect. The crew-cut guy in the T-shirt doubled over in pain. He staggered backward, recovered, and beckoned the skater with a wild expression.

Their dance floated in and out of an alcove below a fire

escape. They surged back and forth along the sidewalk, and finally stumbled into an empty parking spot. Oncoming cars honked and drivers yelled as the fight spilled momentarily into the road.

The men shuffled back onto the sidewalk. The older man lunged and missed. The skater hit back, this time with so much force that his adversary flew up into the air and struck the bottom of the fire escape in a clatter of metal-on-metal. Dazed and winded, he stayed sitting on the ground and rubbed the back of his head where he'd bounced off the metal frame. The skater scanned the area nervously, looked behind him, and bolted past me running south until pedestrians and the crest of the hill obscured him.

The larger man finally stood up, still catching his breath, with his hands on his knees. Another man, weathered, dressed in tattered denim and a dirty plaid shirt stepped forward and tugged on the large man's arm. The guy in the plaid shirt kept tugging as his friend mumbled something to himself that ended in, "You'd *better* run, you little asshole. I ever see you in my bar again, I'm gonna pummel the ever livin' shit outta you."

I waited another moment, hoping he'd come to his senses and leave before cops arrived. The two lingered on the corner curb, the fellow with the crew-cut winded and enraged. Pedestrians resumed their indifferent strolls. Everyone blindly marched past, so I looked straight ahead and walked briskly around them.

No distant sirens wailed only cars and buses rumbled. I had a strong sense that the guy in the dirty plaid shirt stared after me, but I didn't dare turn to face him. I thought I heard someone whisper, *"Ir-eeee-na,"* as though right next to me. My heart pounded in my chest and my stride grew longer until I finally reached the parking lot of the Capital City Motel.

A man in a ratty trench coat with a faded red baseball cap pinning down stringy gray hair sat under a sign for "Steak Dinner ONLY $18.95!" A handkerchief on the pavement in front of him held a few coins. Was steak why he wanted money? Probably not.

I looked at the ground as I passed. I always felt guilty walking by anyone begging because I never gave them money. It wasn't that I didn't believe in it. I was too shy to stop and look a stranger in the eye, especially someone in need.

Back in my room, I sat at my table and found myself face-to-face with my Tarot deck. Did the cards have anything more to show me? In all likelihood, I'd stare at the faded drawings again without incident. I'd get back on a bus and go home, skipping the trip to Chinatown. I wondered what my responsible and respectable half-sister Gemma would say if she caught me playing at divination.

The best approach to the cards was to duplicate what I'd done earlier. Divide the deck into three, flip the top card off each, and simply look at them. I still didn't know what I was doing. From left to right, I flipped over a smiling man holding a wand, a crowned goddess upside down, and an intricate wheel lined with symbols. A trance took over again. With my waking eyes, I saw young and cheerful images of Mom and Darryl putting up wallpaper in our house. Her belly swelled with the late stages of pregnancy.

The scene faded and I saw Mom younger still with a tall rusty-haired man I didn't recognize standing next to rain-soaked ruins. The rusty man placed his hand on an altar. A dark pulse shot up from the ground, through the stone, and into his body. In a blink, Mom and her companion held hands and he opened her palm, placing something in it. Mom's face wrinkled in pain and she tried to pull away but failed.

Suddenly I saw Mom and Darryl sitting on the living room couch, both arguing and gesturing at someone. Their faces wore looks of fear and desperation that hollowed my gut. Then the picture cut to black in a blink. The hotel room reappeared around me. I touched the cards again, lightly at first, then slapping them, frantically trying to restart the vision. I sat at the table for a moment and stared at the paper rectangles in front of me, trying to accept that I wasn't going to see anything more. I scraped the cards back together and looked out the window.

The last conversation I'd had with my parents in person was strained and unpleasant. Darryl told me not to screw around in Victoria because he wasn't going to send money for accommodation or food if I ran out. Mom tried to ease the tension by assuring him I was serious about looking for work. What hurt me was that he'd been right. I hadn't planned to look for work. I'd left home for Victoria because I thought I'd been having psychic visions. I was being irresponsible.

My mind flickered to the moment long ago when I stood in a courtroom with Mom and Darryl watching them sign papers in front of a judge. I think I was about five or six years old. It was one of the few photographs of only me and my parents after Gemma was born. We stood smiling for the camera as Darryl shook the judge's hand. Darryl had just adopted me. Now, I remembered the photograph more than the day itself.

I'd spent my teen years arguing with my parents and being jealous of Gemma. But, I always thought all that resentment would fade and everything would work out. I'd grow up and grow back into step with my family. Questions crowded my mind. Why did I have visions of Victoria? What compelled me onto a bus, only to see a cryptic glimpse of my parents back home? Was I suffering from delusions? Had I been drugged or accidentally poisoned? Did I have a brain tumor? Was it time to throw away the cards? What would happen if I did?

I turned on the television and cycled through re-run sitcoms, news, and game shows. Nothing drew my interest. I couldn't shake the need to complete my journey. Chinatown waited for me right down the street. I'd come here to set foot in the scenes from my visions, to see if a tactile experience would explain why I had visions. I grabbed my hoodie, wallet, and key card.

I strolled casually for about a block, looking up at the canyon of high rises intermittently reflecting the blazing yellow-orange of the afternoon sun. The city looked beautiful in a new way, more than just a cosmopolitan scene. The buildings stretched upward like giant temples inside an ancient city.

I cast my gaze back down to the street. In the flow of pedestrian movement, one body remained still. He looked directly at me – the plaid-clad, greasy-haired friend of the fighting bouncer. His stare was intense, broken only by people passing through the space connecting our eyes.

Fear welled up inside me and overtook my body. I sped back to the motel. The pressure escalated until I reverted to the raw panic of a child worrying that the monsters chasing me from the basement might catch up. I hopped up the stairwell two steps at a time. Sprinting down the interior hall, I whipped my door shut behind me, immediately locking it. Relief swept through me. I'd reached safety.

Chapter 3

I paced around my room, thinking. Should I stay or go? Seeing that oddball man had to be a coincidence. I'd stay.

The evening passed slowly with only sitcoms, local news, and infomercials to keep me company. I ordered a club sandwich from room service and made it last a few hours. As soon as the sun set, I turned off the television and tried to sleep. I shifted in bed from my right side to my left. I flipped back again. I took mindful deep breaths. Nothing helped. I couldn't stop thinking about my visions, about my parents, about the bizarre incident on the street. And that weird man. I listened to the hum of the floorboard heater for what felt like hours before sleep finally silenced my restless mind.

Around three o'clock in the morning, I woke suddenly and sat up, disturbed by a nightmare I couldn't remember. Something malicious had been in the room or just outside. I looked over at the window, out into the monochrome orange-black street. I'd closed the blinds this time, but one of the thick vertical slats was missing. Something flashed past my window! I clamped down on the blanket, gripping it hard as I leaned forward in bed.

The movement blipped by again in my cropped view of the sidewalk. I froze. The figure flashed by once more, larger and closer. My heart thumped in my throat as I forced myself out of bed and over to the window. I peered through the opening in the blinds, panting with fear, waiting. I imagined that a vicious face with fierce red eyes would appear in a blink and scream at me through sharp rotting fangs. How could I defend myself? Why hadn't I found a motel with kitchenette units? Then I'd at least have a knife or two to grab. I had nothing more than my house keys as weapons.

Somehow I knew the thing that passed my window was real, searching for me, and sniffing the air for my scent. I leaned closer, feeling my face throb with my heartbeat. A flash of light blinded me. And then I sat bolt upright, suddenly in bed, again. The orange-tinted darkness around me had less malice in the air now that I'd woken for real.

I made a mental note to tell Bridget about my fascinating experience with lucid dreaming – once I returned to my proper life.

The next morning I woke with a headache. I made a tiny pot of motel coffee. It wasn't because of the nightmare or the headache. I would have made coffee anyway. On every family vacation, we always scavenged the little bottles of shampoo, conditioner, body lotion, and whatever other toiletries and supplies a hotel or motel provided.

Mom was always bitter about the cost of a room. She ranted about 'wanting her money's worth' as she rounded up the room's consumables. I sipped my coffee, but I didn't feel much like packing. Instead, I felt light, fit, and energetic.

The more coffee I drank, the better I felt. After two cups my mood drifted between the hopeful anticipation of Christmas morning and the first day of summer vacation glee. I had the whole city at my feet. I didn't have to rush right back to Prince George.

My loneliness and boredom evaporated. I had a strong sense something fun waited for me downstairs. I felt utterly confused, but not too worried about it. I craved crepes so badly that I almost tasted them. I didn't waste time grooming. I whirled into jeans and a long-sleeved oatmeal-colored waffle shirt and bounded down the stairwell with 110 pounds of thunder.

I reclaimed the booth from my previous breakfast and picked up a menu. I knew I'd order the same meal, but I needed to busy my hands while I waited.

"I thought you'd never come down," said a gravelly voice. A figure slid into my booth. I snapped up from the menu and there he was, the greasy-haired man, calmly sitting across from me. I froze. His frame was dramatically bony up close. Under the oily sheen his hair was a gray-speckled mouse brown. Gray stubble covered the bottom half of his leathery face.

I thought to myself - and I know I did not say it out loud - *Holy shit, it's the lunatic from the street! He's stalking me. He's going to kill me!*

"You do like crepes, don't you? I took the liberty of ordering some. I hope that's all right. I felt pretty sure they're your favorite, but I've been wrong on occasion. The meal has been paid for, including a gratuity. I'm not a lunatic. I'm not stalking you and I mean you no harm." He smiled smugly.

I stared back, speechless.

"Sorry, I realize we haven't been introduced and you're still new to the city. My name is Rubin. And you must be Irina." He extended his hand across the table. His blotchy skin had a reddish-purple tinge.

I shook his sticky hand reluctantly. "It's nice to meet you Rubin, but you've got me at a disadvantage. How do you know me?"

"That isn't important, but not entirely irrelevant," he said cheerfully. "However, I do believe that's also not for me to explain. I wouldn't do the story justice and I'd probably catch hell for talking about it. I *can* ask you to go shopping in Chinatown today. You don't need to worry about getting back on the Greyhound or burning up more money on another night here." He stood. "Be sure to let the front desk know you're staying another night. The room is yours as long as you need it. Enjoy your day." He walked away abruptly.

The crepes arrived, although my grandmotherly waitress was gone, replaced by a weary blonde with a glum expression and bags under her eyes. I smiled, thanked her, and stared at the plate of food as she walked away. Should I call the cops on this guy, Rubin? What would I report? Did he have anything to do with my visions?

I wasn't truly scared any longer. I felt only curiosity about Chinatown. And a strong urge to eat. I shook my head and relented. One soft, spongy bite after another made me increasingly content.

A few more motel guests took seats around me. The pedestrian traffic outside picked up with the start of the work day. I watched as an elderly lady inched along behind an aluminum walker, passed easily by a balding man in a trench coat and a brunette woman with immaculate, bold makeup and a beige suit.

A girl around my age tromped past clinging to the straps of her backpack with both hands. She wore dark jeans under a hoodie with an intricately embroidered treeline and printed night sky. She bounced along as though she was headed to a coffee date with a painfully cool crowd. She belonged in the city, and probably had her own apartment, halfway through a reputable, sensible degree. I could hear Darryl's voice asking when I would find something 'to do' and get on with my life. His words were never angry or loud, just laced with disappointment and frustration. I gulped down the rest of my orange juice, signed the slip the waitress had left to charge the meal to my room, and then slung my bag over my shoulder.

I walked out of the restaurant into the lobby and hesitated. Sketchy street guy did have a point. I knew I'd stay at least one more night, so I stopped at the front desk and let them know.

The sidewalk outside had filled with people. I felt claustrophobic for a moment and seized the opportunity to sit on an empty bench outside an office building next door to the motel. I looked up to clear my head. Clouds rolled across the sky quickly, remaking the ceiling of the world before my eyes in mere moments. It reminded me of the time Mom took Gemma and me camping near 100 Mile House. We'd stopped for the night on our way south to drop Gemma off at the University of British Columbia. Darryl hadn't been able to get time off work, so it was the three of us – as Mom said, 'just us girls.'

We spent a few hours after dinner on an August afternoon sunning ourselves on a large flat rock that jutted out over Horse Lake. The clouds rushed over our heads as though a wind turbine propelled them. But, the air stayed relatively calm and warm – a magical weather combination. When we lost the light, Mom started our campfire and we made s'mores. We talked about nothing and boys and frenemies. We giggled and gushed. For some stupid reason, I chose our rare bonding session as a moment to ask Mom about the start of her relationship with Darryl.

"Why did you and Darryl get married when I was a baby? He couldn't have been an obvious family man." I'd opened an old wound, not even thinking the topic through to its conclusion. I stopped short of adding, *Wasn't it obvious he didn't want to raise someone else's child?*

I remember the look on Mom's face. Her smile dropped and she looked at the campfire thoughtfully. "I got pregnant with Gemma." She let a moment of silence pass. This revelation had occurred to me before, but it hadn't been said aloud. Gemma's confused expression suggested she had not considered this dynamic.

"Darryl does love you girls. Both of you. We use the word 'surprise' not 'accident' when we talk about my second pregnancy. We hadn't been dating for long, but we felt a strong connection. We wanted to try to be a family, so it made sense for Darryl to adopt my first baby. Still, his father gave him a very hard time about marrying me. It didn't help that I was a struggling widow when I found out I'd be having another baby. After the adoption, your grandfather went as far as to change his will cutting Darryl out completely. I won't dignify that man's beliefs by sharing any more detail with you girls. I'm not saying Darryl is a warm, caring man, but there are reasons behind his frustrations in life."

My smile fell as my memory of the warm lakeside rock

refocused on Mom's face discussing Darryl's crappy father. Life made Darryl a jerk, but I got uniquely saddled with his disappointment. He would always look at me like a busted prototype, no matter what I did.

Now, I launched off the urban bench and back onto Victoria's busy main street. I wove through the slow-moving bodies as I sped forward on the pavement. I turned sharply around the corner back to Chinatown. I paused to evaluate the red and yellow dragon street signs on stylized red lamp posts that marked the neighborhood.

I reached the elaborate themed gate and slowed my pace. I lingered at each shop window, waiting for a sign or a feeling to tell me something. I didn't have new information. Sense and reason dictated that I would never know why I'd had visions of Victoria – or why a grubby weirdo started stalking me.

The shops and baskets and trinkets and produce all felt familiar on my second, well, really third viewing. I noticed a tiny brick alley; the one I had seen in my vision. It had its own street sign 'Fan Tan Alley'. I took a step back to look down the narrow corridor. It seemed more European than something inspired by Chinese architecture. I stepped inside and claustrophobia ensued. Three stories of bare brick walls rose on either side. Each shop was small, identified by a hanging sign over the door. I moved slowly to take in the surreal little space as people pushed past me.

I walked past a split door with only the top half open. People in white uniforms with old food stains moved through a loud and steamy restaurant kitchen. Next, a record shop window had handbills plastering the glass, inside and out. A trinket shop overflowed its space with wreaths and charms hanging on racks off its open door. A small biker boutique offered boots and jackets and fishnet stockings in its window. Farther in, more posters clung to the brick around a stairwell opening and a group of shifty kids looked up from their conversation to stare at me briefly. They whispered again and dispersed, laughing.

I frowned and stood stewing over the insult when a wave of incense wafted over me. Across the alley, a tiny windowless shop with lavender on the door had a sign overhead. It was so old and worn that I couldn't read it, but the door sat ajar, the room dimly lit. I barely had room to turn around without my bag bumping rows of liquid-filled glass bottles or snagging cord-strung pendants off their hooks.

"Hello, Miss Proffer. Your order is almost ready. The tea blend is finished, but I still need to prepare the packaging. Have a seat," called out a lovely voice from the back of the store. A curtain of tacky beads obscured a closet-sized storeroom behind the front desk. I saw a figure move.

"Um, I've never been here before, so I haven't ordered anything yet. I just got to Victoria yesterday," I said politely. "Do you happen to know anyone named Rubin?"

"Hang on. We *do* have your order. I'll be right out," she said.

My heart lurched. Had I been given a *roofie* at some point and wandered around town in a stupor?

I looked around the room again. Row upon row of jars labeled with one and two-word herb titles covered the opposite wall. The shop didn't look expensive, but I had no intention of paying for overpriced herbal tea simply because she gave off a mystical vibe, or knew my name – probably through my stalker. I shifted my stance. I shouldn't have come in the first place.

"I don't mean to be rude, but please tell me how you know

me. You're the second person I've met today who knew me in advance." I heard irritation seeping into my words as the shopkeeper ignored me and kept working with perfect serenity.

"Let the tea steep for at least five minutes. If you don't wait long enough–," she stopped short as her phone chimed. She smiled and turned around to answer. Her conversation sounded tense as she responded with "yes" and "no" several times before saying that she was with a customer.

Now I definitely didn't want her tea, but I didn't want to cause a scene. If she wasn't going to tell me anything, I needed to get back to my room and pack – quickly. "I'm sorry. Can I come back later?"

"No need." She handed me the paper bag, "and the bill has already been paid." Free stuff? Again?

I walked back to my motel on a mission. I rounded the corner and marched across the parking lot, bypassing the lobby using the side entrance. I slipped into my room and sat down on the edge of the bed. I tried to work up the motivation to stuff my few articles of stray clothing back into my backpack. I wanted to leave. No, I wanted to feel safe. I also realized that if I left now, it would drive me nuts. I couldn't return to sitting at my parents' kitchen table every morning, wondering what the visions and Rubin's involvement had all meant.

Something had compelled me to come here. Sure, having visions ranked high in the weird department, but it was more than that. Once I'd seen the Harbour, the city, the landscapes, and that man on the beach, a sort of itch grew in my muscles like I had to keep moving until I got here. And I knew in my bones that I could account for all my waking hours. I hadn't blacked out or even accidentally contacted anyone in Victoria.

I stood up and paced around the room, trying to puzzle out what I should do next. Should I call home? And say what? That my job search wasn't going well? Even if what I'd seen about Mom and Darryl meant anything, how could I warn them? I didn't even know what exactly would happen or when. Should I start walking the streets looking for Rubin? How could I get reliable information? It was all still way too vague. My nervous energy escalated and I decided I'd feel better if I packed anyway.

I gathered my clothes, pack of cards, and toiletries onto the table, and dropped my bag onto the chair to fill it. I pulled the bag of tea out and its scent hit me. I'd never liked herbal teas, particularly anything that smelled like flowers. This stuff was different, kind of peaceful, willing my body to betray my mind. I lifted the tape and unfolded the top of the package. The dried fruit and leaves inside looked pretty natural to me. One cup couldn't hurt. It was just tea.

The motel's whitener and sugar basket miraculously included a tea ball, so I filled it, cleaned the coffee maker, and refilled the reservoir. Hot water trickled into the pot and I submerged the ball. The aroma relaxed me. I stopped packing and turned on the television. I found a midday re-run of a 90's sitcom I hated, but I left it on that channel. The show didn't seem so bad.

The snapping gurgling of the coffee maker slowed and the pot filled with a beautiful fuchsia liquid. It smelled like strawberries, but there was more, something nutty and spicy. I poured a cup and sipped slowly. I couldn't remember why I'd been so upset. I didn't need to go home right away. I had only been in Victoria for two days – one day if I wrote off my initial meandering. I'd call Mom tomorrow or maybe send an email. Everything was completely fine. Life would work out for the best.

Chapter 4

I was still drowsily watching the same channel when a knock on my door interrupted the evening news.

"Irina. Hello. … It's Rubin," he said in an awkwardly loud voice from outside in the hall. "Have you eaten yet?"

"No, uh … hang on." I rubbed my face gently to clear my mind. "I'm coming."

I opened the door and he grinned at me, his face grubby, the rest of him as unkempt and sketchy as ever. I considered that he might suffer from a mental illness and empathy took over from unease.

"I'm glad I caught you." He shifted nervously with his hands in his pockets. "Do you like sushi?"

"About as much as I like crepes, but somehow you knew that, didn't you?" I smiled at him and waited for what came next.

"I see you're a bit more settled now. You've had a chance to relax. Good, good. I'd invite myself in, but it's not very appropriate. So how about dinner?"

"As long as it's not a date, sure. Why not? Just give me a moment to get ready." I smiled again. I reached for my backpack but thought better of it and pulled out my wallet alone. I fished out my petal-pink lip gloss and slicked some on, pocketing the container afterward. I drew a black border above the eyelashes on my upper eyelid sand dusted on a bit of earth-brown eye shadow. I ran my brush through my hair and evaluated the results in the wall mirror. I looked passable, but not great. Oh well.

Rubin led me back towards downtown and we walked in silence, past Chinatown and along the main drag until we turned north onto a street of antique shops and curio boutiques. Window displays overflowed with flower-patterned china, polished silver trays, and aged coin collections. Vintage clothing, followed used books, after baked goods. It was the sort of neighborhood in which having high tea would seem completely normal.

As we moved away from the ocean, I smelled freshly cut grass and the scent of blooming flowers. We passed a cathedral with a small landscaped park in front, complete with a walking path and a memorial obelisk at the center. A small elderly lady sat hunched on a wood bench scattering birdseed for a small flock of pigeons at her feet. The oak trees that towered over her had already regained boughs full of vivid green leaves. The sun had almost reached the horizon and the trees glowed under warm light. The surrounding lush lawn was alive with bright yellow dandelions, tiny perky violets, and delicate white snowdrops that quivered in the breeze. The sky shifted from radiant gold and orange to a soft purple and royal blue with wisps of hot pink cloud. A cold gust of wind lifted the hair on my arms.

"So, I expect you still have quite a few questions about why our city appeals to you so deeply and why I know so much about you," said Rubin.

"Actually … the drawing power of the Capital is subsiding. So are my worries, for that matter. I felt so uncomfortable that I was getting ready to leave again. But that crazy tea your friend gave me must have a magical zen ingredient because I feel so much better now. Calm in fact."

"Magical zen? I guess you *could* think of it that way." He frowned and rubbed his chin. "So I can answer some questions – and I will – but I don't want to offend you when I hold back. It's not my place to tell you everything, you understand."

I looked over at him and marveled at how well-spoken he was, now that I listened properly. His clumped hair and weathered skin had distracted me from the fact that he spoke intelligently and, more importantly, appeared completely lucid. "No, I don't understand, but that's partly the point of having dinner tonight, isn't it?"

"Let's get our table and we'll talk more." Rubin gestured towards a large wooden door to our left, set in from the sidewalk and partially obscured by an awning bearing a faded yin-yang symbol.

"Are you sure this is a Japanese restaurant? I thought that symbol was Chinese."

"I'm sure this is the right place. After you," he said, gesturing again towards the entrance.

I followed him down the slate stone path and past the thick door with an oversized carved wood handle which he held open for me.

A beautiful woman in a light pink kimono and bone-straight black hair that flowed down to her waist smiled, bowed, and showed us to a compact booth at the back of the dark restaurant. She handed us two leather-bound menus, gave us another small bow, and left.

"So, I think we need to start with an explanation for why you gawked at me on the street yesterday. And what was the story with that fight on the street? A hellava, big scary dude and a skater fought – and then afterward you smoothed things over with aforementioned scary dude." I hoped to catch him off guard with my bluntness.

"Yes, that was an unfortunate incident, but both parties have put it behind them." He didn't seem the tiniest bit jarred or put on the spot.

"Excuse me, sir, are you ready to order now?" The waitress quietly reappeared next to our table.

"I'll have a dirty martini. No ice and no olives," said Rubin.

The waitress looked at him, confused. "Uh, so, you want a dirty martini, but no olives?" she said cautiously.

"No *ice* and no olives," he confirmed.

"A martini doesn't come with ice," she said, thoroughly perplexed.

"Well then, there's no problem, is there?" he said matter-of-factly.

"Do you still want olive juice?" she asked.

"With*out* the olives," said Rubin.

"Rubin," I interrupted, "that's what a dirty martini is. You know that, right?"

"Have you ever wondered what makes olives dirty?" he said, fervently curious.

"Maybe have something non-alcoholic," I suggested.

"Good idea!" He beamed at me. "How about some sake instead? We're going out later and I want a twinkle in my eyes when we get there."

I covered my face with both hands for a moment, then I asked the waitress for a pot of green tea. I pointed to a mixed sushi platter on the menu and ordered for both of us.

"Okay, never mind the story behind the fight."

"What would you like to talk about next?" He crossed his arms.

"You stared at me in the street yesterday. How do you know who I am?" I asked, satisfied that I'd hit the heart of the matter.

"Ah, unfortunately, I still can't properly answer that one – yet."

"I see. Well … How did you know where to find me?"

"Excellent. I can answer that. I read minds," he said proudly, hastily adding, "and sometimes influence people."

The pink lady brought two trays of assorted sushi and placed one in front of each of us.

"Of course you can," I said sarcastically. "Why hadn't I figured that out myself? You're one of those mind-reading stalkers."

"No, I'm not stalking you. We've already covered that too. I merely introduced myself to a like-minded person. I took an interest in you because you're like me, being that you have a unique talent of your own."

I shoved a yam roll into my mouth and swallowed hard, pushing the entire roll awkwardly down my throat.

"I think the problem is that you don't know very much about yourself yet. I've got a business card for you, assuming you'll want to find gainful employment. Even though you have accommodation, you'll still need some funds. And something meaningful to do with your time."

"Oh yeah, I meant to ask about that too. What do you mean

by taken care of? I paid for my room and I'm pretty sure they took my money. I'm expecting them to charge me again when I leave."

"The front desk at the motel knows not to charge you. Best if you leave it at that for now."

Rubin pulled a crisp white business card out of his threadbare wallet. In green writing, INNOVIRO INDUSTRIES shouted at me beside a logo of three snakes twisted into a recycling icon.

I ate another piece of sushi and took the card from him.

"I think once you apply for work, you'll move in the right direction to get all the answers you'd like," he said. "I'd try the administration department since I'm pretty sure they have an opening. Have patience with the process. The Human Resources director expects you tomorrow morning."

I sipped my lightly steaming tea and watched as Rubin ate. What kind of administration job did he have in mind for me? How much did Rubin, and in turn Innoviro Industries, know about me? He ate quickly, barely chewing as the rolls bulged in his throat. I selected a piece of raw tuna from my plate, dipped it carefully in soy sauce and wedged it into my mouth as Rubin plucked up his last roll.

He smeared it generously with wasabi, swallowed it whole, and gulped the last of his tea. In spite of his slow start, he'd eaten as though he expected his food to be yanked away at any moment. I smirked to myself thinking that his eating habits and personal appearance were the only two things about him that fit together.

"Shall we go out on the town?" he asked casually.

"What? Is that what you meant when you said we were going out later?" I said, shocked as I set down my tea cup.

"Club-hopping. That's what you call it when you go out with Bridget, isn't it?"

"I think you need to give it a rest with the mind-reading stuff. You're seriously creeping me out. Whatever the hell was in that relaxing berry tea you hooked me up with isn't going to stretch that far."

"Fair enough. Quite right. But drinks and dancing? Is that out of the question? For the record, I'm not trying to date you. I want you to get a feel for the city and meet a few more people. The more you see now, the better. You don't want to spend another boring night in your hotel room, do you? No, of course not. And it's not like you'll be alone with me or anything like that. It'll be somewhere public. I vote for The Looking Glass. It's my favorite club."

"At this point, I'm not even going to bother objecting or asking more questions." I laughed nervously and added, "I guess you're fairly safe. Of course, that's assuming I read people as well as I think I can."

I followed Rubin out of the restaurant. He'd spoken to our waitress but hadn't paid her. Was this woman a friend of his? He didn't look like he had much money, whether he wanted to pay or not. I'd have to get around to that money question again, but unless cops started to chase us because we hadn't paid for our meal, I had more pressing concerns. We walked slowly back to the downtown core.

"Wait, Rubin. Can I ask one more thing? You only answered one question at dinner."

"I wasn't restricting my answers to the dinner table, so go right ahead."

"You mentioned that I'm 'talented' and if I take it as truth that you read minds, you know I've seen things with my Tarot cards. Why? How come I saw what I did? It's never happened before, so I'm not sure it's me instead of something special about that deck of cards."

"Well, it seems to me that those cards were merely a trigger, but that topic strays into taboo territory. I'll say that as you get older, and use your gift more frequently, it will develop like any other talent. It is part of *you*."

I felt better. It was comforting to know that I wasn't part of some trick of fate. I hadn't just picked up a magic deck of cards that would have struck anyone with visions. But if I could 'see' real life, real-world things, did I have to worry about what I saw? More disturbing than seeing a strange mystery man or a random landscape in my mind was the image of my parents, afraid and angry on our living room couch. My gut told me the near future held a nasty shock for them and instinctively, I wanted to stop it. I contemplated calling to check on them.

"I doubt there is anything wrong with your parents, but as before, please consider the job opening I mentioned. It is the next step. Remember that some of what your mind shows you is the past and some of it is the future. Not all your visions may be from pivotal moments in time. We don't know enough about precognition or remote viewing yet." Rubin watched me as I glared at the sidewalk. "But if you'd like to call home right now, feel free to use my phone."

I stopped and looked back at him. Having someone pluck thoughts out of my head took longer to adjust to in actual practice. He wasn't willing or able to rein it in for my benefit. I opened my mouth to say something but sighed instead and accepted the phone he handed me. I tapped my home number on the screen and relief washed over me when Mom answered.

Rubin waited patiently as she launched into a tirade about

the fact that I hadn't called home soon enough. I shared the news about my job lead. I got in one comment about their lack of enthusiasm for my trip, but Mom was too angry about not hearing from me to listen to me in the moment. I mumbled something about having to give a friend's phone back and ended the call. Rubin smiled politely and pocketed his phone.

Chapter 5

We walked in silence again, re-tracing our route from the restaurant and passing my motel as we wound through the streets. Rubin's route took us into a light industrial area. We approached a run-down building, thumping with bass. I saw a sign designed to resemble a broken mirror with the words "The Looking Glass" placed between the broken shards.

As we got closer, I noticed the size of the line outside and I groaned. The prospect of being seen with Rubin partaking in the slightest semblance of a date-like outing embarrassed me. And then I remembered he could probably hear my catty reaction and heat flooded my cheeks. He'd been nothing but nice and I still had bitchy thoughts in my head.

"We don't have to stay here."

I let guilt overtake me, hoping he'd feel it. "I'm very grateful that you're taking me out. I definitely would have been bored back at the motel," I said as sincerely as I could manage.

Rubin smiled and kept walking past the end of the line-up.

I hesitated for a step, lifted my eyebrows, and followed. Were we going to walk right past this entire stream of people? I grinned. Everything else pointed to his unlikely VIP status. Why not a club too?

The bouncer's gaze flitted briefly over Rubin and hovered on me. He looked me up and down as he raised his hand to stop me. It hit me. This bouncer was the man I'd seen in the street fight Rubin watched the other day. He intimidated me even more up close. His massive muscular arms had thick, dark scars from under his T-shirt cuffs to his wrists.

"Casey, she's with me," said Rubin as I prepared to defend myself verbally.

I gave a small wave, feeling like a complete dork as the people waiting near the entrance glared at us when we walked up to the doors ahead of them.

At Casey's nod, I nudged my way gently through a crowd of punk and goth twenty-somethings that made my Prince George friends seem exactly that – PG hicks. Inside the club, I came face-to-face with a boy sporting a tall blue Mohawk, more vibrant than my streaks had ever been. His forehead had three metal cone studs protruding from barely healed openings. I'd heard of dermal anchors before, but this was my first up-close look. He glared at me and put a cigarette in his mouth as I passed.

I caught up to Rubin as he leaned toward the bartender shouting multiple drink orders. I waited behind him, scanning the room. It was pointless to look for people. In this club, on the other side of the province, I couldn't find a table of familiar faces. Rubin tapped me on the shoulder and passed me a screwdriver. I thanked him, noting that his ability might come in handy in a loud, crowded place. I wouldn't hear him back, but at a bare minimum, he'd know what drink I wanted.

For a moment, I felt trendy and out of reach to my former hometown betters who still hadn't seen a club this edgy. Then, I realized that all the tables in the dingy bar were full leaving my strange friend and I stuck in an awkward limbo between having ordered and choosing a place to hang out.

A pair of mid-twenties boys caught sight of us from the upper level. They waved to Rubin. They were sitting at a tiny tall table next to the dance floor. There was no room for us to sit. I followed Rubin over, preparing to linger as indifferently as I could manage if they only wanted to talk to him.

"Rubin! What the hell are you doing out tonight? And with a date!" said the muscular, scruffy, blond skater boy. The other half of yesterday's fight! I could tell he was joking with Rubin, but I blushed anyway.

"Cole, nice to see you. Keeping out of trouble, I hope. And Jonah, I see you're both having a fun night on the town," said Rubin.

Cole had dark eyes and a five-o-clock shadow, making him look grouchy regardless of his enthusiasm. He rubbed his right hand through his crew cut and shook his head at Rubin.

"Dude, nobody talks like that – 'night-on-the-town'. We're getting wasted. We both had a long, shitty day at work. I've been working on a tectonic event simulation that crashed again. Can you believe it? But seriously, what are you doing here? And who's the chick?"

Flashes of Cole's fight popped into my mind as he spoke. His friend Jonah looked almost as uncomfortable with his surroundings as I did. A crisp striped collared shirt and gelled black hair made him look much more professional than anyone else frequenting The Looking Glass.

"This is Irina. She's new in town and a guest at the Capital City Motel," Rubin shouted over the louder song that had just started.

"Ah, old copper-top," said Cole. He turned to me and said, "How do you like the city's most notorious brothel?"

"Cole!" barked Rubin.

"It's okay; he's kidding," added Jonah. "That motel is known for its karaoke bar, but that's about it." He looked at me with light, vivid aqua eyes. His irises practically glowed against his smooth pale skin, and dark glossy hair. He smiled crookedly.

"Uh, I think I need another drink," I said as Rubin pulled my empty glass from my hand. "Oh yeah. I guess you knew that," I said, but he had slipped into the crowd.

"So, Irina, what brings you to Victoria?" asked Cole.

I looked at him, then at Jonah as I considered telling them the truth. They knew Rubin and were obviously 'talented' too. Still, I didn't want to risk it.

"I'm looking for work. I'm from Prince George and the job market up there is only awesome if you're in a trade. Rubin offered to hook me up with a job at a place called Inno-something-or-other. He's been pretty cool." I hoped to avoid adding an explanation of how I'd met Rubin. Even if they knew what he could do, it felt sketchy to admit that I let some stranger show me the city.

"Innoviro Industries! That's where we work!" said Cole, beaming. His square stubble-covered jaw softened substantially when he smiled.

"Seriously? Small world, eh. Is it a good place to work?" I asked.

"You could say that." Cole grinned and looked at Jonah who rolled his eyes.

"Yes, Innoviro is a good place to work. You shouldn't listen to anything this guy says in most cases." Jonah gestured with the end of his imported beer bottle. Jonah looked around the bar as Cole said something into the ear of a waitress. "What kind of job are you applying for?"

"I don't have much experience. Mostly working at a car dealership as an assistant go-for type. Rubin suggested something in admin." The buzz of my drink diminished. "Speaking of Rubin, where is he?"

"Probably chatting and making friends as usual," said Cole, speaking into his pint. "But never mind him. We've got shots to do!" he said as the waitress returned with a tray full of miniature glasses. She transferred them to the table. Unlike Rubin, Cole handed over a twenty-dollar bill.

"To your new life in Victoria," said Jonah, lifting a shot glass. Cole did the same and we downed hot cinnamon liquid. They each grabbed their second shot and gulped it, so I did the same. I tried to steady myself as I surveyed the collection of empty glasses on the table.

"Let's go dance before the posers invade." Cole shifted off his chair. At that moment, my friend with the blue hair walked past us. "It's started already. Look at this guy. He thinks he's a freak. He wishes!"

A girl with black hair in a black coat waved at Cole and he darted off after her. Jonah smiled at me and gestured towards the dance floor. I had my liquid courage back, so I led the way.

The Looking Glass felt like the kind of club where disorganized flailing was the dance of choice, so I wasn't too out of place. I'd never learned to dance back home and I didn't have the kind of figure that moved well without much effort. I wasn't overweight, but it took more than a hip wiggle to make me look sexy – especially while wearing a hoodie and jeans.

We twisted away to a couple of mainstream hard rock songs. Then hopped along with excessively nasal punk I didn't recognize. The exercise hit me quickly and I overheated. I unzipped my hoodie as gracefully as I could, glad that I had on a reasonably clean T-shirt. I tried to limit my eye contact with Jonah to a few casual glances. But it was hard to look away.

"Are you wearing contact lenses? Your eyes are so bright," I said and blushed, again.

"No, that's all natural. Well, sort-of." He smiled.

I didn't want to pry, so I left it at that. What if he could read my mind too? Damn it! Oh well, too late.

We kept dancing until the music changed to slow and steady electronic beats. Trent Reznor's croon came out of the speakers nearby. Mom had always been a Nine Inch Nails fan and their songs conjured fuzzy childhood memories of evenings when our house hopped with raucous partiers. Jonah held out his hand and I took it. He pulled me against his body, breathing heavily. I wasn't the only one feeling the cinnamon shots. I put my arms around his neck and rested my head on his chest and we danced in slow circles with the other couples in the dwindling crowd until Rubin put his hand on my arm.

Chapter 6

Traffic outside the Capital City Motel wasn't just congested. It put the volume of Victoria's opulent vehicles on display. Having worked at a car dealership, I noticed every blue and white pie, concentric rings, pouncing wildcat, and three-pointed star that passed the window where I sat waiting for my crepes.

My weary blonde waitress offered 'my usual' along with a cup of coffee. Intuition told me that she wanted me to know that she was looking after me, rather than being too lazy to bring a menu. I was flattered but picked at the rolled pancakes when they arrived. I stirred my coffee over and over. I couldn't shake my irritation about being stalked by Rubin and not having learned much from anyone yet. And the shame of being hungover glazed every emotion in my mind. I'd bathed and redone my makeup but I still felt wrung-out.

I continued stirring my coffee. Jonah probably pegged me for a hick lightweight after the way I'd made an ass of myself clinging to him and gawking at him. I acted like a child petting an animal for too long when Rubin pulled me away and insisted on walking me to the motel.

I let my coffee spoon drip briefly before I set it down on my napkin. I reached into my bag, fished out my wallet, and set it in the middle of the table where the waitress would notice it. I remained uncomfortable with not paying for my room and board without a decent explanation. I pulled the card for Innoviro Industries out of my wallet and turned it over in my hand. If I got a job there and still didn't learn anything, I would at least have a paycheck. If I had a regular income, I could rent an apartment where I wasn't being watched.

I wondered if Innoviro was a scam. For all I knew, I would walk into some dive and wind up with a needle in my arm, getting pimped out the next day. I shook my head at my sense of melodrama. Victoria wasn't exactly a hub of human trafficking as far as I knew. I could try the cards again and maybe coax another vision or two out of them. My stomach lurched with helplessness and guilt as I recalled the image of my parents' distress in our living room.

My worst-case scenario for Innoviro did sound a bit extreme. I wanted to believe that Rubin was genuinely trying to help me for a solid, albeit unknown reason. I had established two pseudo-facts. Firstly, I hadn't seen anything bad involving Rubin in any visions so he was probably decent and secondly, Innoviro must be a legitimate company if I'd met actual employees.

Jonah I trusted, even if he did unnerve me with those piercing blue eyes. Cole, on the other hand, clearly had powerful violence inside, although he'd resolved the matter with that bouncer if he sat comfortably in the bar all night. I frowned at the business card, thinking that Rubin shouldn't have left me with such an unstable person, especially knowing I'd witnessed that temper and extreme strength in action.

"Are the crepes no good? Can I get you something different?" said the waitress, watching my expression as she paused at my table.

"Sorry, I'm sure they're fine. I'm hung-over and I've got a lot on my mind."

"I can imagine," she said as she walked away.

I frowned. Was she part of Rubin's network? If she was, I didn't want to know. I tried to calm down as I cut off forkfuls of crepe, just to put something on my stomach before I started the day.

I found the Innoviro office easily, and I'd unknowingly passed right beneath it when I walked around the courtyard on my first day. I hadn't noticed it because I had been looking at beads, candy, and trendy clothes. Even the below-ground basement level drew my attention with snacks, toys, and home decor. The top level of boring blind-filled windows had floated right over my radar.

A smooth stainless steel door shone under a die-cut sign that read, 'Innoviro Industries' with the slogan 'Shaping the World of Tomorrow' in smaller letters. I considered the sign. The prospect of working for a sophisticated corporation intimidated me. I wondered what to say to whomever I found when I entered. I didn't even have a resume. Looking for work had been a line for my parents. I took the business card out of my wallet and opened the door.

"Hello, welcome to Innoviro Industries," said a silky voice before I'd gotten the door closed again after me. "How can I help you?"

The voice came from a beautiful woman in a lavender

cashmere sweater and a French roll swept behind her head. I'd never made half that effort for a shift at the dealership. This receptionist was no more than a few years older than me, but her expression radiated class and confidence. I looked around the office. It was gray and glass – disappointingly normal, except for a vault-style door at the end of a short hallway.

"I'm here to apply for a job in your administration department. A friend of mine, Rubin, gave me your card." I handed over the small piece of paper embossed with my sweaty thumbprint.

Her beautiful face took on a look of pity and concern. "Oh. Um, I'm very sorry, but I don't think we have any openings at the moment," she said slowly, sizing me up much the way last night's bouncer had.

I stood my ground. I'd changed into my most presentable clothes – a set of brown corduroys and a long-sleeve gray collared top. I wore my own hair pulled into a plain, but tidy ponytail. With my free hand, I fidgeted with the wisps hanging loose around my face, wracking my brain for something to say when a door clicked down the hall.

A tall, slim man wearing a crisp light blue dress shirt and charcoal pants walked into the room and smiled. In the fluorescent light, his pale skin blended with his shirt.

"Melissa, I hate to interrupt," he said slowly, as smooth as silk, "but I could have sworn I heard this young lady asking about employment."

"Yes, sir, that's correct. I offered to keep her resume on file since we're not hiring."

"Actually, I've been thinking about hiring a new assistant," he said cheerfully. She looked as though he'd slapped her in the face. He continued, "We keep you quite busy and I need someone to handle more of my personal matters." He turned to me and asked, "Does a role like that hold any interest for you, young lady?"

He didn't even know my name yet and I didn't know his, but the man seemed prepared to offer me a job. I thought of Rubin and I felt torn between my desire to trust them and my instinctive suspicions. I felt conflicted about being anyone's personal assistant, whether I was qualified for the job or not. Being a go-fer had been part of my job before – the more humiliating part. I hated having to fetch coffee and lunch orders, make other people's phone calls, send other people's emails, call for couriers and cabs, maintain office supply inventory, and generally do tiny menial tasks the person who assigned it to me should have been doing for him or herself.

"My name is Ivan. I have the privilege of signing a few checks around here. Why don't you step into my office? We'll go over the details and make sure we're a fit for each other," he said.

I took his attempt at modesty to mean that the company was small and the job not too illustrious. I liked that he acted humble rather than domineering, so I nodded and set my bag down on one of the front room's angular black chairs. I let Melissa take my jacket and followed Ivan back to his office. The letters on his door read, "Ivan Krylov" in thin black letters. There was no job title.

"Please have a seat." He gestured toward a plush leather chair positioned in front of his desk.

I sat down and folded my hands in my lap. Ivan took his time finishing whatever task he had underway on his computer. I fidgeted, wringing my hands as he calmly clicked and typed. I busied myself taking in my surroundings. Ivan's office was hardly pretentious. On the wall to my left, he had a large, colorful, modern acrylic painting depicting an aerial view of the city's Inner Harbour. Behind his chair, a bay window looked out over the street. From where I sat, I could only see the top of the building across the way. On my right, a partition separated his desk from a small kitchenette.

"So," he said, swiveling to face me. "What brings you to Innoviro Industries today? Tell me a bit about yourself."

"I'm from Prince George. My name is Irina Proffer. Sorry, I should have started with that," I blushed but continued. "I'm new to Victoria. I came here to … have a vacation and I wasn't looking for work. I planned mostly to wander. But I met a man named Rubin and he suggested I apply here if I decided to stay in Victoria for a while and needed a job. Not that I'd expect anyone to give me a job only because I need one. I don't have a degree, but I'm qualified. I have office administration experience from a car dealership back home. I can give you contact information, but I don't have a resume on me. Normally I'd bring a resume of course." I forced myself to stop talking before I did more damage.

"Rubin is a good friend, so if he's referred you, I'm quite pleased." Ivan examined a piece of paper on his desk and I regretted even more deeply that I didn't have a resume. "I'll give you an overview of our work here at Innoviro. This is a research firm. We are retained by private companies, ranging from pharmaceutical designers to electronic technology developers, and even a few federal meteorological installations. We conduct tests to ensure that our partners are creating safe, well-designed products. Sort of like a tutor for tech manufacturers." Ivan paused and smiled.

I still had a shot at the job, which made me even more

nervous. I couldn't think of a single question to ask. None of his explanations of what Innoviro did made any sense to me. Used cars – no problem. Advanced scientific testing – that's biting off a handful more than I could chew. He had to be humoring me based on his level of professional tact. I took a deep breath. A graceful exit was the most dignified choice at this point.

"What I'm looking for in an assistant is, I'm ashamed to say, mostly personal. Since I started Innoviro six years ago, we've experienced a phase of hyper-growth, adding offices in several other cities, and I can't keep up with the demands on my time. Melissa's role is to take care of Innoviro's administrative needs and to run our Victoria office. To put it bluntly, I'm looking for someone to run my errands, help me manage my schedule, and book appointments. You'd take care of the minor stuff that slows down my day." He chuckled briefly and then looked down as he continued, "It's not stimulating or exciting work. But I hope that whoever we bring on board for this position can grow within the company once my schedule slows down enough that I can look after myself again."

I wanted to launch into a speech, making my case for the job. A sensible question finally came to mind. "Wow. The job is pretty much what I expected. But, the stuff you work on here is way out of my league. I don't want to pretend I'm something I'm not. I have no academic background in science or business. Are you sure I will be able to grow within the company? Won't I need additional training?"

"We do look for *some* post-secondary education, within one of the academic sciences or from a technical institute's lab tech program. However ... as this particular job relates to my personal needs, I think someone with less training is an asset. I want an assistant to do the job the way I ask, rather than someone who tries to perform the role from a textbook. When it's time for a promotion, you'll have learned everything you need to know."

I still had no idea what I was getting into - or better yet, why me? But Ivan made his sale. I wanted to work for him. "Think of me as a blank slate." I smiled nervously. "I'm a hard worker, I'm smart, and I learn fast. I know that sounds kind of generic, but it's true. Point me at whatever you need done and I'll get on it. If I don't know how to do something, I always figure it out."

"You do seem like a bright girl. But I should also let you know that we demand the full attention of our employees and ask for passion, dedication, and loyalty. I want employees who are willing to 'drink the Kool-Aid' so to speak. We also have a zero social media policy for ALL our employees."

"Sounds good to me. I'm loyal and I can skip the social media scene." I was compelled to wrap up the meeting before I rambled my way back out of the job. "Do you need me to fill out an application? Should I leave the number for my motel with Melissa?"

"I don't think that's necessary. I'm happy to get the paper-work started on hiring you today. Congratulations; the job belongs to you if you want it."

"Great! That's so awesome!" I blushed and steadied myself. "I mean, thank you for the opportunity."

Ivan grinned again and shook my hand. His icy iron grip caught me off guard, but I pumped back as firmly as I could. He instructed Melissa to print and pass me forms for both Innoviro human resources and government taxes. I filled them out hunched over the coffee table near the reception desk. Ivan asked me to come back first thing the next day. Melissa's dejected expression had no effect on him.

I returned the papers and collected my jacket as other employees emerged from that vault door, probably to go for lunch. I scanned their faces, looking for Jonah or Cole, but neither of them appeared. Seeing Jonah again was bound to happen, so I smiled anyway.

The walk home felt effortless like I'd lived in Victoria all my life and belonged. I left the market and crossed over to the alley that connected to Chinatown. I had no intention of dropping in on the tea lady, but I wanted to enjoy the quaint brick close that bore no resemblance to the stark industrial landscape of my hometown.

As I slipped into the alley, I thought I heard a faint jingling. I stopped and it was gone. I started walking again and I heard it again. I smirked to myself, thinking that the noise came from the magic 8-ball keychain clipped to one of the top zippers of my backpack. Tension slid off me and I let the chain tinkle with each step. I imagined the rubber triangle inside the ball divining for the bricks on the ground.

Chapter 7

I had to tell Mom the good news, but it was too soon for a purchase as big as a smartphone. I was devastated when I lost my old phone, especially in such a stupid and predictable way as gesturing next to a snow bank. I hadn't stopped picturing someone finding my phone, covered in dirt, in the gutter during the spring thaw.

I felt incredibly downtrodden without a phone, but I couldn't let my parents see the depths of my need. Darryl had said good riddance with his usual awkward gruffness. Mom clicked her tongue and said I needed to get back in the game if I wanted luxuries like a new phone. She and I had different definitions of the word 'luxury'.

Reliving my mom's lecture gave me a stomach ache. Did she think I was incapable of getting it together? I dreaded hearing her voice. My chest constricted from tension. But then I remembered the earful I'd already gotten for not calling fast enough after arriving in Victoria. The phone in my motel room would be expensive. And maybe even monitored? A small miracle; I saw a payphone while exploring downtown. One of the few payphones I imagined that worked in BC sat in front of the auto repair garage on the corner of my motel's side street. A sign over top of the payphone proudly declared that the phone was maintained courtesy of the garage.

So I headed home via that parking lot. When I picked up the receiver the plastic felt sticky and cold against my ear as I listened to the dial tone and plugged coins into the abused metal box.

"Hello?" Mom answered, with her usual lack of enthusiasm.

"Mom, it's me. I got a job!"

"Sweetie, that's wonderful. Well done!"

She sounded happy for me, but distracted and a little exasperated. I promised to buy a phone or at least get on a plan when I got my first paycheck. I said I expected to be able to email once I had a desk and a computer. A recorded operator cut me off, announcing that I had to insert another dollar to continue the call. I didn't have any more change so I cursed into the receiver and slammed the phone back on its hook.

I wanted to tell Mom so much more. I wanted to share my discoveries and worries, but I couldn't make any of it believable for her if I didn't fully understand it myself. I stood next to the phone booth, frustrated, torn between going on to my room and marching to the nearest ATM. I could grab some cash, buy some gum, and have change for another call in less than 20 minutes.

I looked down the street and then back at the garage wall in time to glimpse a shadow gliding across the painted pale green brick. The dark shape slipped around the corner into the alleyway behind the building before I could get a good look. I felt the frown lines on my forehead deepen.

I slowly put one foot in front of the other, rationalizing that I only needed to confirm that I hadn't seen a shadow cast by nothing. Something would be there in the alley and it would be benign, like a balloon on a string. The air grew cold and my lungs complained. I couldn't resist satisfying my curiosity, a weakness that got more dangerous by the day.

The narrow alley allowed one person to walk between an overgrown chain link fence and a mildew-stained brick wall. The tight dead-end space contained nothing more than a few rotting wood pallets strewn around grease-coated concrete. The garage roof shaded the alley as the sun sank behind the other side. Nothing stirred as I entered.

My breath puffed clouds that dissolved behind me after each step. An overwhelming dread gripped me in the eerily still air. I marched to the end of the alley and something grabbed my collar.

I felt a scream inside, but no sound came out. Something thick and strong clamped my mouth shut. I wrestled, fighting to free myself or to twist and at least see my attacker. The grip on my jacket collar lifted me off the ground. I fought harder, flailing kicks in every direction.

"We're watching you," a deep raspy voice growled into my ear. I tried to twist around again. "We know who you are. We know *what* you are. And we expect you to keep quiet." His hot breath reeked of garlic and tobacco.

I tried to say something as I struggled. I tried to make a noise to draw help. Pain demanded my attention. The zipper of my coat dug into my neck, choking me as tiny plastic teeth bit the skin of my throat. I fell to the ground with a gasp, landing on the balls of my feet before crumpling to the side. Fresh pain seared my ankles. The urge to run overpowered my instinct to recover and I limped onto the sidewalk. I jogged in pain until I reached the motel parking lot, slowing to a brisk walk to avoid drawing attention to myself as I sped up the stairs to my room.

The key card shook in my hand as I rattled the handle. I flung the door shut behind me. I collapsed into a chair and stared down at the table. My backpack sat across from me as if to greet me with a deadpan reminder that it would be easier – and safer – to leave. I pushed back my hair, trying to gather my thoughts. Who or what had just attacked me? How could I find out? Rubin? Or would he send me back to Innoviro? Should I stick to my plan and go to work there?

My instincts shifted from flight to fight. Anger surged through me. The kind of righteous anger when someone shoves you to the ground for no reason. The bitter humiliation that comes from not defending yourself.

I didn't have any way to contact Rubin, but I still had my cards. I fished the cracked paper packet out of my backpack and emptied the deck onto the table. They looked so unassuming now. The old paper looked dull in the sunlight. I shuffled them, calmly concentrating, willing the cards to relinquish something useful from their two-dimensional scenes.

As I laid down a row of three cards, I only glanced at the paper images before the pictures in my head flooded my field of vision. I saw my mystery man-boy again, this time standing in the same Chinatown tea shop where Rubin had sent me. He spoke with the same eccentric lady I'd met, but the conversation was muted and I didn't hear a word.

They moved too slowly and the image blurred in my mind.

I concentrated and it came back with intensity. I saw through the boy's eyes. He looked over his shoulder to a figure outside the window. Handbills and posters obscured the figure's face. He collected his own brown paper bag and turned to leave. I felt myself walk through the doorway with him, looking around the alley as he did. We turned to face the man waiting for him. It was unmistakably my new boss, Ivan.

The reflex to back away gripped me. I felt myself stepping backward in the alley and standing up from my chair at the same time. I had snapped back to my hotel room. I saw nothing about what I'd bumped into on the way home, but now I knew Innoviro was definitely part of my future.

I slipped out of my work clothes, smudged with dirt from my roll on the pavement, and pulled on my sweatpants and a T-shirt. I had one more outfit I could wear to work. Tomorrow, I could get some new or at least better clothes. I'd try to track down Jonah and Cole, the latter for protection as I recalled him slugging that huge bouncer in the gut.

Morning came with the unpleasant ringing of Darryl's wind-up pocket alarm clock. Yet one more reason to get a phone, I thought, as I reached for the obnoxiously loud bell.

As soon as I remembered my plans to find Jonah and Cole at work, I couldn't wait to get out the door. I skipped the diner and got a croissant for breakfast on the way to Innoviro. I finished the pastry and dusted my hands as I walked up the last flight of stairs to the posh steel door.

Melissa already sat at her desk. She glanced at me briefly and returned to writing something on a notepad. I wondered what her to-do list looked like and if it contained an item for *'get Irina fired'* possibly coded with language like *'take out the trash'* or similar.

"Ivan's not in yet, but he asked me to give you a tour of the office." Melissa stood. She refused to break eye contact with her notepad.

"Follow me. It's a short tour. You won't have access to the labs below until you've passed your three-month probation," she said. "You'll probably never see any of our international offices, so I won't even bother talking about those."

I followed, nodding and saying, 'OK' as optimistically as I could each time she pointed something out in a flat, joyless tone. I looked around for signs of other staff, hoping for Jonah or Cole to pass. Utter silence, except for our footsteps and the ticking of fluorescent lights overhead, left me disappointed.

Melissa circled back to her desk and instructed me to wait in the lounge for Ivan to arrive. "Task-wise, I have no idea what he has in mind for you, but I can't let you browse." She watched her screen, clacking away on her keyboard, but I could tell she had me in her peripheral vision.

Fortunately, only minutes passed until Ivan arrived and cheerfully invited me to follow him to his office. I felt the exciting rush of a fresh start. My life had the potential to evolve into anything – exciting challenges, fascinating projects, rewarding achievements. Despite my sheer gratitude for having a job, I knew this role probably couldn't offer any of those things. My expectations were confirmed with a THUD when Ivan set his briefcase down and asked me to go to the coffee shop around the corner for his soy latte and a cranberry breakfast scone.

As the day wore on, Ivan's assignments continued to live up to the job title of personal assistant. I typed up scrawled notes from a prior meeting. I picked up his dry cleaning, called his salon to make a hair and facial appointment, organized his office closet, and reviewed his day book to circle droppable tasks or in his words, 'weed out the non-essentials' when it came to his daily activities. At four o'clock I called him a courier, then a cab, requesting that it arrive precisely at four-thirty.

Ivan's last task of the day transcended demeaning and reached the realm of bizarre. While he selected files to carry home in his briefcase, he instructed me to find a nearby pet shop and purchase two mice. This would have puzzled me if I hadn't been directed to the kitchenette inside his office that morning to apply cream cheese to his crumbly scone (an extremely tedious task if you've never attempted it) and pour his coffee into a mug. The kitchenette I saw during my interview had been half concealed by a partition of Russian illustrations. Hidden behind the partition sat a cabinet and on top of that, a well-appointed terrarium containing a large coiled snake. Ivan told me his name was Chester.

Knowing what lay ahead for the mice, I insisted the pet shop's attendant select the mice himself. I wanted it to be an impartial twist of fate for the furry creatures. When I got back I expected to find Ivan waiting in his office – until I saw that the clock on the wall pointed to ten after five. Ivan had left in his cab and I found a hand-written note with two capsules instructing me to feed a pill to each mouse, and then feed one unfortunate rodent to Chester immediately. Part two was to place the second temporary survivor into a smaller cage in the cupboard below Chester's sacred perch.

I don't have strong feelings about snakes, apart from caution regarding poisonous species. It was part of my live-and-let-live philosophy that had always worked out well. Chester on the other hand, quickly became my exception. His giant, polished wet eyes held me in a trance as we stared at each other. I hadn't noticed my face inching towards the glass until I felt a hand on my shoulder.

"I've been wondering if I'd bump into you around here," said Jonah's voice as I yelped in shock. "I guess you're not allowed down to the tombs yet."

His vibrant blue eyes sparkled as though lit internally. He must know how unusual he looked and make regular allowances for people who stare too long.

"Feel like grabbing some dinner?" he asked.

I nodded with a smile.

Chapter 8

Jonah zipped through Innoviro's underground parking and quickly rounded the corner onto Wharf Street. Heading south, the Inner Harbour unfolded in a panorama starting with the vine-covered Empress Hotel, the art deco Royal BC Museum, and the domes of BC's Provincial Parliament. The distinctive landmarks gave way to modern swanky hotels at the far edge of the Harbour. As we passed, I looked up at each building. Old-world Europe and contemporary American culture walked hand in hand here.

We reached the end of the Harbour and the coastline opened up around the corner. I saw a sign for ferries to the US in front of a giant concrete breakwater and a pub decorated with a helm wheel and a mural with starfish and orcas. The hazy soft blues of the ocean and sky were broken by the jagged edges of American snow-capped mountains on the horizon. The seaside sidewalk had a mix of young families, dog walkers, and spry seniors in trendy windbreakers.

"You know what they say about the people here in Victoria,

right?" said Jonah, as he watched me watch everyone else.

"No, I can't say that I do. More money than they know what to do with?"

"True, but not as bad as Vancouver. Ever heard of the saying 'newlyweds and nearly deads' or as my mom says, 'God's waiting room.'"

"Kind of a dark way to look at things, isn't it?"

"My mom's a dark lady, but hilarious. I hope you don't mind, but I invited Cole and his sister. You'll love this little restaurant. It's got awesome food and live music, but not too hipster-ish," said Jonah.

Something dropped in my chest. If Cole and his sister came along, we were a group of friends going for dinner. I felt silly for thinking that we were on a date. We turned another corner and Jonah pulled the car over next to a brick building with a 50's style neon sign that read 'Cymbals' next to a caricature of a drum set. I followed Jonah through the wrought iron gate and looked up at the oak tree on the lawn next to the patio. Tiny fresh leaves and new buds covered the gnarled old tree. It was also home to dozens and dozens of sneakers, canvas shoes, skate shoes, oxfords – any kind of shoe with laces to tie together.

The air felt warm enough to linger, so I walked over to the tree and looked upward. I smiled. I reached up to one of the lower branches and touched one of the shoes. The yard and the tree melted away. I saw the face of a girl with faintly bluish skin and platinum hair. She turned and I saw two leather-like wings flex and relax. Her shirt had been cut to make room for her wings which stretched out past the frayed edges of the fabric. She was standing in a sewer or catacomb.

Faces milled around the winged girl. It wasn't quite like a

party, maybe more like a camp. An older lady standing next to the winged girl reached down to the ground. She pinched the concrete and plucked something, maybe a stone, off the surface. The stone wriggled. It was a camouflaged beetle, exactly like the one I'd seen on my first day in the city. She lifted the beetle to her mouth and I reeled back.

The yard outside Cymbals surrounded me again in a blink. Jonah stared at me. I noticed my arm still reaching for the shoes and withdrew it.

"Are you all right?"

I heard fear in his voice.

"Rubin mentioned that you were psychic, but I never knew what it looked like in person. I mean, I've never witnessed anyone 'see' something if that makes sense."

"Oh, I … what *does* it look like? It's still pretty new for me. I've always been alone when that happens, but I hadn't even wondered what somebody watching me gets to see."

"You looked sort of, gone. And then your eyes rolled back for a moment. I thought you were having a seizure."

I looked around the yard and fortunately, we were alone. Still, I didn't want to keep talking about this stuff where we could be overheard. More importantly, what was Rubin doing sharing my personal information while giving me his best poker face?

"Let's go inside. I'm hungry." I didn't feel like socializing, but I needed to eat.

Cole waved from a table on the other side of the building. Sitting next to him, a girl with purple dreadlocks looked up from her purse and smiled.

The restaurant was loud with the chatter of many conversations. Dim candlelight, a few glass chandeliers, and an antique-looking piano in the corner set a romantic atmosphere that sparked another twinge of embarrassment. On the other hand, the abstract and industrial mixed-media wall décor had me looking around for art and film students. Aside from a few biker bars, the edgiest hangout I knew of in Prince George was an indie coffee shop – and it had only been open for a few years when I left.

We made our way around and between tables. Everyone in the restaurant looked like an artist or an intellectual. I felt like an ugly duckling in my plain, boring clothes, but I was glad for the first time since starting my new job that not all of the blue dye had gone from my hair. Jonah reached the table and pulled out a chair for me. We sat down and Cole scowled.

"Dude, what's up with the timeline fail? We've been here for like, half an hour," said Cole.

"Ignore his attitude. I'm Faith," the girl said as she extended her hand to me and grinned happily. The flickering light glinted off a stud in her nose and a ring in her eyebrow. She wore metallic makeup on her eyes and mouth. She had the same coffee-brown eyes as Cole. I couldn't tell if it was her striking features or the unusual eyeliner and lipstick, but she looked eclectic. As we shook hands, her gaze shifted over to Jonah.

We looked at our menus in awkward silence, waiting for a server, and sipping our water. I sighed and put down my menu. I could feel Cole's eyes on me as I watched Faith stare at Jonah, the only person still looking at his menu. I gave in and glanced back at Cole briefly with a small smile. This was all heading in the wrong direction. The time for tact expired along with my patience.

"So I take it we're all mutants here," I said casually.

Jonah sprayed water onto his menu and coughed. Cole looked at me urgently. Faith's mouth made a small 'O' under her confused frown.

"Seriously." I looked around for another beat. "I came here, to Victoria, because I started having visions of this place and wanted answers. All I've gotten is cryptic nonsense. Other than meeting *you* people, I've learned next to nothing. Rubin is all vague double-talk. It's getting old. I want to know what you all know."

Jonah looked at me and took a breath as if to say something. He decided against it and looked around our corner of the restaurant. Nobody paid any attention to us. He placed his hand over the droplets of water on his laminated menu. The water coalesced into puddles under his palm. As he concentrated on the small pool, it lifted off the menu and spread into a donut shape. The circle broke and the stream became a spiral, getting thinner and thinner until it evaporated into steam, absorbed into Jonah's hand.

Faith's frown turned into a smile as she looked at Jonah. She picked up one of the unlit candles on our table and pinched the wick between her thumb and forefinger. As she released it a flame sprang to life.

"Well, I'm not breaking this table, that's for damn sure," said Cole.

"That's okay. I saw your street fight with the Looking Glass bouncer when I first got to town," I said. Cole rolled his eyes, but I couldn't worry about his temper. I wanted to keep talking about Innoviro and Ivan. "So, now that we're making progress, albeit moving into some surreal comic book world, tell me, what's the deal with Innoviro. What the hell does this company do? For real." I felt my adrenaline rise.

"I'm not risking my job so you can get a head start on whatever Ivan has in mind for you. You're acting like there's something bad going on here. He helps people like us." Cole looked over at Jonah. "For some of us, being different *is* a health risk."

"Leave it alone!" said Jonah.

Faith frowned again. "You've met Rubin. He's like a recruiter. He told you that much at least, didn't he? He works with Ivan to find people like us and help if they need it."

"And what if I don't need help?" I said.

"You may help others. We're not all different in the same way. Some of us were born this way and some were ... made," said Faith.

"Ivan will talk to you about all of this soon enough. We're not allowed to and I think the reasons for that will start to be obvious. It's not the kind of research the government likes. You can't put this kind of stuff in a job posting and you definitely can't chat about it at parties." Jonah looked around the room again.

"So they're doing tests on people." I felt the unease in my gut churning faster. "On us."

"It's not like that. We *are* doing research and development work, but it varies. Sometimes we're looking at mutation in other animals or plants. We look at weather and geography to understand how a person's gifts are advantageous or dangerous, depending on where and how they live. Imagine me living in a desert, for example. And we're not catastrophically testing on people. Sometimes we'll take a small tissue or fluid sample from a person, but nothing barbaric," said Jonah. "We've also got to make money. Innoviro takes research contracts from public and private firms for anything from environmental research to mining and industrial development. Ivan keeps a low profile for his work under the guise of confidentiality for his legitimate clients."

"Are you guys even qualified for this? Or are you all older and more educated than you look?"

"Hey, we're not screwing around here! Jonah and I were recruited directly from our graduate programs. I was working on a master's in geology and Jonah had nearly finished his thesis in microbiology. Don't you think research like this is best conducted by someone who understands it firsthand? Could you imagine convincing a serious scientist to take this on, instead of a real career? You'd have to divulge every secret Innoviro has to even have a conversation, let alone get a commitment." The table crunched under Cole's grip.

"And how about you?" I nodded at Faith, "Are you some kind of brain surgeon?"

"I'm an IT technician. I specialize in network administration and hardware integration."

"Wow. I feel like a complete dunce." I had nothing unique or meaningful to contribute to Innoviro. Nothing but a tissue sample.

"Don't be intimidated. Remember that you were recruited for a reason. You probably won't get to know everything the company does. We don't discuss the details of our work with anyone but our supervisors," said Faith.

"Lots of projects are shared on a need-to-know basis. But it's not bad. You'll understand more when Ivan gives you a full tour. Let it happen on his schedule," said Jonah.

"I can go along to get along, but you've got to understand how this looks from my point of view, getting drawn to a strange city by visions – which are an entirely new phenomenon to me. Have I mentioned yet that I got jumped the other night?"

"What?" said Cole and Jonah in unison.

"And you know why I didn't get a look at him?" I said.

The boys had quizzical looks on their faces, but Faith looked anxious.

"Because there was nothing to look at," I said. "Some enormous *thing* that I couldn't see picked me up off the ground and threatened me."

"You need to tell Rubin. Or Ivan, but not everyone in this restaurant." Faith scanned the room tensely.

"Fine." I lowered my voice. "But I don't have a way to get a hold of Rubin. If he was keeping tabs on me, listening in, where was he? Did he know I'd be fine, half-choked by an invisible monster?"

"I'm sure he *is* looking out for you. It's his job to keep us safe," said Jonah.

Our waitress arrived with a platter of salsa and fresh tortilla chips.

Chapter 9

Cole insisted on driving me back to the motel. Even though it was dark, he wanted to take the scenic route. He took the seaside road Jonah had taken to get to Cymbals. However, instead of heading south, the way we'd come, Cole went north.

The restless Pacific Ocean lapped at the sea wall on my right, brilliantly lit by a bright white moon. The tide was out leaving expansive stretches of driftwood, sand, and stone in front of foam-trimmed inky surf. A handful of stars twinkled overhead as I took in the wall of cliffside homes on the other side of the road.

The drive felt more like something off a British postcard than the far side of Canada's West Coast. We rounded another corner and came to a gap in the residential landscape. As we approached the thick wall of dark cedars, I saw gravestones in the gaps between each trunk. The graveyard sat patiently in the dark. Cole pulled over on the gravel shoulder across the street.

"This is Ross Bay cemetery. There's a whole bunch of touristy crap downtown, but the cemetery is one of the more interesting spots."

The graveyard whispered at us as giant evergreen branches and other dark shapes undulated in the powerful coastal wind. On the other side of the road, the ocean lapped at the beach below, glittering with reflected pieces of moonlight.

Cole looked at me, and back at the cemetery before he pulled a U-turn back onto the road. He must have noticed the apprehensive look on my face. "I realize it's a bit sketchy to bring a girl here at night. You don't know me. But, there is cool shit to see there. We could come back during the day and take a look at the statues and carvings. Or we could go for a drive and find other stuff worth checking out. If you wanna take some classes up at the university, that's something to see. There's a college here too. If you don't have a car, you're stuck riding the bus to see more of the city than downtown. There are more beaches, a couple of castles, and loads of parks. I could show you around if you're into that."

I hesitated, but Cole sounded so sincere. I didn't want to give him the idea I was interested in a date, but I didn't want to be rude, especially since I did need to explore more of the capital region to track down all my visions.

Yet, Cole had the worst combination of strength and temper I'd ever seen. I remembered *"a master's in geology"* and the idea still didn't fit. I thought about the crunch of our dinner table under his grip. And then the memory of being hoisted in the air behind a garage popped into my head. Whatever else Cole might be, a makeshift bodyguard was in my best interest.

"I'd like to do a little sightseeing. I wouldn't want to be any trouble though. I don't need to rush back to PG, but I'm not sure if I want to live here for long. I can't shake the fear that takes over when I think of that guy who jumped me."

"Don't worry, you're safe with me. And it's no trouble to take you around town. Maybe after you see the best parts of the city, you'll want to stay."

We passed under a white-orange streetlight and the glow highlighted a dimple in his cheek when he smiled. Cole grew on me with his calmer, more charming side.

By the time we got back to the motel, my eyelids felt heavy. I noticed a figure standing at the bottom of the outdoor stairwell. Rubin waved at us and Cole waved back. Exhaustion poured over me. Where *had* Rubin been last night? What would he say about my hanging out with co-workers? I didn't want to share my thoughts with him, so I tried to clear my mind. I thanked Cole for the ride and hopped out. He paused, eyeing Rubin before he drove away.

"You're out a bit late for a work night, aren't you?" said Rubin lightly.

"It's Friday."

"No reason you can't get some work done tomorrow," he said in his infuriating matter-of-fact tone.

"The office is closed, so I wasn't planning to work." I walked past him up the stairs. I heard his footsteps behind me.

"I meant work of another sort. It's time we found you a proper apartment. I'm not convinced that your assailant from the other night hasn't been following you."

"So you did know! And you waited a DAY to check on me? Thanks, I'm overwhelmed by your concern. But since I haven't cashed my first paycheck, I kind of hoped I could keep this room a bit longer," I said. "Then again, I still have enough money to make it back to Prince George and at this point, heading home looks pretty good."

"Innoviro prefers that you stay here in Victoria. The company paid for this room and we will cover your apartment as well. We cover room and board for all employees. I'm surprised Melissa hasn't mentioned this yet. I see your new friends didn't bring it up either. Discussing inappropriate topics instead from the sounds of it."

"Get out of my head! I'm tired as hell and you show up here to … what, kick me out?" I felt my fatigue turning into frustration and anger.

"You're not being kicked out. And I understand that you're tired, but I'm afraid this can't wait."

I sighed and invited him in to make arrangements to look at apartments.

The next morning, Rubin waited for me again when I came down to the diner for breakfast. I wasn't surprised to find him eating dry white toast and drinking black coffee. Naturally, he'd ordered me a plate of crepes.

"Does anyone ever get used to you knowing their every thought?" I asked sarcastically.

"It goes in phases." He spread jam on his toast. "Disbelief, awe, fear, and irritation, usually leading to avoidance."

I felt gratitude for his honesty and resolved not to do that to him.

"Yes, eventually, you will avoid me."

"We'll see about that. So what do you have lined up for us to look at?"

"I'm placing you in one of the company-owned properties, with a focus on our more secure buildings, in light of the circumstances."

"Do you know who my attacker was?"

"I believe you were assaulted by an ex-employee. We cannot be certain, but as I'm sure you'll realize - as you begin to work more closely with Ivan - that we are a very special organization, dealing with impressive technology. Unfortunately, not everyone we welcome into our little family is worthy of staying for the long haul."

"What do you mean by that? Was he fired? Were you testing on him and something went wrong?"

Rubin shot me a dark look. "We do nothing reckless, malicious, or irresponsible and I won't have you making statements that so much as imply we do," he said angrily. I felt my body tense like I was in trouble. "But returning to your accommodation situation, I have several buildings in mind. You won't have unlimited freedom. I'm afraid that's no longer possible. However, these are lovely living spaces."

I stared back at him, still frozen in my seat, trying to determine if I had been threatened. I wanted to know why he'd spoken to me like that. But security-oriented apartments would soothe my immediate fears. After all, Rubin was probably being his eccentric self. And if Innoviro had the money and would foot the bill, I wanted to see what they offered. Maybe psychics were quite rare and they wanted to make sure I felt content and comfortable.

"Protecting staff that are in danger is the right thing to do. You must understand that the danger I'm talking about doesn't come from the company." He bit off a piece of toast, chewed, and swallowed. "Or from me."

"How long has the company been around? How long have you worked there?"

"If you recall our earlier conversations, I'm not at liberty to answer every one of your questions. You're starting to get a sense of where and how you'll find all the answers you're looking for, so I think we're best served by moving on to today's appointments."

I smiled and nodded. I ate my crepes as Rubin outlined the tour of the city to view three different apartments.

Our first stop was in a neighborhood near the cemetery Cole showed me. We were still fairly close to the ocean in an upscale neighborhood. I saw a sign for a bus stop ahead where the sidewalk curved into a driveway which led to a gated entrance to underground parking. The tower above us was easily the largest on the street. Rubin said, "I agree that you should familiarize yourself with the city and if Cole wants to take you, I suggest you accept the offer."

Damn it, Rubin, I'm going to lose my voice if you never let me say anything out loud. And for god's sake, give me some privacy! Or at least pretend! Now I get what you meant about people avoiding you.

"I apologize. However, I am pleased that you're still within the irritation phase."

I glared at him.

Rubin stopped the car, but the glossy black gate didn't move. He produced a remote from his coat pocket and pressed the only button. The gate retracted upwards along the parking garage roof.

"This is the Oak Bay Tower. There are eighteen floors, each containing six two-bedroom apartments. If you select this building, it's likely you'll never use the underground parking. Since you don't have a vehicle, the building's management will not issue you a remote button." Rubin pulled into a parking spot marked VISITOR with white stenciled letters.

I followed him through the dank concrete garage into the stairwell and up to the building's lobby. He walked briskly to a panel of buttons near the large glass doors by the entrance.

"You gain access to the building with a key card. Each unique card is programmed for both the main door and the apartment of the cardholder. Once inside, you enter a security code here. Forget to enter this code and your key card will not open the door to your apartment."

I watched as another tenant entered the building using the procedure Rubin described. I felt the crease in my forehead deepen. I couldn't imagine needing or wanting this level of security.

"I think this is a bit too intense for me. Are the other buildings this secure?"

"More so. The next building on our tour has an armed doorman. Not to worry, you'll never need to tip him." Rubin entered a code into the panel.

"Somehow I don't think tipping would be my first concern in that scenario."

We got into the elevator. We reached the top floor and walked along a white corridor with dark slate floors. We looked very out of place in such posh surroundings. Rubin swiped the card at apartment 1806. The suite was simple but elegant. A regular-sized two-bedroom apartment. The dining area had a basic table and chair set. The living room had a microfiber couch. Modern art hung on the wall. I could have brought my backpack and made myself at home with one trip to the grocery store. But a half-hour bus ride from work? Not ideal.

For the next apartment, we went back downtown, to a brand new building I recognized from my first day in the city. It had a distinctive atrium connecting two towers. The second apartment was much more beautiful with a leather sofa set and stainless steel appliances. I felt heat coming from the floor. But the square footage was noticeably smaller. Sure enough, the lobby included a doorman, but he didn't look armed with more than an awful uniform. This building also had a receptionist and a front desk like a hotel. No matter how normal-looking, I couldn't get past the prospect of someone carrying a gun where I lived. Rubin suggested we should see all three apartments regardless.

For the last building, we drove through downtown and crossed the blue iron girder bridge near the Market Square. We followed the left fork in the road along the coast of Esquimalt. We parked next to a mid-century brown tower with wood siding. The bottom few feet of the exterior had a coating of moss and mildew creeping up from the ground. I wasn't sure what kind of security it provided, apart from being far from downtown.

Rubin pulled a key from his pocket and unlocked a mailbox on the side of the building. He took out two copper and glass pendants hung on brown leather cords. He placed one around my neck and the other on his own. It wasn't the weirdest thing I'd seen so far.

The décor reminded me of a slightly more modern version of my grandmother's house. The velveteen sofa and chenille chair looked dated, but charming. I sat down on the sofa and sunk in, like Goldilocks on Baby Bear's bed. Rubin smiled at me and I quickly stood up to continue the tour. At the end of the living room, the floor continued into an enclosed balcony sunroom adorned with ferns and a banana plant. I saw the Olympic Mountains in the distance. In the foreground,

Victoria's Inner Harbour lay to the left, slightly distorted by a curve in the thick glass. In front of me stretched a coastline of blue-green trees. A cruise ship came into view on the water.

"I like this one. Definitely. If it's up to me, I'll take this apartment," I said.

"Fair enough. However, the security system here is slightly different. If Esther isn't home, we can't get your 'key' to the building." Rubin held out his copper pendant.

We returned to the lobby and I followed him down a long hallway with kitschy orange, yellow, and brown geometric carpet. He knocked on the door and asked me to wait outside. I didn't hear or see anything and a few short minutes later, Rubin emerged with new shiny copper pendants.

"Wear this around your neck at all times while you're in the building. You have an additional pendant for guest use. I realize this seems ridiculous to you but take it seriously. I have no interest in having to undo a curse on you or anyone you choose to invite to visit. There are no other keys here, although you can lock the deadbolt from the inside while you're home. And like the other apartments, your accommodation includes a weekly housekeeping visit."

Rubin placed the new pendant around my neck before removing the original one. I held the little copper oval and twisted it around so I could see the marking under the glass. It looked like a 'Y' but the bottom stroke came up through the 'V'. The shape reminded me of a fork.

"Is there anything else I need to know? I'll take your word for it if I'm supposed to burn incense in the morning, chant before bed, or anything else," I said.

Rubin smiled. "Let's get your belongings from the motel. Assuming you're ready to move in tonight?"

I nodded and followed him back out the front door.

apartment buildings were punctuated by a dingy salon, a check-cashing office, a few low-budget convenience stores, and several boarded-up buildings with lettering peeled off the signage.

I watched the Inner Harbour get larger while the bus rolled down the road towards the bright blue iron bridge marking the entrance to the city's core. I needed a phone and work-appropriate clothes to become a true city girl. My first paycheck could handle those purchases. Next, I would invest in a laptop. Not having access to a computer at home bothered me. Since nearly one hundred percent of my income was at my disposal, aside from food and now a bus pass, I thought about what to do with my savings. Why save up for school when I already had the kind of job an education was supposed to deliver? Other than travel, which I couldn't take on for long periods while keeping my job, what else did I want to buy? I'd never been in a position to consider the question.

To make sure Ivan's morning coffee wasn't cold by the time he arrived, I had to kill some time before stopping at the cafe below Innoviro. I walked around the block and back while pedestrian volume increased. Tourist season, at least for thrifty vacationers, was starting to take hold. Nobody vacationed in Prince George aside from visiting family or using the city as a launch point for hunting or fishing trips. I wasn't accustomed to seeing people wander aimlessly.

I followed their example and lingered at a few shop windows, allowing myself to picture near-future shopping trips. How long could I work for Innoviro? Was I moving to Victoria for good?

I thought about Jonah and Cole and Faith being a part of my life. And I remembered the image of my parents. That vision. I couldn't think about it without a nagging need to know what it meant and how the story ended. Why had my mind's eye plucked that particular scene out of my timeline? I had to figure out whether it was legitimately something from the future. If so, what was significant about that argument?

I visualized getting back on the overnight bus and then bursting in the door, panicked and out of breath, frantic to see if they were all right. When they discovered that I left a good job, for nothing more than a dream about their well-being, my mom would frown, concerned and disappointed while Darryl would make some remark about my finding a creative new way to screw up my life.

I sighed. Things between my stepdad and me had grown more tense since I graduated from high school, but he wasn't a monster. He just wasn't at peace with my refusal to make decisions, or grow up, or move on to adulthood. Like he said, there was a time for childish behavior and my time was past. He wanted to see me in school or with a job that challenged my mind, not one that barely tapped my brain like the car dealership.

I looked at my reflection in the window of a hat boutique. The top of my reflected head lined up with a blue denim newsboy hat. I smiled noting the seams and partial pocket on top of the hat. If it hadn't been made of recycled jeans, it was meant to look that way. I saw the price tag and my smile fell. I kept walking. Shopping could wait.

I would keep working at Innoviro, and learn more about my abilities and how to control them. Once I grew more comfortable with Ivan, I could ask him for help. Maybe if I volunteered for testing, they'd teach me in return. Could I find a way to make a vision happen on command? Was it possible to learn more about a person or a place when I needed or wanted additional information? I'd certainly use my gift for the company if I could use it for myself too.

I assured myself I made all the right choices as I set Ivan's cup of coffee down on his desk. I hung my jacket on my chair and turned on my computer. The little alcove down the hall where Ivan had set up my desk was semi-private and had a window looking out onto the street. I sat with my back to the window, which I preferred, because it meant I had privacy regarding my monitor.

It was noticeably quieter on this side of the building and I had a view of the courtyard. Ivan's window looked out over Johnson Street, including the bridge and a large slice of the Harbour. I wasn't envious. I knew I was damn lucky to be employed at a sophisticated company and even more fortunate they'd sought me out in the first place.

I wasn't sure yet what my tasks were for the day - or for the rest of the week. So a Google search on 'psychic skills' felt like a responsible way to start my day. I quickly saw what a silly plan it was to conduct research like this online. All kinds of scams and nonsense crap popped up as the top search results. No thank-you to the 'reading' from a random website. What would they read? My electronic essence? Seriously. I tried a more academic approach and went to the website for Greater Victoria's public library. Maybe someone who had taken the time to write a book on the subject earned more credibility. I had clicked on a link titled 'Treasures of the Psychic Realm' when a knock on the wall next to me made me flinch.

"Irina, I wonder if I could have some of your time this morning," Ivan said, not phrasing it as a question. All I'd done so far was run his errands. But, at least he acted politely. My last boss snapped his orders at me.

I followed him to his office. "What can I do? Your coffee isn't cold, is it?"

It looked like he hadn't touched his soy vanilla latte. He looked confused for a second, and then said, "No, the coffee is fine. I wanted to take you on a little tour of the building. I meant to do it last week, but I had a few fires to put out." He looked at the copper and glass oval hanging around my neck and smiled. "I see Rubin was successful in getting you settled."

"Yes, I'm very happy with the new place. I have to say, I've never heard of an employer paying for accommodation *and* offering a wage. I feel like a …" I caught myself before I said 'princess' and my cheeks flushed. "It feels like everything is happening so fast."

"Rubin mentioned to me that you've been getting to know some of your co-workers and doing your best to learn more about Innoviro. I think it's time to have a more serious discussion about what we do here and why we've brought you on board."

I blushed. It had never occurred to me that my evening at Cymbals stood any chance of getting back to my boss. Was he put out? Or disappointed? My stomach sank.

"I *was* doing some research on my ability this morning – only because I wasn't sure what to work on today and I wanted to stay productive."

"That's very thoughtful of you." He showed no emotion with a perfect poker face and then smiled again. It looked odd, an unnatural smile. Was he disguising disappointment or contempt? I wondered if I'd ever feel comfortable around him. It occurred to me that he must have some kind of mutation as well.

What could it be? Was he like Rubin, able to read my thoughts?

He walked briskly to the end of the hall and the mysterious steel door. I hustled to keep up with him. I'd gotten used to seeing people pass my desk, coming and going through that door without knowing who they were, where they were going beyond the door, or what they did for Innoviro. The door opened to a small foyer containing a painting, a planter, and one elevator door. I followed Ivan into the elevator which played a folk-sounding flute and piano tune. I almost laughed and asked where he'd found the *Muzak*, but I refrained.

Ivan didn't say anything. He pushed a combination of numbers on the panel. The elevator moved downwards. I expected to go down several floors, but I had no idea how far down we went. The numbers on the wall looked more like a vintage phone interface than an elevator panel. Nothing indicated where the elevator was or where it was going, no digital display, no lights. I wondered how many levels the building had. I was sure I wouldn't see all of them.

The elevator finally stopped with a ding and the door opened. A white hallway stretched in front of us with pale tile floors and more stainless steel doors. We walked partway down the hall until we reached a window looking into a large lab.

"Okay, starting off our tour this morning, we're looking at Innoviro's main research and development testing area. We won't disturb the more sensitive specialized labs on this floor. As I'm sure you've come to understand, much of the testing we do here relates to genetic research. We also experiment with viral strains, bacteria, plant matter, and other substances that affect people like us differently than other humans. We also do research in the areas of climatology and geology."

As Ivan spoke, I realized I'd been holding my breath as I gawked at the handful of lab coat and goggle-wearing individuals who were all going about their work, mixing liquid-filled beakers, extracting droplets, entering data on keyboards, and God knows what else. I had no frame of reference to understand. I didn't recognize anyone.

"The testing we're viewing here relates to a contract we're fulfilling for a cosmetic company developing a new form of sunscreen. The approach is two-fold. First, we will deliver accurate test results to our client regarding toxicity levels of their formula. Many manufacturers of chemical products sold for mass consumption achieve a higher level of credibility by participating in the kind of independent testing we provide. Second, every time we take on a new project, we concurrently gather data for our purposes." Ivan paused to gauge my comprehension.

"In the case of this sunscreen, we're assessing the client's formulas to determine if they're effective and safe for the general public. But we also want ideas for health solutions to benefit our more photo-sensitive employees and subjects. What I mean by 'subject' is someone we deal with that doesn't directly work for us. Not every person we discover with a genetic gift will receive employment with Innoviro, but we intend to help everyone we can. And not to worry, collecting this data is perfectly legal."

"Even if it's not legal, it has to be done, right?" I blurted out and slapped my hand over my mouth. "Sorry, I know we're doing everything by the book, but I understand what Jonah and Cole were saying. This is sensitive work that most scientists wouldn't even believe." I immediately regretted confirming that I had been discussing Innoviro's secrets with other employees. "But, they weren't giving me any details about their work or anything like that!" I needed to stop talking.

"That's okay. I want you to become part of our team and develop an understanding of our work. I don't expect you to be involved in the science of what we do, but I'd like to help you understand your gift as much as possible. I think an important part of living with a mutation is specific knowledge. In your case, your genetic variation is located almost exclusively in your brain, which is difficult and time-consuming to investigate. Fortunately, we've been successful in examining psychics and telepaths post-mortem, so we already know quite a bit."

I felt my eyes widening from the full impact of his words. I remembered Cole's insistence that all Innoviro's human testing had strict safety standards. How much information would the company share with me and how quickly? What exactly would I provide in return?

"This is a lot to take in, but not to worry, we are completely prepared to train you and to develop your role here at Innoviro." Ivan walked towards the end of the hall and I followed. We passed more identical steel doors. I noticed Roman numerals on each door. We reached the unmarked metal door at the end of the hall and Ivan pushed down on the long bar handle.

The stairwell behind the door led up a narrow brick hallway. A fluorescent pot light in the ceiling outside the doorway threw off a bit of light, but the passage got darker as we walked upward and only dim natural light glimmered. As we climbed, I noticed dampness in the air and a musty smell growing fouler as we got closer to the top.

"I know you've already seen some new and strange things in the last month, but I want to prepare you for the people you're about to see. These catacombs are a haven of sorts for people whose gifts or mutations are more extreme. For physical and or emotional reasons, these people don't feel they're able to lead normal lives, integrated into society. I'm cautioning you because it can be embarrassing to gasp or stare."

"Thanks, I appreciate that. I'm not the sort of person who stares, but I have a feeling you're about to show me things I've never seen."

"I don't want to alarm you with the conditions here. Innoviro has made every effort to make these people comfortable, but you can understand that some individuals reject anything they might view as charity."

"So they're camping out in a sewer?"

"Put bluntly, yes. Rubin keeps an eye on this area for me. He makes every effort to fit in, although he has an apartment of his own."

"Will he be there today?"

"Probably not. I've sent him on an out-of-town errand and he's gone by now."

We reached an arch at the top of the stairs. I followed him through the open doorway and the unpleasant chill that had been wafting down the stairs evolved into a forceful reek. Decaying fish, seaweed, salt, excrement, and diesel fuel made the seaside sewer location unmistakable.

The sound of running water and muffled voices increased as we walked along a wet sidewalk that hugged the wall of the expanding tunnel. The corridor opened into a central room, very dimly lit by small shafts of sunlight high above and a few small fires in barrels and makeshift pits. I tried to guess what street we were under and where. How did a place like this remain undisturbed? I'd seen a shelter a few blocks north along the waterfront at the point where downtown transitioned to a light industrial area. If someone living in a sewer frequented a doorway in that neighborhood, they would probably blend effortlessly.

We paused at the edge of the room, unnoticed so far by the community in front of us. In total, roughly two dozen figures stood, leaned on the wall, or sat on lawn chairs and milk crates. Tents lined an open landing on the far side of the room. The moat around that little concrete island would have been charming if it didn't have noticeable flotsam and bits of foam throughout. Other than being a hidden tent city, nothing looked out of the ordinary. I kept scanning the room, straining my eyes in the poor light. Did Ivan plan to introduce me to anyone?

Then I recognized the bouncer from the bar. Casey! That was his name. He was having an animated, yet friendly-looking conversation with a small woman around my size. He gestured with his arms, shook them, and the unbelievable happened. His scars opened wide and another set of arms flipped out. Casey's gigantic muscular arms became four slim-sized arms in the blink of an eye. If I hadn't been watching, I wouldn't have known what happened. A surreal mythological character stood where a man once was. The woman he was talking to laughed and a giant red forked tongue rolled out and flicked the air. Something ruffled along the side of her neck and disappeared again like her skin had fissures that opened and shut seamlessly.

Ivan put his hand on my shoulder and I jolted. I'd been

staring. In my mind, I whispered that I was so sorry. No words came out. He gestured ahead and I followed as we approached an abandoned cardboard shelter consisting of a large floor piece and a smaller open box propped up behind it. It made my heart ache to think of someone sleeping and passing long, lonely, hungry hours on scraps of cardboard like this.

As my foot connected with the cardboard floor, the sewer dissolved around me and I was transported to the ocean beach from my earlier vision. Suddenly I stood behind my mystery man. He walked on the sand ahead of me next to a giant wave. The sea curled down, crashing into calm bubbling fingers on the sand. As I watched the back of his head, he turned and looked directly at me with a glass-eyed expression that chilled me. My reflex to step backward yanked me off the beach and brought me right back into the sewer with my feet on bare concrete again. Ivan looked at me intently. "What did you see?"

"That man. I saw him before I came to Victoria. I had a vision of him and I can't tell you exactly why, but it was extremely compelling. Before I got on the Greyhound and came down here, I had seen other parts of the city. But, with this guy, it was like we had a connection, even though I had never met or even seen him in my life." I lowered my voice as I caught my tone and volume amplifying.

"Would you recognize the setting around him, if you saw it again in real life?"

"I think so."

"Good," Ivan replied firmly. "Very good. I hoped that bringing you down here would force a stronger connection. This," he gestured at the cardboard shelter, "is where Ilya slept.

He's my son and he's missing."

I gasped. It made total sense now, why I'd seen the young man with Ivan. If I found Ilya, I might finally figure out what my visions meant. Most of them, anyway.

Ivan said it was easier to leave by passing through the sewer instead of going back to Innoviro. We took another stairwell to an alley while Ivan talked about Ilya. He sounded so far away mere paces ahead of me.

Chapter 11

His face had been fading from my mind, but now I had a clearer picture than ever. And I had a name. Ilya. I connected to him for a reason. But what was it? I'd come here with wild notions of finding him, along with whatever insight came with him. My priorities had completely changed, which made sense on the surface. Regardless, guilt gnawed at me. Everything had become about building my new life and Ilya was obviously in trouble, maybe even in pain.

Ivan and I emerged from the sewer stairwell in another hidden corridor, much like Fan Tan Alley, only quieter. A steel door thudded shut behind us and I looked up to see a faded yellow sign in Chinese characters hanging over a tiny herbal remedy shop. The alley smelled of spicy incense. On our right office windows sported closed blinds. To the left, a metal fire escape zigzagged up the side of a brick building. Around the corner, a dark tunnel led to muffled traffic and the voices of pedestrians.

"Irina, I want you to take the rest of the day off. You've got a lot to process now and I don't think you'll be any good to us with so much on your mind."

"I feel bad, but I think you're right." I laughed nervously.

"I want you to consider one more thing before you come back to work tomorrow morning. You remember what I said about the research we've been able to do on psychic brain activity?"

"Yes. It's hard to forget something like that."

"Our research has produced an experimental drug. My motives are selfish, but I think any man would do the same to find his son. I'm hoping you'll consent to receiving this drug. It's a serum that I believe can enhance your abilities."

"Enhance how? What would change?"

"We can accelerate your skills to a level you'd take years to reach naturally, if ever. Ilya has been missing for two months now. If you feel connected to him, there has to be a reason. His gift is extra-sensory, like yours, but somewhat different. He's more like Rubin, but stronger and capable of creating illusions. He should be able to get out of trouble on his own. The fact that he hasn't come home makes me certain something fairly serious has happened. Understandably, I don't want to turn to the police and risk an investigation that exposes my work or any of the many people who rely on Innoviro for discretion. I think you are our best hope to find him, and if you do, I think we can solve more than one mystery."

Ivan stopped talking and we stared at each other for a long moment. His face was as motionless as a mask; an artist's rendition of fortitude. I broke eye contact and looked around the alley, but we were still alone.

"I don't know what to say. I understand *why* you're asking, but I get the *what* part too and that's pretty scary. I've never done any regular drugs, never mind mind-altering stuff. I mean, I've smoked a little weed, but this is different." I couldn't bring myself to confess that I'd recently contemplated this exact exchange of resources between me and Innoviro.

"I know this is huge and that you're already overwhelmed. Take some time and think about it. Know that your job is NOT at stake. If you decide not to take the drug, we'll still keep trying. I'm grateful for whatever help you can offer."

I nodded, thanked him, and walked slowly out towards the street noise of Chinatown. I wasn't worried he would change his mind about giving me time off, but it felt odd. I had only the car dealership to compare as an employment situation and they were as different as night and day. Most people wouldn't have sent me off to think just because things got stressful. Then again, I didn't exactly have much experience with decent employers.

My last (and only other) boss had been arrested for theft and fraud. Lucky for me, the police decided I was an innocent dupe during the investigation, or Darryl never would have let me hear the end of it. I smiled at my improving luck in jumping from one end of the workplace quality spectrum to the other.

I started walking up the hill, in the direction of my old motel room, contemplating how I could make the most of a day off. I slowed my pace to think. I went in the direction of the old service station where I'd been attacked. Maybe I had something useful to do today after all. I started walking faster and faster as I hit the intersection ahead, turned right, crossed again left, and nearly speed-marching, I covered the parking lot in only a handful of paces.

I rounded the corner to the alley head-first with my heart

thudding between my ears. The attack and ensuing fear refreshed like a wound pulled open. I slapped my hand onto the peeling paint of the brick wall and willed myself to stand motionless. I let the attack play back in my mind, begging the wall for an image of the man – or thing – I couldn't see with my naked eyes. Nothing came.

A gust of chilly ocean air cut through the alley and I flinched. A rumbling engine got louder and an old pickup truck pulled into the alley. A grizzled mechanic yelled at me to get out of the way as his rig passed a few feet behind me. He parked by a garage door and I heard the creak-squeak of his rusty door. Panic took over and I bolted back towards Innoviro.

As soon as I got back among the Chinatown pedestrians, I slowed my pace. Another reason to re-appear at Innoviro suddenly hit me. Mice! I'd forgotten Chester's weekly supply and he was due for another feeding today. I veered over to the pet store. Despite the security at my apartment, I felt safer at Innoviro, even though I knew the truck driver wasn't my assailant. For starters, he wasn't at least seven feet tall.

Walking down the street with living food items bothered me less than it had the first time. I smirked at my diminishing remorse about their fate. Ilya still had my guilt's attention, so someone else would have to mourn the mice. I swung open the main door, cradling the box in my other hand as I maneuvered through the opening. I instinctively looked over to the front desk.

Melissa's eyes met mine. "He gives you the day off and you don't even take it. If you kiss his ass too much, it'll backfire, you know."

I stared at her as the door thudded shut.

"Ivan left for Vancouver anyway, so he's not here to see you working," Melissa went on, "Shouldn't you know that, being his *personal* assistant and all?"

"I'm dropping off Chester's mice. I was supposed to get them this afternoon 'cause he's all out and needs to eat."

The lab door at the end of the hall opened and several people in lab coats exited and walked towards me. I saw Jonah's face and I felt a rush of excitement. He looked downright handsome in his lab coat. His dark hair and ocean-blue eyes stood out against the white of his coat.

He waved at me and smiled back. "Have you had lunch yet?"

I opened my mouth to answer, but Melissa's voice cut me off. "She's not working today. Ivan gave her the day off." Her tone dripped with bitterness. "But, you can have lunch with me."

"Ah, well, I guess-" Jonah struggled.

"Lunch sounds perfect." I cut off the conversation between them. "I'm dropping off a couple of mice for Chester. Let me give him one now and put the other away."

I sped into Ivan's office and dropped one mouse in Chester's terrarium, and another in the small shavings-lined plastic cage on the shelf.

Jonah held the front door for me while Melissa scowled. I nodded at her as I passed. I hopped quickly down the stairs, eager to put some distance between us and Melissa's ears.

We reached the corridor to the street and I relaxed. "I need to talk. Can we pick a lunch spot where we'll have some privacy?"

"I heard that Ivan took you down to the catacombs this morning."

"So you know what I want to talk about."

"No, but I have some ideas. There's a little Indian cafe

around the corner." Jonah pointed at Wharf Street in the direction of the Inner Harbour. "It's dark and the booths are very private."

We rounded the corner and turned up the hill to find the restaurant exactly where it was supposed to be. As Jonah promised, it was a dark little storefront with three rows of booths along the wall.

A cheerful woman in a bright green and gold sari sat us at the back of the restaurant, perfectly concealed from the rest of the world. We ordered chai and the curried chicken lunch special that Jonah recommended. After the waitress left, he sipped his tea, looking at me patiently.

"Okay, here's the deal. Ivan wants me to take a drug. Probably an injection. Probably several of them." Suddenly, I felt terrified that I said the wrong thing to the wrong person. I had to trust someone in Victoria that I could relate to and talk to, or this bizarre new life would not work for long. I hoped with every cell in my body that my 'someone' could be Jonah. "It's to make my visions of his missing son stronger."

"So he told you about Ilya?"

"It's more than that. Did you ever meet this guy, Ilya?"

"Sure, we all knew him. He didn't technically work for Innoviro, but he came around a bit to talk to Ivan."

"The visions I started having in Prince George, the one that truly compelled me to come to Victoria, was of Ilya. Something about him and the look on his face … I knew I *HAD* to come here. Ivan says his gift is like Rubin's because he can read minds, but Ilya is stronger and capable of creating illusions. So maybe he reached out to me. If this guy 'sent' a vision, is he responsible for all of it? Or maybe Rubin was involved from the get-go, driving my need to get here. Who knows, but now I feel like finding Ilya is something I'm meant to do. It's a huge leap though, letting a man I hardly know put an experimental drug in my veins." I looked down at the table and noticed I gripped the edge with white-knuckled fingers.

"So you're afraid to take the drug?" Jonah's expression suggested he absorbed some of my tension.

"Shouldn't I have some reservations? Wouldn't you?"

"I've been working for Ivan a lot longer, so I know from experience that he's not the malicious sort. But he takes risks. Everything we do is experimental and that's risky. I'm not going to tell you to do what he says, but if it were me, I would. I have before," he said, getting quieter.

We exchanged a look and I told him with my eyes that I wasn't judging him. "Is that something you want to talk about? Or can you?"

"I wasn't born with … the way I am. At university, I did some monumentally stupid shit with a virus and I got deathly sick. Ivan found me in the hospital in Vancouver and he offered me treatments to stabilize what I'd done to myself. It's not extreme to say he saved my life."

"The more I learn about Ivan, the more it sounds like he's some kind of saint. How can I *not* help his son?"

"I wish I could make this easier, Irina, but it sounds like time is a factor."

"If it were any other medical treatment, I'd get a second opinion or do some research. But this isn't exactly something I can look up on Wikipedia, is it?"

"How about this? I'll look around a bit this afternoon. I'll ask a few people if I can. Maybe I can find out specifically what Ivan referenced so you've got a bit more information before you decide."

"I don't want you to get into trouble over this."

"I won't do anything stupid. Do you know how to find the Harbourside Pub?"

I nodded. It was down the road from my new apartment.

"Meet me there at eight o'clock tonight. And hopefully, I'll provide some reassurance." Jonah reached out and held my hand.

Blood rushed up into my cheeks and I looked away.

After we had left the restaurant and said goodbye, I made a pit stop at a cell phone store. I'd promised myself a laptop and a phone with my first paycheck, which sat idly in my bank account. It was finally time to make big purchases. For the phone, I had modest criteria – something sleek, but not the latest, biggest model.

All I needed was a phone plan for texting along with a search engine and a map. A great camera would be nice too. I said 'no' to several monthly plans in favor of a pay-as-you-go system until I set up a credit card. It was inconvenient but cheap and, in case I ran out of money again, the most sensible choice.

On the next block over I made my way to a mid-size computer store I'd walked past several times. I already knew what not to bother with, and what I really needed. I wanted more than a netbook, but I didn't need hard-core processing capabilities or enough storage for huge applications. I wouldn't make movies or mix music or play RAM-sucking video games. I didn't want an inflated warranty either. I left the store pleased with a middle-of-the-road laptop and made my way straight home.

I set the bag from the phone store down on my small dining table and brought my laptop into the living room. My first major task was to figure out how to connect myself to the building's wireless network. Rubin had provided the password when I moved in, but I was surprised at how easily I connected. The laptop automatically detected the network and asked me for a password. In minutes, I resumed my search for information on psychic phenomena. Not much else mattered.

I checked my email, but there was nothing new. The prospect of doing research exhausted me after such an eventful day. I wasn't even sure where to start, beyond replicating my earlier Google search. I sat back for a moment to stretch my legs. It had been a long day, but I had a lot to show for it, including plans for the evening that made me giddy. I closed my eyes and breathed deeply. My good day wasn't over yet.

Excited nerves made me restless. I pictured Jonah's face, specifically, his magnetic ocean-blue eyes. No, his smile – and his wavy black hair. I let the memory of dancing with him overtake my mind. I snuggled into my couch and let myself dream of his strong arms around me again. It might happen soon. I jumped up, grabbed my Tarot cards, and created a spread while I pictured Jonah's face.

Chapter 12

I woke up on my couch staring at the rain screensaver I'd chosen at the computer store. I looked at the clock on the wall. It was somewhere between eight-forty-five and nine o'clock. The clock only had dots for each quarter hour. Either way, I was late to meet Jonah. I leaped off the couch, quickly scanned the room for my purse, grabbed it, and slung it on in one motion.

Checking my reflection in the hall mirror, I ran for the front door. I pressed the elevator button, but after a few seconds, I turned and raced down the stairs. At the bottom, I flung the door open and found myself at the side entrance. I hit the pavement running and almost made it to the front sidewalk before I heard my name.

"You're lucky. I know where you live," said Jonah with a sly smile as I reached him at the front door.

I stood in front of him, panting. He grinned and I felt a flush of heat in my cheeks. "I fell asleep! I'm sorry," I blurted, embarrassed. "I didn't forget, I promise!"

"It's okay. I stopped by the pub and it's hopping busy. I don't want to wait for a table. I should have thought of that."

"There's a cute little ice cream stand down at the sea wall, near the park. How about ice cream?"

Great, ice cream. Good and childish. Why couldn't I make note of some hip bistro or fusion joint? And *did* I want that drink, mostly to soothe my nerves? I wanted Jonah to have several drinks and relax a bit too. Now that I had committed to staying in Victoria, I could commit to having a boyfriend. Whether or not he felt the same was debatable.

Adam, my last boyfriend had been a short-lived situation. He was tall and slim with light blonde hair and an angular, but attractive face. He was smart enough to keep up an interesting conversation, but not so accomplished that I felt intimidated. Adam hadn't shown a strong interest in me, but he flirted with me at a bush party one night. The next day, I called and invited him out for coffee. I felt like I'd taken charge. We dated for about two months until fall came and he left for trade school in Alberta. Only a few weeks passed before he called to tell me he'd met someone else and had no plans to return to Prince George.

Jonah hadn't shown a strong interest in me either. So why was I staring up at his bright eyes with so much anticipation?

"I'd love to get ice cream." He smiled. "I think I know the place you mean. You know I haven't had ice cream in years."

Of course he hadn't had ice cream in years. He'd been dating grown-ups. I decided to roll with it anyway. A booze-free setting was better for learning whatever he managed to dig up about Ivan's drug programs. After all, that's why he wanted to meet me for a drink. He was keeping a promise and ideally helping me cooperate with our boss.

Jonah followed me toward the park entrance. We turned down the paved path that bordered the park fence and the apartment building next to mine. The ice cream stand was shaped like a large blackberry and had a few moms with children milling around its service counter. We waited for our turn while an indecisive toddler chose between an ice cream sandwich and a scoop of chocolate. When it was our turn, the adolescent boy behind the counter quickly produced our plain vanilla soft-serve cones. We walked towards the ocean under a gentle breeze. As we walked, I concentrated on licking off all the frilled edges from my tower of ice cream.

"So I poked around at work this afternoon," Jonah said. "I checked some of the obvious drives and folders. My workstation has a relatively high permissions level, but anything worth looking at is password protected."

"I understand. Don't dig too deep. I don't want you to get in trouble on my account," I said with as much sincerity as I could muster through my frustration.

"I would have asked around, but I don't know anyone in pharmacology all that well. I'm sure Ivan has documentation and testing records on whatever drug he wants to give you. If you ask him, I think he'll share the information. He won't want you to participate in anything you're uncomfortable doing."

We walked a bit farther in silence. I had assumed Jonah would find something, at least a mention of the drug, within the files at Innoviro. How could something either guarded or fresh out of the lab, be a trustworthy substance I should let them inject into my veins? Even if Ivan showed me charts and research findings, what insight could I gain from them?

Jonah and I rounded a corner. The path diverged around

a ring of shrubs and a large arbutus tree. On the one side, the path jutted out to a viewpoint looking over to the Inner Harbour. On the other, a bench sat tucked into a semicircle of overgrown juniper bushes. The sun had nearly dropped behind the hills in Esquimalt, casting vivid yellow-orange light onto downtown. Bright pink clouds floated like cotton candy in the sky. If we kept going the Harbour would greet us in its gown of twinkling lights. My sunroom balcony had that view at every sunset. I turned towards the bench. I suddenly felt like I needed a break.

Jonah sat down next to me. He touched the side of my mouth and I jumped.

"Sorry; you had some ice cream …" he said sheepishly.

I wished I was the kind of girl who carried a mirror in my purse, but I knew better than to bother searching. I looked out at the ocean and the pink pieces of light floating on the water.

"You look tense."

His arm slipped behind my back as I kept staring ahead. I turned to answer and found myself nose-to-nose with him. I tried to think of something to say as he tilted his head and leaned in, touching my lips with his. I'd forgotten how sweet a gentle kiss could be and I reached out to hold him. The gesture encouraged him. He wrapped his free arm around me and with the other hand gently cradled my neck.

His tongue found mine. My hand slid up from his shoulder, along the back of his neck, into his soft hair as I wrapped my other arm around his waist. He moved around me, lowering his hand from my neck to my breast. Heat surged through my body with a wave of physical need. And suddenly something was different.

My mouth went dry. I felt tired, even sleepy. A pounding pain started inside my head. I couldn't breathe …

I regained consciousness, suddenly back in my apartment, lying flat on my couch. Jonah sat on my coffee table. His elbows rested on his knees with his hands clasped as he stared intently at me. Fortunately, he had thought to go through my purse and find my guest pendant, so we didn't set off some sort of alarm.

I still didn't know exactly what would happen if someone came in here without a special amulet. Would that person contract a freak illness? Or injury of another sort? I made a mental note to ask Ivan or Rubin exactly what tea and runes had to do with a high-tech science lab.

I sat up, feeling as though I'd been asleep longer than Sleeping Beauty. I blinked painfully.

Jonah looked nervous and angry as he wrung his hands. "Oh thank God!" He reached out and then retracted his arm before touching me.

"Did I … pass out or something?" The sudden thought that I'd been drugged made my stomach drop like a stone. Jonah handed me a glass of water he had ready at his side.

"No, not really," Jonah said cautiously. "It's my fault. I thought since you were different, varied, like me, you'd be immune. I was so sure!" He spoke more to himself than to me.

"You don't think there was something in that ice cream, do you?" I said, after a sip of water.

"No, it *was* my fault. But I would never drug you – or hurt you! Shit. This is complicated," he said as he stood. "I sort of drained you. You know the human body is mostly water, right?"

I frowned again but nodded.

"Remember in the restaurant when I moved that water on the menu and absorbed it with my hand?"

"Sure, I get it. You can manipulate water," I said groggily.

"It's more than telekinesis though. Ivan calls it 'aquakinesis' which I think is stupid because there's more to it than that. My body feeds off water. I'm constantly drawing it in from the air around me. And it's getting worse. It's why I need to live in a humid climate, near water if possible." He paced to the far side of my living room. "I'm so sorry." He darted towards the door and I heard it slam a half-second later.

I tried to get up off the couch and my head swam. I lay back down on the comfortable plush cushions. I tried to say something and nearly choked. I grabbed my glass of water and downed the entire thing. I wanted to run after Jonah, but it took all my energy to adjust myself on the couch. My eyelids grew heavier and heavier. I gave in, and let sleep take me.

Chapter 13

My apartment was full of bright sunlight that Saturday morning. And I had a throbbing headache knocking around my skull, worse than any hangover. My memory of the night before flooded back.

I saw Jonah's face and remembered the kiss, accompanied by a stab of self-pity. Did this mean I could never kiss Jonah, let alone do anything more intimate? His inability to touch another person must have been the reason he'd let Ivan experiment on him already.

I went to the kitchen and made a pot of coffee. Knowing the coffee wouldn't help dehydration, I chugged another glass of water while the coffee brewed. I sat at my kitchen table to wait, prying my laptop open. I loved how quickly it booted up and I grinned even in my miserable state. I clicked on the curled-up orange Firefox logo and I typed 'aquakinesis' into Google. I found an entry in the Urban Dictionary that read, *'The ability to manipulate water, create water or to change the state of water.'*

That didn't sound so bad. And not a recipe for draining the life out of people. Something had gone wrong because he had done it to himself, unnaturally. I would probably never understand the science, not for Jonah's work, Cole's, Ivan's, or anyone else inside the walls at Innoviro. Not in a way that would serve a purpose.

The only thing left to look for was my gift, though I knew I couldn't get real answers from the Internet. I typed 'precognition' into the search engine and hit the Enter key after a moment's hesitation. A Wikipedia entry came up first, so I opened the page without skimming the rest of my results.

'In parapsychology, precognition, also called future sight, and second sight, is a type of extrasensory perception that would involve the acquisition or effect of future information that cannot be deduced from presently available and normally acquired sense-based information or laws of physics and/or nature.'

I knew I'd also seen past events in my visions, so again, there was more going on than a website could reveal. What did I think was going to happen, anyway? If I bought a computer of my own and searched in private, some new resource would turn up or a miraculous insight would unravel in my mind? These answers weren't up for grabs online and I had to accept that.

I snapped the laptop shut on Wikipedia. Only Ivan could help me. I'd have to be brave, ask, and trust him to find out what I wanted to know. The saying 'curiosity killed the cat' flitted through my mind and I felt the now familiar hopelessness of failing to make sense of the bizarre tangle of my new life.

After I clicked on my television, I remembered the bag on my dining table. I hadn't set up my phone yet. I could do something practical that had a measurable result. Suddenly I wanted to hear my mom's voice very badly. I grabbed the bag and opened the box. The manual with the phone was a thick text-heavy booklet, but after impatiently re-reading the first few pages, I figured out how to activate the phone and add the pre-paid phone card money. In less than half an hour I had transferred my collection of phone numbers from sticky notes, receipts in my purse, and from my memory, into my shiny new device.

I revisited one of the first numbers I'd programmed – my parents' home phone in Prince George. My finger hovered over the icon with the green symbol of a receiver. Would Mom get angry, again? Or would Darryl answer the phone and quiz me about the quality and stability of my new job? I pressed the red receiver symbol instead.

Fat lot of good a phone would do me if I had nobody to call. I scrolled through the rest of the address book I'd just created and stalled on a strange name. I had Faith's number and I decided to call it. I didn't really know what I planned to say, or if I'd have the guts to ask her about the pharmacology department, but the idea sounded reasonable so I dialed. And she answered on the first ring.

"Hi Faith, it's Irina. I hope I didn't catch you ..." but she was so excited to hear my voice, I didn't get a chance to finish. She'd been waiting to hear from me. She wanted to know if I'd come to watch her game. Faith was on Victoria's only roller derby team and they were playing a team from Vancouver that evening. I had only a general idea of what roller derby involved – roller skates and a rink.

Faith must have thought I had enough knowledge to enjoy the game, but I also got the impression she wanted to put butts in seats and would have asked a girl on the street to watch. I didn't know Faith apart from one meal and a few nods at work. But I usually read people fairly accurately. Was that part of my gift? She did sound sincere in wanting me to come out. I refocused on Faith's instructions to get the details I needed.

I agreed to meet her at the Esquimalt Arena, which was not far from my apartment. In the meantime, I needed groceries, breakfast, and then a well-earned hot shower.

I lived less than a block from a run-down, but reliable supermarket. Victoria reminded me with subtle nuances how long the city had been standing. Compared to Prince George, Victoria was the Old World and the streets of suburban Esquimalt were no exception. As I walked down the street away from my building, towards the supermarket, I noted in more detail how the structures around me documented the passage of time. I passed restored heritage houses from the early 1900's as well as weathered 60's and 70's complexes not yet ready for rescue. One large glass and metal tower contrasted the original bricks and vines of the neighborhood.

Street signs bore the poppy-based insignia of Canadian veterans, marking the area as belonging to the military, much as the red dragon signs on Fisgard pointed me down to Chinatown.

I reached the dated plaza with the vintage supermarket and walked through the automatic doors into the artificially chilly air of the Garden City Grocer. It felt like walking into a slice of my childhood. From the kitsch cartoon wall signage for each department right down to the brown and sand-speckled flooring, the interior of the store hadn't changed for decades. I grabbed a plastic basket, feeling like a kid in a candy shop instead of a near twenty-something in a supermarket.

Food shopping for only me was liberating, now that I had settled into my life and had time to appreciate small things. Fortunately, the products on Garden City's shelves were up-to-the-minute. I got the brand of tortillas I liked. I got the expensive ice cream sandwiches Darryl used to forbid. Everything I bought was mine. Nobody else was going to eat my food or complain about my choices. I walked home contemplating how little it took to sate me.

My shower, on the other hand, was a bit more unnerving. I hadn't paid attention to my body while getting dressed. I hadn't looked at my reflection when I twisted my hair into a clip. As I prepared to disrobe again, I watched myself in the bathroom mirror, unclipping my hair and removing my jeans and T-shirt. I saw the marks left by Jonah's touch, or more specifically, his 'variation'.

I noticed that everyone at Innoviro used the word 'variation' and it sounded dispassionate, until now. My lips were parched and now that I looked closely, the skin around my mouth looked burned. Streaks on my back resembled bruises. He had burned me right through my clothes! I took off the cotton bra I'd slept in and evaluated the raw red hand print on my left breast. I wished I hadn't looked first. I got into the shower and rushed through my soap and shampoo routine with the sharp stinging pain of my wounds chasing me the whole time.

I fought the urge to cry, getting progressively angrier at the unfairness of my situation. I replayed my hazy recollection of his rant last night. He'd done this to girls before, obviously not intentionally, but he could have said something. If he warned me, would it have gone any differently? Had he ever touched me before? He probably couldn't touch anyone, at least not for any duration. Was it emotion or excitement that brought out his ability? Was he angry at me now? Why hadn't I heard from him? I should be the angry one, covered in wounds and all. I wondered if Jonah's friends knew this part of his 'variation.' I decided not to discuss the incident with Faith. I didn't know her well enough yet.

As I finished getting dressed and applying my standard minimal amount of eye shadow and mascara, I came to the lip-gloss step and paused. I sized up my mouth's reflection in my hand mirror. I added a few dabs of concealer around my mouth. I thought the burn was still noticeable, but I'd stand up to a quick review without questions.

I took a deep breath, shouldered my purse, and set my mind on auto-pilot. As I walked down the building's stairwell, I committed to watching Faith's game without dwelling on injections or variations or strange lost boys.

Chapter 14

I arrived at the arena early to look for Faith and say hello before the match began. I hoped she'd introduce me to some of her other spectators so I'd have someone to sit with during the game. At a bare minimum, people would see me talking with her before I went to sit by myself. I didn't like eating in a restaurant or going to a public movie theatre alone. The idea made me feel pitiful, as though the other people around me would all immediately notice my alone status and label me weird, dorky, and probably friendless. It also occurred to me that Jonah could show up, and I wanted to make sure he knew I'd come at Faith's invitation, not because I was trying to track him.

I walked through the front doors and immediately saw the ticket table Faith had described, complete with a sign for "Will Call" tickets. I scanned the small lobby for signs of Faith's distinctive purple dreads. I picked out a few of her teammates and it dawned on me that she had a specific reason for choosing purple to color her hair. Their bright violet sleeveless jerseys bore the name "UnbearaBelles" over a logo depicting ball bearings spilling out the side of a broken roller skate wheel. *Clever*, I thought with a wry smile.

Faith herself was nowhere in sight, so after I collected my ticket, I walked around the arena. It was obviously a hockey arena during the winter months. Springy rubber flooring looked like many blades had passed back and forth across it. Old sweat lingered in the mildly humid air. I walked up to the plywood border of the concrete rink and watched through scuffed plexiglass as the skaters warmed up, gliding back and forth around the oval in endless leisurely laps. Watching them stretch their legs in yoga-like twists reminded me of their daintier ice skating counterparts – a guaranteed unwelcome comparison. Like Faith, and to a lesser degree, me, these girls were all a bit edgy, as though they'd show up for an all-female Fight Club accessorized with glitter and stockings. I felt a pang of longing to have my blue streaks back to their original vibrancy.

"Faith told me she'd invited you, but she wasn't sure you'd show," said a familiar voice behind me.

I felt my shoulders flinch. I'd been concentrating harder than I realized.

"Sorry, I didn't mean to startle you." Cole placed his hand on my shoulder. He left his hand on me as he moved to my other side. I must have needed the hug because I didn't want to move even though my instincts warned me that I sent the wrong signal. An earthy unmistakably masculine scent, probably nothing more than his deodorant, wafted past and I relaxed. I knew now I wouldn't be hugging Jonah any time soon. I had to resist the urge to lean my head to the left and rest it on Cole's shoulder in return. I'd had my fill of bad ideas for the weekend.

"Are you okay?" Cole asked when I still hadn't said anything.

"Oh, sure. I had a long day. A long week is more like it."

"Yeah, I talked to Jonah."

"What?" I recoiled in shock. I felt furrows deepening on my forehead.

"He's worried that you're freaked out – and clearly you are. But you're not alone. You won't be the first of us to do trial injections. " Cole's eyes were full of compassion.

"Oh that." I relaxed my shoulders. A girl in bright red and pitch black skated right past the boards and my attention whipped back out to the rink.

"Have you got something more important going on at the moment?"

"No, that's pretty much it," I said. "I was just thinking about …" I paused to think of something other than welts on my body. "Home and my life in Prince George." I lied extremely poorly and I hoped Cole couldn't tell.

"Did Faith tell you she reserved a spot for you in the VIP section?"

I assumed he wanted to change the subject. "No, I don't think so, but I'm guessing you can point me in the right direction." I forced a smile.

"What, do I stink? You're sitting with me unless you'd rather not." Cole grinned to show me he was joking. He put his hand on my waist, guiding me towards the first stairwell in the bleachers. We climbed and shuffled down to a cluster of roped-off rows, directly behind the players' seating. If someone had told me back in Prince George that I'd be sitting in a VIP section at something sporty I would have thought they'd been visiting a parallel universe.

Hockey in PG was like football in the American South. The sport created hometown heroes and devoted fans, while the oddballs who couldn't get into it might as well have disappeared. Not that primo seating in a hockey rink was the strangest development in my world, but it made me suddenly glad I was starting to lead a bigger, weirder life.

We continued watching the growing number of girls skating practice laps, and Faith's purple dreads finally appeared on the rink, albeit crushed under a round white helmet that matched her teammates.

Cole instructed me on the rules of roller derby. Each team had five girls on the track for every round, although twice as many remained on the benches along the boards. We, Victoria, wore purple and white while the girls in black and red uniforms were from Vancouver, which I'd already noticed from posters on the walls and handmade signs throughout the crowd.

Two players from either side had special roles. One girl was assigned a spandex helmet cover with a star. She was the Jammer and the player who could score for her team. Another girl was assigned a striped cap and her role was the Pivot, leader of the remaining three girls, or the Blockers. Each team's coach re-assigned the key roles, strategically mixing up the rotation with every round.

The goal during each round or 'Jam' was for the Jammer to weave through the entire crowd and make it back across the starting line, ideally ahead of the other team's Jammer as well. A wiry stubble-covered man in a silver leisure suit was their coach, more in costume than in uniform. I watched as he handed the star cover to Faith and she snapped it onto her helmet like a shower cap. I wasn't confident I could follow the action, but then the whistle blew and I watched the cluster of skaters down on the rink spring into action.

The elbowing and body-checking began immediately as the girls rolled forward. Faith wrestled her way out of the crowd and pumped her legs hard to gain a strong lead. Another skater in a referee uniform blew her whistle and pointed at Faith, seconds before she arrived back at the starting line to cheers from the crowd. She made a sweeping jazz-hands gesture over her hips and Cole told me she had called off that particular Jam. If she didn't think she could stay in the lead and continue scoring, it was her best strategic move.

Faith's lithe, muscular figure and agile skating skills earned her a few assignments as Jammer, naturally also making her a target for the other girls. Like football, several Blockers received their roles because they were well endowed for the shoulder and hip checking required.

After several more Jams as a Blocker, Faith wore her spandex star again. Seconds after the whistle blew, she was ejected from the pack with a grimace that revealed her vibrant purple mouth guard. Her skate caught something on the floor as she sailed out of bounds and tumbled to the ground. I hadn't noticed any paramedics on site, but suddenly two knelt next to Faith, one supporting her neck on her farthest side, the other obscuring the rest of my view.

"Is she all right? Should we go down there?" I asked.

Cole's face wrinkled with concern but not outright panic. "No, and they wouldn't let us on the track if we did. That's why the paramedics are here for every bout. If she's not okay, they won't let her back in the game. And they'll take her to the hospital if she needs to go."

"Is this normal? I hadn't expected so much violence."

"Yeah, but that's why they're padded from head to toe, and why they have to wear those gross mouth guards. Faith says they nearly gag some players, but you'll get booted off the rink without one. Girls used to lose teeth, and way worse."

"We should do something for her." I wanted to show my empathy, even if it was useless at the moment.

"We'll take her for a drink when the game is finished. That'll be good enough. Look, they're letting her up," Cole said, still frowning.

And the paramedics stepped away. Faith waved to several sections of the crowd, smiling behind purple plastic, showing everyone what a good sport she was. Then she skated gingerly back to her team's bench where she spent the rest of the game.

Knowing Faith wasn't likely to play again curbed my interest in the action at first, but as I watched, I saw an admirable level of sportsmanship. Every girl on both teams genuinely cared about Faith. They all whooped and hollered when she'd been green-lighted to stay on the bench instead of making a trip to the hospital.

Several girls gave her a thumbs-up as they glided past between Jams. Even the large Vancouver girl who'd written "I EAT BELLES FOR BREAKFAST" in capital letters on her ample belly skated over to Faith and playfully jabbed her shoulder. I was suddenly ashamed I hadn't given Faith a chance before tonight. I'd definitely buy her that drink.

Cole and I waited for the crowd to thin before we made our way to the rink. Faith stood with a group of her teammates laughing riotously and I felt thoroughly out of my element. These girls would not want to hang out with a mouse from up North.

"Irina!" shouted Faith from behind a wall of girls. "Guys, this is my brother's soon-to-be girlfriend." The girls all grinned.

"Can it, Faith," glowered Cole.

"Never mind that. How are you? You took a big hit," I said, grateful for a reason to change the subject.

"Oh, she's fine," said a girl with pink braids.

"She'll be more fine once we get a couple-few tequila shots into her!" said the tall Blocker next to Faith.

"Woot! Let's get going, ladies!" said Faith.

Chapter 15

The actual hangover I earned with Faith and Cole nearly wore off by Monday morning, but I still felt tired and extremely sorry for myself. Not only did I buy Faith a 'feel-better-soon' pint of draft beer at the bar down the street from the skating rink, but Cole had continued buying us various cocktails until we could barely keep our eyes open. I spent most of Sunday throwing up in the privacy of my apartment, mercifully alone. Taking an anti-nauseant by late afternoon was probably the only thing that saved me from having to call in sick on Monday. I'd also thought to call Ivan and let him know that, yes, I would participate in the trial injections he wanted. One decision to come out of my ridiculous weekend could do some good.

When I found a glossy, well-made-up, very corporate-looking woman in a black dress suit sitting at my desk, I didn't have the energy to feign polite patience. I stared at her, openly sizing up her ironed espresso hair and sculpted matte rose lips. She smelled of a musky Chanel-type perfume. She also radiated superiority as she continued typing on my keyboard, glaring a hole into my monitor. Despite her harsh exterior, she looked familiar, although I'd never seen her before.

"I'm Ivan's sister, Tatiana. I'm here to give you your first shot. You're late." She only looked up to meet my gaze with her last sentence. Like Ivan, she had only the merest hint of an accent. I briefly speculated on how long ago they'd left Russia, 20 years, maybe 30. And then I looked at the clock on the wall behind me. It read "9:02" in bright red digital letters. I turned back to Tatiana, opening my mouth to defend myself.

Her eyes filled with disdain. "Follow me downstairs."

Tatiana plucked her clutch purse off the top of my desk after closing whatever windows or files she had been viewing. If I thought Melissa acted hard, she emitted only a whiff of what this woman gave off. It wasn't mere Chanel. Her attitude blended 'heartless bitch' with a kick of arrogance. I followed her nevertheless.

She walked directly to the elevator and punched in a code as Ivan had done to take us to the lower level. The silence between us thickened, but I refused to give in and make small talk. That would irritate this woman even more. Shouldn't she at least be pleasant? After all, *I* was the one doing the company—and Ivan—a huge favor by letting her stick me with a potentially dangerous shot.

"We're in room B109. Go wait for me there," said Tatiana.

I gave her a forced, thin-lipped smile and marched past her down the hall. I let myself into B109 and found a room that looked like a doctor's exam room. I sat on the black stool where I knew Tatiana expected to sit, my little act of rebellion. She kept me waiting for what seemed like an hour, much like any doctor. I'd left my phone upstairs in my jacket pocket and

I had no way to tell how slowly time actually passed.

Tatiana appeared with a syringe full of lavender-colored liquid. She wore safety glasses and had her hair tied back in a low ponytail. If I didn't know better, I'd think she expected something explosive to happen. I trusted Ivan, so I forced myself to hang on to that belief rather than dwelling on the risks. She removed her blazer and as she turned her back to me, I saw a snippet of writing on her shoulder blades partially visible through her semi-translucent white shirt. The characters looked like something Middle Eastern or South Asian, but I was more interested in picturing Tatiana's wilder tattoo-friendly days.

She asked me to expose a hip, so I did. She gestured for me to lean onto the paper-covered patient bed and I did that too. Not only had she gotten me off the doctor's stool, which she immediately sat on, but she'd managed to get me into a compromising position. Fortunately for me, fear overrode humiliation. Before I could crack a joke, she stabbed my right buttock and I flinched. A few seconds later she jerked out the needle.

"Go straight back up to your desk and take it easy for the rest of the morning. Don't drink any more coffee. If you have any reaction, including new visions or dreams, report them to Ivan immediately. I'll leave the elevator unlocked for you." She snapped her latex gloves as she peeled them off, dumping them and the syringe into a plastic receptacle with the unmistakable biohazard logo on the side. She left the room without another word.

I felt fine, but I had a project waiting for me upstairs, specifically the organization of Innoviro's spring picnic. A stupid, almost pointless task compared to whatever Tatiana

– or any other Innoviro employee - would do for the rest of the day. But I'd stay busy, which was a mercy if Ivan wasn't coming in to give me anything else to work on.

Tatiana took her time coming back up from the basement. I'd already come and gone from my lunch break when the elevator door opened to her talking on her phone.

"… it was the strongest dose. … You want results don't you? … There isn't time to screw around here. You still want them both?"

She walked right past Melissa and straight out the front door without so much as a nod. Melissa looked slighted and I felt a brief moment of satisfaction until she caught me staring at her and glared back at me.

I didn't see Cole, Faith, or Jonah for the rest of the day. I didn't feel much different after the injection, except for a sore ass. So after work, I went home to sulk on my couch and watch hours of television, to calm down and take my mind away for a while. And then I tried to change into the only nightgown I had. The gown was a long T-shirt and a hand-me-down from Mom. I hadn't factored the garment's origins into the decision to put it on. I'd already been wearing it for a few years, so it felt more like mine.

I picked it up out of the top drawer in my bedroom dresser. I popped my head through the neck opening and my bedroom disappeared around me. I was instantly flung into the corner of my parents' living room. The image of them appeared crisper and more vivid than previous visions, as though I stood there with them, watching them argue with their unseen guest.

Darryl's expression looked much more like rage in this clearer version of the scene. I noticed the lines on his face along with the pores and pockmarks on his cheeks as he mouthed words of anger I couldn't hear. Mom had her head in her hands and then lifted her face. Tears streamed down her cheeks, streaked with watery black traces of her mascara. Her eyelashes clumped from absorbing her tears. I saw hopelessness mingling with despair on her face and I felt a momentary lurch of repulsion. I recovered my focus and tried to concentrate on zooming out and seeing who they were addressing.

It was as though I was hung up on some undetectable barrier, right on the edge of the scene. I couldn't see the shadow outside my peripheral vision, the other figure in the argument. I fought harder, trying to turn my gaze. I concentrated more still, attempting to make out some distinguishing features, but it was a blur. The shadow's hand lifted as I looked back at my parents. Their expressions turned from anger and frustration to shock and pain. In a flash, they both slumped backward to a pose that knocked my heart against ribs.

I stepped forward with my arm outstretched only to find myself jolted back to my apartment hallway. My parents looked like they were either unconscious or dead. But I knew better than that. My gift served no purpose if it wasn't warning me, providing a chance to stave off tragedy. That scene depicted their future. I felt certain of that.

I peeled the nightgown off and stood there in my panties, staring hard into the mirror at the end of the hall. My body retained the welts and burns from my encounter with Jonah. My face filled with fear, and then a new idea hit me. It was a safe bet that the lavender liquid had done its job.

What would happen if I used my cards now? Could I get ahead of whatever pursued me? And force that shadow threatening my parents to reveal itself? The variant world and the threat to my parents had to be connected.

I no longer believed the cards themselves were at all special, but they had triggered something all those weeks ago. I went back into my bedroom and pulled on my old sweatpants and pajama T-shirt. Then I returned to my living room and removed the deck from their new home in the end table drawer next to my couch. If I figured out what lay ahead, I could warn my parents and stop it. As soon as I had the answer, I would call home, hear Mom's voice, and give her vital, life-saving information. If she didn't believe me, I could always call Gemma. If nobody listened, I could go home to Prince George and straighten out this mess.

Remembering that users of Tarot cards typically held a question in mind, I quietly asked myself, *"What has been hunting me?"* I removed the cards from their package and asked again several times as I shuffled. While I flipped the cards together over and over, I pictured the alley where I'd been hoisted up by some invisible menace. I pictured the dark street outside my old motel room and the red eyes that still chilled me. I turned over the top card, placing it face up on the coffee table in front of me.

Nothing happened as I stared down at the image of a ladder with a trio of star coins blooming on a vine. I turned over another card and another. I stared at images of a robed man holding a wand over his head and a hooded old man holding a lantern. I felt a sharp pain in my temple and my vision blurred. I blinked and a new vision began.

I saw Ivan sitting at a glass table in a glass-enclosed apartment looking down on Victoria's Inner Harbour. The sun set rapidly and the windows became dark indigo mirrors.

The dark glass walls reflected a sparsely decorated modern apartment. He owned little more than a glass coffee table, an L-shaped cream-colored couch, and an abstract painting mounted over his fireplace. In the dark negative space on the window walls, lights from the city below twinkled like fireflies.

Ivan sat comfortably in his chair, not taking in his lavish surroundings, but focused on an indiscernible point in space. He murmured something I couldn't make out. It wasn't English and I didn't think it sounded Russian. Whole words eluded my ears preventing a guess at what language he was speaking instead. My gaze drifted downward, coming into line with what Ivan saw through his eyes. I felt nearer to him, but the sound of his voice was still distant and indistinct. I looked around at the floor-to-ceiling glass wall across from where Ivan sat. Red eyes stared back, nestled in the silhouette of a cobra-headed humanoid creature. I couldn't make out exact features, but the eyes looked back – at me – as though the creature knew I was there. The eyes that I'd dreamed were stalking me outside my old room at the Capital City Motel glared from within the reflection on that window. And they were full of pure hate.

The urge to scream seized my whole being, but like a dream, no sound came. I was paralyzed. I willed my mind to back away from the vicious and eerily calm reflection. As I pushed, harder, and harder, I was finally sucked back to my silent apartment. I knew instantly that I was safe, or at least alone, and that I'd only had a vision. Still, the fight-or-flight instinct gripped me and I jumped up from the table to check that my door was locked. I locked the balcony's sliding door and closed the drapes.

I turned on my television. A useless gesture, but the noise always comforted me. I used to do it when I was home alone or if I'd watched a scary movie. It felt like having company in the house. Watching images and hearing voices took my mind off whatever dark and horrible thing had scared me. Of course, this was the first time I'd ever been scared by a real 'thing-that-goes-bump-in-the-night' sort of creature. I believed it was real with no other evidence than the visual echoes in my mind.

As I walked down the hall to get a blanket from the closet, I noticed my hands shaking. No, my whole body was shaking. I wondered if I should call anyone. And say what? I couldn't call Mom in my worked-up state. Without real answers, I would only frighten her. For now, I'd sleep on the couch and let the television keep me company all night.

* * *

The rest of the work week dragged on, seeming like each day lasted forever. I waved to Jonah awkwardly when I passed him upstairs. Cole came to my desk wanting to set up another driving tour date. I stalled him by complaining about the effects of my shot. I wasn't entirely lying, but it was mostly psychological trauma. I imagined scenarios in which my name came up in conversation between the two men.

I played out scenes of Jonah telling Cole about kissing me and the latter punching a hole through a concrete wall of his lab. I alternated versions. Jonah pretended that nothing happened, encouraging Cole to take me driving to distract me. I toyed with the idea of trying to spark a vision and get the answer 'my' way. I decided against petty personal drama when something genuinely important crossed my desk.

Chapter 16

Ivan brought several of Ilya's possessions for me to touch; a scarf, a pair of sunglasses, and an old shirt. Repeated sessions with these items kept my thoughts centered on Ilya and I continued having dreams. I wasn't sure if things I saw in my sleep were accurate visions, but I reported everything to Ivan each morning, disappointing him with variations of scenes I'd already witnessed.

Ilya walking down the beach, talking to other variants, wandering Chinatown and the market around Innoviro. I told Ivan every new detail, however minor, with one exception. I told him nothing about seeing his apartment and a reptilian demon. Until I understood that disturbing scene, my instincts insisted I keep it entirely to myself.

After I had related roughly a dozen images and sensations that led nowhere, Ivan felt certain I needed another injection, maybe several to have a breakthrough. I consented with reluctance. I wanted to help find Ilya, but I also had a strong inclination that the other visions I'd had were important too, that I had seen them for a reason. The shots still frightened me and Tatiana wasn't fun, but if I could endure and help Ilya, more answers could come. The only saving grace was that Tatiana had left for a business trip and it would be another week before she could inject me again.

Friday afternoon arrived and I was the second to last person left in the office. Until Melissa gave me a stern warning to stay upstairs since her early departure made me the last person at Innoviro that day. It was the start of the May long weekend, so naturally, most people had plans. I briefly considered leaving town myself. I still had a sense of unease about the fate of my parents in the not-too-distant future. I had called home and made small talk with Mom after even fewer words with Darryl. Even so, talking to them set my mind at ease, although I still didn't know how to warn them. What could I say? Don't talk to strangers? Wasn't that their line? Besides, neither of them sounded truly interested in my new job. Darryl seemed glad to have me out of the house. Or was that my angst?

I re-focused, reminding myself that the only way to prevent any future danger was to figure out who or what that shadow was and stop it, permanently. Finding Ilya could lead to that shadow. Maybe that was destined to happen - I was meant to rescue this man and he'd help me save my parents. I wanted Ivan to come back to tell me more about his injections and about Ilya, regardless of how personal he found my questions.

I had a right to know what sort of person Ilya was, how he had gone missing, and what made him so important to Innoviro, apart from being the boss's son. It was just my intuition, but I believed Ivan wanted Ilya home for more than his piece of mind. It didn't feel appropriate to call Ivan again without a real reason. I'd already consented to the injections.

Getting the other details had to be done casually, and subtly, two conversational strategies that had never come easily to me.

The silence in the office deepened and I heard the front wall clock ticking and the white noise of my computer's motors. The clock on my screen read "2:56 PM" in the bottom right corner. This could be the only opportunity in the near future for me to go downstairs alone. I stood almost no chance of finding any files on the office computer network, but downstairs held the promise of learning something useful – about Ilya, or my injections, or even better, a hint at what Innoviro did beyond 'testing' and 'research'.

I'd caught a glimpse of the security camera feed on Ivan's monitor once by accident. He must have known I'd seen it but hadn't reacted with alarm. So security was a precaution, something he'd only review if items went missing or if there was a curious incident. If I went downstairs, I'd have to leave no trace to motivate a review of security footage. I slung my purse on my shoulder. If anyone came in, it would look as though I'd left for the day too. Truancy was preferable to breaching a secure area. Especially with everyone else already AWOL for the weekend.

I walked out to the front room, looking for signs of life. I locked the front door's deadbolt. As I walked toward the elevator, I called "Hello?" ahead of me, more to set my mind at ease than because I expected a reply. I opened the steel door, entered the foyer, and pressed the down arrow button to call the elevator. I heard no noise, but in less than a minute, the brushed stainless doors slid open revealing the innocuous compartment with its one bland flower painting. I stepped inside and concentrated on staying calm as I waited for the door to close.

My focus paid off and through my closed eyelids I saw one of Tatiana's matte rose acrylic nails pushing a sequence of buttons. I pulled back with mind and body to find myself standing in front of the elevator panel. I duplicated the code she pressed and the floor jarred slightly as I felt the downward lurch in my stomach. Only a few beats later, the door slid open again and I placed my hand on the gap in the wall to keep it ajar.

"Hello?" I called out again, and as expected, I heard no reply. My heart thudded audibly in my chest accompanied by a ringing in my ears. If I suddenly met anyone, what should I say? I'd been at Innoviro too long to play dumb. I was looking for someone – Cole? Jonah? But why?

I'd never come looking for either of them. I stood frozen in the elevator, wanting an excuse ready before I stepped out, but nothing came and time passed. I had to act or go back. I put one foot in front of the other until I had my hand on the door Tatiana had reached for as I passed her on the way to B109. The door had a line of numbered buttons below the knob. I concentrated and again saw that acrylic fingernail punch in another code.

I copied Tatiana again. The door opened and I slipped in immediately. I positioned the door a hair from closed. I wanted to be able to hear the elevator bell while leaving the hallway looking as inconspicuous as possible. Skimming the room, I saw a wall of refrigerated glass doors. The vials and sample jars were too numerous to count. A row of plain white cupboard doors and a stainless steel counter on the other side of the room revealed even less. I had to concentrate and think fast.

And then I noticed the filing cabinet at the back of the room. An unassuming gray tower of simple metal drawers looked like the right spot for files on patients – or subjects. Each drawer had a label: A – E, F – J, and so on through the alphabet. I opened the drawer for P – T and sure enough, "Proffer, Irina" stared up at me in black felt on the tab of one manila file. I pulled it out of the hanging folder and flicked it open. To my surprise, the file included a copy of the photograph on my ID badge. I hated the shot and I sulked as I continued reading.

The first page had the biographical information I'd expected; height, weight, birth date, hair and eye colors. Then a few more curious notes leaped off the page.

Variation: precognition, remote viewing

Genetic Status: pre-natal intervention

Enhancement Status: ongoing, TE-9306 5ml

What did pre-natal mean in connection to genetic status? If I developed psychic abilities before I was born, how the hell would anyone at Innoviro know that? I needed to confront Ivan. There was no choice now. He either knew more about me than he'd ever let on or he was injecting me with who-knows-what based on assumptions. These injections were dangerous shit. I'd have to make up an excuse for needing more information, aside from confessing to breaking into the company lab.

I turned my attention back to the wall of vials and jars. Pure morbid curiosity held me in that room, peering into the bottles of liquid, straining to read the labels. They were all coded with letters and numbers, similar to the chemical noted in my file. And then my gaze landed on an entirely different cabinet.

Every jar of liquid behind the next glass door held some grotesque specimen of flesh or bone. A container that glinted mildly in the dim fluorescent light turned out to be fish scales on closer inspection. What looked like a shard of wood was a bone fragment with exposed marrow. Another container displayed a lumpy chunk of flesh that was simply unrecognizable.

As I continued reading each label, I noted that the biological specimens had several grading categories. The bone shard was marked "Modification: CB5608" and a green highlighter had marked the text. I couldn't read several others as the bottles weren't all facing out. The fish scales were marked with a different grade, "Modification: FD7394" highlighted in yellow and circled with red felt. I wondered how fish scales could be less friendly than bone. I knew better than to touch any bottles in a strange experimental lab, but I instinctively placed my hand on the polished chrome handle of the fridge door.

I saw Tatiana working diligently in front of a Bunsen burner. She had various medical instruments spread out on her workspace, including the lumpy flesh specimen from the cabinet. In a flash, she injected a clear liquid into a big beefy bicep. I concentrated, trying to zoom out and see the face above Tatiana's subject's arm. Instead, my eyes focused on the specimen jar's label. I made out the words "photon chameleon" and "UNSTABLE" in alarming red letters. Tatiana's elegant hand made a note on her clipboard that read: "Refraction rate improved to 99%. Mortality risk at transition elevated to 75% above baseline."

The elevator bell sent a jolt through me and I released the door handle like a hot potato. I crept back towards the open filing cabinet drawer and closed it very carefully. I slipped into the gap between the filing cabinet and the wall. The space between the cold metal and the corner of the room barely fit one small girl. I pressed my back against the wall, hardly breathing as I waited for my inevitable discovery.

"Fucking interns," I heard a technician named Brad curse before he pulled the door closed from the hall outside. My whole body prickled with tension as I waited. I took time to calm myself down and then I waited some more. I wanted to be sure the man had gone again or settled into whatever room he entered.

I briefly considered simply stepping into the bright hallway and trying to act casual, as though I had a right to be coming out of a restricted lab I'd never been given the security code to access. While I waited, an overwhelming feeling overtook me – that Ivan's research on genetic 'variations' was not intended to help people like me, Jonah, Cole, Faith, or anyone period.

I'd started to suspect his motives were much more selfish, although I couldn't pinpoint his underlying objective. Could it be anything other than money? Manipulating human DNA would be endlessly lucrative if he'd figured out how to initiate and control the process, or possibly even turn on traits by request. How far could the research go and how quickly since he had willing human test subjects? Getting back upstairs unseen was now a matter of self-preservation rather than the concealment of a simple act of insubordination.

I tried to picture the hall. At least a half dozen doors were out there and one corridor I'd never explored. Brad could be anywhere, even back upstairs, but nobody ever left the building through the sewer as far as I knew. If I remembered the hallway correctly, only one of the rooms between me and the door to the sewer had an observation window. It was the lab I'd seen a collection of white coats in during my tour with

Ivan and the pane of glass looking in was wide and tall. Had the light been on in there when I came down?

Damn it! I'd have to take my chances that Brad wasn't in that large lab room.

I crept towards the door and carefully turned the knob. I ventured a scan of the hall and I couldn't see or hear anyone. I slipped out into the hall, closing the door equally gently. My sneakers made no noise, but I heard my breath and the thudding of my heart. I tried to walk casually towards the sewer exit at the end of the hall.

As I approached the window on my left-hand side, I ventured a glance, still trying to stay cool. My eyes met Brad's almost instantly. Whether he heard me or looked up in a moment of horrible coincidence I wasn't sure. He frowned and I waved with my right hand. Suddenly I realized I still held my medical file, but the folder eased Brad's tension, giving me enough camouflage of belonging. He waved back and gave me a confused smile.

My mouth was dry, my heart raced, and I squinted in the bright fluorescent light. I stayed my course and pushed the long metal bar on the door at the end of the hall. Before the door closed again behind me, a red light in the ceiling of the outdoor stairwell began flashing and the beep-beep-beep of an alarm came from the lab behind me.

Out of pure instinct, I ran. The grating beat of drums and guitars blasted out of cheap speakers from the cavern ahead. It occurred to me that the variants in the sewer might be more inclined to kill or capture me than to let me pass. Praying for darkness, I kept going, up and up the stairs and through the winding corridor. I noticed a narrow hall on my left. I didn't know how much farther it was to the main sewer where I'd seen the make-shift tent city. Was the narrow hall a dead end? At least I'd have somewhere to hide if it wasn't an escape route. So, I took it, head down.

Someone – or something – muttered behind me. How far behind, I couldn't tell. An Innoviro employee? A sewer-dweller? A rat? The undecipherable sound echoed, bouncing around me as I marched faster and faster.

Chapter 17

The narrow concrete hallway leading away from the catacombs was barely wide enough to jog through without bumping the walls. I lifted my purse strap and slung it across my chest to stop the bag from bouncing against the rough stone. The lab alarm beeped faintly behind me.

The tunnel went on and on and on, curving slightly the whole way. As I neared a pronounced turn, the glow of light ahead gave me hope that I was heading somewhere. Soon I smelled the urban ocean. Salt, seaweed, and diesel fuel grew stronger.

I splashed through shallow puddles that quickly merged and deepened. I waded into ankle-deep water before I knew it. Icy ocean water flooded my thick black skate shoes and soaked my corduroys as my feet got heavier. My ankles throbbed with stabbing pain. My teeth chattered. My body shook. I trudged on, hoping the water wouldn't get any deeper or that I wouldn't meet a locked iron grate.

I rounded another corner. The blinding light of an overcast sky streamed in through a large round opening. I was in a slime-covered culvert and it must have been low tide. I risked a brief stop, panting from the intensity of running through water. When I looked at the path ahead I saw a ghostly figure.

Instinctively, I screamed as I reeled backward and nearly fell ass-first into the shallow ocean. I locked eyes with the translucent apparition and realized it was Ilya. He was pointing at something. His silent image mouthed something I couldn't understand, but I followed the line of his pointer finger. I saw nothing but a misty line of hills in the distance.

His expression grew urgent as I looked back and forth between him and the foggy blue-green landscape on the horizon. The image flickered out of existence and I snapped back to the moment. I had to keep moving. I waded out of the tunnel and around the corner of the culvert onto a temporarily exposed wet pebble beach made even more difficult to navigate by a slimy layer of algae. I was below the sea wall of a hotel, near a boat launch dock on the far side of the Inner Harbour. I made my way to the rusty ladder that reached down the side of the dock. The structure reeked of the seaweed and fuel soaked into the barnacle-encrusted wood pillars. I tucked my file folder under my arm and clambered up the slick metal rungs.

I walked casually off the dock and reached the road quickly, trying to act normal. My feet squished and squeaked with each step. Aside from my sopping sneakers and soaked pant cuffs, I didn't look out of the ordinary. So I walked to the nearest bus stop and waited, physically and mentally uncomfortable until an unfamiliar bus pulled up, labeled simply 'Oak Bay'. I got on, swiped my transit card, and slipped into the first empty seat. I'd get off again as soon as I recognized the area.

Within minutes I came to one of the stops for the Esquimalt route that would take me home. Another stroke of luck brought a connecting bus in another few minutes. As I stared out the window through the blue iron beams of the bridge, I thought about what had happened point by point. I'd stolen a file, encountered Brad, and set off an alarm before running off through the sewer. The likelihood I still had a job was small.

Could they or would they press charges for theft? Setting aside professional and legal consequences, I still had to consider the ramifications of one small line in my file. 'Genetic Status: pre-natal.' I couldn't shake the idea that Innoviro had known about me long before I followed my visions to Victoria.

I decided to go back to Prince George. And why not leave immediately? I'd go home, pack, and put this city in my rear-view mirror. Sure, I was leaving the best job I'd ever had, but it also was the most fundamentally screwed. A pang of regret came as I looked at the time on my phone. It had been less than an hour since I decided to go snooping in the lab, so sure I'd find some piece of information to set my mind at ease about Innoviro and my participation in their experiments. I thought about Walter and his crimes at the car dealership and I laughed out loud. Several other bus passengers stared at me, but it didn't faze me. I reeled from the rush of my escape.

After the world's fastest packing job, I made it back downtown again with plenty of time to make the eight o'clock Coastal Coach passenger bus to Vancouver. I could have purchased a connecting Greyhound ticket to Prince George, but I wanted to see how much more the comfort of a Via Rail train would cost me once I arrived at the Vancouver bus depot. Getting off the Island would be enough.

My laptop got heavier with every step, so I put my backpack in a storage locker and walked back out onto the sidewalk. I had almost three hours to kill. I could sit down to a meal, but that wouldn't suck up enough time, so I continued around the corner to wander for a bit.

I nearly walked right into a girl sitting cross-legged on the sidewalk behind a cap full of change and a flimsy piece of cardboard. She sat on a folded blanket, her tangled hair tied back. Her colorful, tattoo-covered arms looked vivid alongside her dingy, faded T-shirt. She gazed at me, unmoved by my shock at nearly walking into her. She continued holding her sign: *Please stop being nice to me. I'm not a nice person. I have nowhere to go and nothing to eat. I don't deserve your help.*

Normally, I'd offer my standard remorseful 'No, I'm sorry,' response, but I didn't know what to make of her cryptic attempt at reverse psychology. But, her bright, crisp tattoos. They were almost hypnotic and I couldn't look away. I saw movement! I caught a smirk on her face and I broke eye contact as I resumed my march.

I wouldn't feel safe until I was on that bus rolling quickly out of the city's core. A long three hours lay ahead. I veered into the gardens on my right. The landscaped lawn between Victoria's bus depot and the Harbour-front Empress Hotel was a quiet and conveniently crowded place to wait until I got hungry enough to grab some dinner, and then finally board my bus.

I sat on a chilly wood bench and looked back at the sidewalk. The corner of the building concealed the tattooed girl. I stared for a long minute to see if she would come after me. Nothing happened and I relaxed a bit. I pulled *The Chrysalids* from my scuffed purse. On Jonah's recommendation, I'd picked up the novel at a used book store on Johnson Street a few days ago. I looked forward to reading it, particularly now that I had a personal context to relate to the story about mutants hiding their differences from mainstream society. I hadn't made my way through more than two pages when a tall – no immense - figure walked into my peripheral vision. I closed the book and saw Rubin walking alongside a giant. They strode rapidly towards me.

"You cannot leave town, Miss Proffer. Not without talking to me first," Rubin said darkly.

"Wow, you don't miss a beat. 'Hi, how are you Irina? Great? That's nice, me too," I said sarcastically.

The giant glowered at me. His long forehead and thick eyebrows made the angular lines of his face seem outright menacing. He was at least seven feet tall. I shifted in my seat as I realized he was both tall enough and strong enough to lift me several feet off the ground. If he could disappear, this man could easily be my attacker.

"Who's your friend? Aren't you going to introduce us?" I said.

"Irina, this is Hugo. He also works for Innoviro," said Rubin. "Now, I know why you're leaving and it doesn't matter. Ivan won't punish you for this afternoon's indiscretion and … your parents aren't waiting for you at home."

"What? How do you know where my parents are?" A creeping sense of dread pawed at my sides. Anger surged in me and I grabbed Rubin's forearm. A nauseous wave hit, but I held on, transported to my parents' living room.

Darryl yelled, gesturing the way I'd seen in my vision. "Listen, buddy, I don't know what more to say here. We've never met you before and you're telling us that our daughter works for your company and that because of her job, you want us to cut off contact?"

"We're supposed to take your word that she's fine? After only a handful of phone calls? Is this what Irina wants?" Mom demanded.

"All I can tell you, Mr. and Mrs. Proffer, is that Irina has relocated permanently and she requires time and space to focus on her work," said Rubin's voice.

I couldn't see him, but suddenly realized his voice came from me, inside my vision. I saw the conversation through his eyes.

"You're not making any sense! What have you done to our daughter?" cried Mom.

"I've had about enough of you, man," Darryl said. "Get out of my house, and I mean NOW!"

"I'm afraid that's not possible. Mrs. Proffer, you know why I can't leave, don't you? Don't you understand who I work for? It doesn't matter in the end. We're not done here yet," said Rubin. His hand swung out into my field of vision and my parents both went silent. They struggled against an unseen constriction but quickly fell back on the couch, stiff and still.

I let go of Rubin's arm and staggered backward, dropping onto the bench behind me. I leaned forward and vomited.

"It was you!" I shouted as soon as I recovered my breath. "You're the shadow in my house! Has it already happened? What did you do to them? Why?"

"I'm sorry, Irina, it was an accident. My task was to wipe their memories of you, and to seek out your connections in Prince George, co-workers, teachers, and friends, removing their memories as well. And with the exception of your friend Bridget, I got them all. With your parents, it went wrong.

I had to do more digging in their minds. I've wiped many memories before and it's never been fatal," Rubin said in a slow, calm tone. "If you go back to Prince George now, you'll waste valuable time …"

Rubin's voice faded as I turned and marched methodically back into the bus depot lobby. Tears rolled down my cheeks and sobs escaped. There wasn't enough tea in the world to calm me down after this. I felt all the eyes in the room on me as I fumbled through my jacket pockets frantically searching for my locker key. It was no use. I'd come back for my bag later.

I couldn't go home, but I knew Faith lived in a bohemian neighborhood slightly north of downtown. I'd seen a bus labeled 'Fernwood' along Douglas Street. As soon as I was on my way to her house, I'd call to make sure she was home. If she wasn't there I'd sit outside her building until she came back.

As I walked and Rubin's news continued to sink in, I gave in to the grief and let my crying escalate, rippling through my body. I didn't want to believe it, but I knew my parents had really died. Why hadn't I seen the whole vision earlier? Was there ever any chance to save them? Why hadn't I gone home the first time I saw them arguing with someone? If I had put my parents, my *true* family, first, there would be nothing to regret now.

After only moments of standing alone at a bus stop up the street, I felt a giant hand clamp down on my mouth. Another wrapped around my throat. The grip held me in place, but as my eyes darted around, there were no hands or arms in sight. One mystery was solved; Hugo had been my attacker from the gas station parking lot. And I had related the whole incident to Rubin. Obviously, he'd known immediately who I'd encountered. Maybe he had even ordered it. Maybe Ivan had. My heart raced faster.

"We're going to get into the back of Rubin's car," said that familiar gravelly voice. "I suggest you don't fight me or I may squeeze too hard."

On cue, Rubin pulled up in front of the bus stop. Hugo's giant meaty hands forced me forward. I knew I was trapped, so I reached for the car door handle myself. After shoving me into the car, Hugo pushed in beside me. His hunched form seeped back into reality like a rapidly soaking stain. I ignored him and focused on Rubin's eyes in the rear-view mirror.

"Why my parents? What did they do to deserve having their memory wiped?"

"Ivan thought it best that you cut off ties to your previous life," Rubin said. "I sensed some homesickness in you and I advised him accordingly. The series of procedures Ivan asked me to perform has been done for many variants before. When you join Innoviro, you step into a world that requires boundaries and protection. It's for the good of the work we do, for the people we work with, and for our clients."

"So you went up there to scramble their brains so they'd forget I ever existed? Just in case they felt like coming for a visit and met my mutant friends and saw my mystically protected apartment!"

"Essentially, yes," said Rubin.

"What about my sister? She wasn't in Prince George and she'll start asking about me."

"No, Irina, I'm afraid she won't."

"What? You killed her too?"

"Thankfully I visited her beforehand and nothing went

wrong." Rubin tried his best to sound soothing as he turned off the main drag onto the road that funneled traffic out of the Inner Harbour and up the coast. He continued along the edge of the Harbour until the road curved and the coastline opened up ahead. "Families or other interconnected parties need to be wiped very close together so as not to cause confusion or regression. I took my time with the rest of your life so I could leave your parents to the end."

"So, what will Gemma think happened to me?"

"She now believes she is an only child. All traces of you were removed from your parents' house. And courtesy of several Innoviro IT staff, no record of your birth certificate, Social Insurance Number, high school transcripts, or driver's license will be found when the police investigate your parents' death. They will simply inform Gemma that her parents died of accidental carbon monoxide poisoning," said Rubin.

"So you and Ivan have this shit all figured out. You're going to clean up after yourselves as though I never existed!" I looked over at the waterfront sidewalk on our left. A smiling middle-aged couple escorted their golden retriever. A mother pushed a stroller, accompanied by a little girl skipping.

"Of course not, Irina. How can you think that? I am deeply sorry for what happened and I know Ivan will be too. He's not going to care that you peeked at your medical file. Come with me and we'll get you back into the lab so you can proceed with your injections. You can still help find Ilya."

"Well, there's no need for that search anymore either. I'm pretty sure he's already dead," I said, with slight satisfaction. I felt sick again as soon as the idea reached completion. No matter what Rubin or Ivan had done, Ilya deserved better. I still felt like I knew him.

"Have you had a fruitful vision now?"

"You could say that. I saw his ghost. He tried to tell me something, but I couldn't hear the words. It was Ilya though." After a pause, I added, "But, now that I'm thinking of it, why can't *you* hear him? You picked up on me the moment I got to town. Why can't you put your 'feelers' out for Ilya?"

"The fact that I can't is one of the elements that has Ivan so worried. I'm puzzled by it myself. However, I highly doubt you saw Ilya's ghost. He is capable of using astral projection. Did he communicate anything, any gesture or message at all?"

I reviewed my mental picture of looking back and forth between Ilya's urgent expression, his outstretched arm, and the blue-green hills on the horizon. I quickly remembered my present company and blotted the hills out of my mind, instead reliving the terrible scene from my parents' living room.

"If you think I'm ever going to help you or Ivan again, in any way, you can both go fuck yourselves. You killed my parents! You're a monster! You think I care anything about Ilya compared to my own family!"

"Irina, you must understand that there is more at stake for Innoviro than your personal life. You're going to have to stay with us until you've calmed yourself. We can go to my apartment." Rubin made an abrupt left onto a residential street and then spoke to Hugo, "I think our employer will want to get involved at this point."

Hugo nodded silently, slid a phone out of his pocket and started typing deftly in spite of his meaty fingers. While Hugo concentrated on his text message Rubin came to a halt behind a handful of cars stopped at a red light.

I seized the moment and flung open the car door. I heaved myself out towards the road and landed on cold damp grass.

I rolled across loose twigs and debris. We'd been traveling along a road on the border of Beacon Hill Park. I didn't stand a chance on foot for long, but I hastily remembered that the park had many tourist attractions including flower gardens and a petting zoo. Neither of the men wanted to follow me into a crowd of civilians. I heaved myself up and sprinted in the direction of the zoo.

Chapter 18

I'd gambled correctly that Rubin and Hugo would steer clear of a crowded children's petting zoo. Whether they drew a moral or a tactical line, they didn't seem to be following me. Continuing to Faith's was out of the question now. I couldn't risk that Rubin knew my plan. He may have seen those blue-green hills in my mind, ready to intercept me no matter what route I took or whose help I enlisted. I had to think of something. I couldn't stroll around the edge of a petting zoo all day.

As I walked slowly along the park's main path, wracking my brain for how to direct my feet, another wave of grief hit me. The image of Mom and Darryl dropping lifelessly onto our couch played over and over in my mind. The sadness tightened its grip on my heart and I felt powerless to keep moving. It was all I could do to keep putting one foot in front of the other. I saw a bench and sat. I lay down on my side, tucked in my legs, and turned to face the back of the bench. The wood was hard and cold with the damp of mildew and old rain. I was not comfortable, but I couldn't move. I let the tears resume and continue pouring off my face. I cradled myself helplessly.

It seemed like an hour passed before I cleared my head enough to sit up and take stock of my surroundings again. I dried off my face with the sleeves of my jacket. My parents were gone, but Gemma was safe, for now. The only outcome that could give any meaning to this disastrous period of my life would be saving Ilya. If he was still alive, I had to help him. After I found Ilya and told him who I was and what had happened, maybe he could help me get revenge. We could gut Innoviro and ruin Rubin and Ivan!

What I needed was backup – an extra pair of hands and heads. Rubin could likely read my mind from a distance making my only currently viable option to do nothing. And what was the worst Rubin could do? Other than killing me too, he'd already taken away my life and my family.

I phoned Faith. No answer. I left a voice message for her and then for Cole, all the while thinking of a brick wall for Rubin's sake. I'd seen that tactic in an old movie. I couldn't keep up the brick wall constantly, but I hoped to keep enough concrete details out of Rubin's grubby head.

When I dialed Jonah's number, I had no trouble becoming distracted from my plan. The images of burn-like wounds reflected at me in my bathroom and hallway mirrors were still mentally and physically painful. I blushed again, now thinking of Rubin seeing my body and knowing how I got injured. As I was about to hang up, Jonah finally answered his phone and agreed to meet me at the tourist diner at the edge of the park.

I ran to the diner and flung myself into a corner booth. I suddenly realized that I must seem like a meth addict pursued by mental demons. I took a deep breath, returned to the front counter, and ordered myself a sundae. I treated myself to butterscotch syrup and a waffle bowl with it, knowing it would taste like wax with so much grief and rage in my system. By the time Jonah and Cole sauntered into the diner, I pushed cold butterscotch, waffle crumbs, and melted cream around a small glass plate.

"Thanks for finally showing!" I glared at them as they approached. "We need to drive up the coast immediately. Those blue-green hills north of the city."

"Uh, you want to give us a reason?" said Jonah.

Cole frowned, looking back and forth between Jonah and me. "Or a more specific destination than the Sooke Hills?"

I noticed the tension in Cole's body and I remembered what his grip did to a table top. Had Jonah finally told him about us?

"Ilya is out there, somewhere, and I know he needs my help, our help. I don't want Rubin making an appearance. I want to talk to Ilya and find out what's been happening to him – and more importantly, why he hasn't come home."

I told my story, relating my intensifying reaction to my injection, the cryptic contents of my file, the disturbing biological samples at the lab, my jog through the catacomb tunnels and finally the confrontation with Rubin and Hugo. I reached the part where I learned about my parents' deaths and the floodgates of emotion opened again. The few other patrons in the diner all looked back at our table, but I didn't care.

"Irina, I'm so sorry," Jonah said. "I don't know what else to say. But how can you be sure about any of this? Rubin's never hurt anyone. This has to be a mistake. And labs can feel creepy. Specimens reserved for testing are usually pretty grim looking."

"Jonah's right. Rubin isn't a violent guy." Cole frowned. "Plus, you *were* in a restricted lab. No wonder you saw things that freaked you out. I think you're overreacting."

I hadn't expected them to question my story. I had lost my parents to a ruthless psychopath and having to convince someone it happened was excruciating. I reminded myself that they'd been working for Ivan and Innoviro for several years. They believed in their work, and by extension, their boss.

Finding out you work for a malicious monster would be a tough pill to swallow. When I watched Walter get arrested, I stared in shock, slightly disappointed that his downfall didn't feel more satisfying. Instead, I felt fear and unease. Ivan's crimes were much, much worse and my apprehension scaled up accordingly.

I took a deep breath and focused enough to talk again. "I can't prove here and now that my parents are gone. And I can't prove that Innoviro is doing something terrible. But I *know* that something is wrong. Why would he go to the trouble of having my existence wiped out of the minds of everyone I've ever come in contact with? Rubin made it sound like they do this often! Ivan is doing more than erring on the side of caution with his secrecy. At least consider it!"

"It's not that we don't believe you." Jonah's voice slowed to a soothing tone. "I think you're misunderstanding things. You were okay with Ivan's gene therapy. It seems like you got spooked after looking behind the proverbial curtain. If I'd just seen my parents die in an accident, I'm sure the entire world would look completely messed up."

"I am not fucking imagining this! Everything else I've seen has come true, and I'm not overreacting or exaggerating! Rubin admitted killing my parents!" Tears pooled in my eyes again.

Frustrated, I grabbed Jonah's hand. "Here, I'll show you how right I can be," I put my thumb and forefinger on the silver ring he wore on his middle finger and tried to clear my mind. I hoped with every fiber of my being to see something that had already happened, an incident I could relate for immediate verification.

I saw Jonah slow dancing with a girl in a silver dress, her hair sculpted into a fiery red French roll. Smoky charcoal powder framed her eyes in sharp contrast to her porcelain skin. Her smooth and slender frame moved gracefully above her sparkling high heels.

In another setting, I'd think I was looking at a prom, but from the low light and chest-high tables, it looked like a bar, although not one I'd seen. After a few more moments, the girl dropped to the ground like a wilted lily. Her arms had the tell-tale red blisters where Jonah had been touching her. Within moments, the other people on the dance floor had noticed the scene and started shouting at Jonah.

The look of panic on his face was much more intense than I'd seen the other night. He glanced furtively at the crowd, back to her limp body, and again at the people shouting at him. One man took hold of Jonah's arm while the girl recovered herself and glared up at Jonah with a look of outrage and disbelief. Heat grew in my own hand where I gripped Jonah's ring, so I let go and opened my eyes to the diner.

"There was a redhead – she must have been the first girl you burned after experimenting on yourself. She's the reason you said yes to Ivan's treatment, wasn't she? She looked so hurt and betrayed. Were you afraid when that guy grabbed you?"

Jonah glared at me. I blushed with remorse. I still had feelings for him and I knew he'd never hurt anyone intentionally. I looked down at the table, and then up at Cole's face. I reached out and he took my hand.

The first image I saw was of Cole pushing a little kindergarten-age boy on a swing at a public park. He appeared no more than eleven or twelve years old himself. The boy giggled as Cole pushed him higher, and higher, and higher. One last shove sent the boy flying in the air. He screamed and landed in a nearby swimming pool with a crack, followed by a splash. I dropped his hand with a jolt.

"Oh my God! That little boy on the swing! He could have been-" I stopped myself as I processed the look on Cole's face. Jonah's frustration was nothing compared to the rage I saw in Cole, and from the alarm in Jonah's eyes, I realized that Cole had probably been guarding that incident carefully to make sure it stayed in his past. Cole had been living with his variation for a long time, long enough to grow bitter and resentful.

"I'm sorry, we don't ever have to talk about that again," I rambled while thinking about how to change the subject. The silence at our table got heavier and heavier.

"Okay, say we go out to Sooke to find Ilya. We can't just drive around town," Jonah pointed out. "Even if we focused on the hills, we'd be looking for a needle in a haystack."

"Can you try again? Concentrate harder?" said Cole.

"I don't know. I'm trying not to think of it because I'm pretty sure Rubin's listening in. I don't know how much he hears or sees. The only saving grace is that for some reason Ilya has blocked Rubin out somehow."

"Has Faith ever mentioned that she dated Ilya? It didn't last very long, but she probably has something of his for you to touch," said Jonah.

"That might work. I saw my parents when I touched my Mom's old nightgown, and again when I grabbed Rubin's arm." I gulped, suppressing hurt.

"I'm not excited about dragging my sister into this," said Cole.

"We're *all* in this already," I said. "Whatever is going on here, every employee of Innoviro, maybe even every variant the company has ever come into contact with could be a part of it."

My phone rang and I saw Faith's number on the screen. The universe was finally on our side. I answered and discovered she'd been at roller derby practice. Now, that she'd listened to my message she was already on her way to my place. I redirected her to the Harbour downtown. Even if Rubin showed up, it was too public for another incident.

Chapter 19

I found Faith dancing in front of a saxophone busker. His seat and small audience were wedged between a caricaturist on one side and a potter on the other, each with crowds of their own, oohing and ahhing at their wares. I'd prayed for a bustling Inner Harbour. I was relieved to have one small element of my twisted day work in my favor.

The hot pink-orange glow of a nearby sunset intensified as I watched Faith bop and sway to the music, her dreadlocks flipping and rolling around her head. Everything in the Harbour looked bright and warm and comforting. For a moment my situation revealed itself as surreal – I sought a pyrokinetic girl so I could locate a telepath with my own psychic abilities, in order to avenge my parents' murders.

I couldn't dwell on my bizarre situation. Cole and Jonah waited in the car and I worried that Rubin was listening, to me or to all of us. The underlying panic of constant surveillance wouldn't abate. I tapped Faith's shoulder quickly to avoid launching an unrelated vision.

"Hey, honey! I've been wondering where you were." Her bright eyes and light smile made my eyes water again.

I hadn't told her about my parents in my message. I didn't want to tell the story again in a crowd. "Did you bring something of Ilya's for me?" I said.

"You bet. This little trinket is perfect for what you need." She lifted a Swiss army knife from her pocket. "He used to play around with this thing all the time, so I'd always expected him to come and get it back at some point. I felt like a dork the longer he left it because I figured he'd rather never come to my place again than get his knife back. But, when he started living in the sewer below the market-." She looked down at the ground, her smile gone.

I nodded as I reached out and took the folded knife from her hand. Nothing happened. I rubbed the side to be sure and unfolded several tools. Still nothing happened. My pulse quickened and my stomach twisted. "It's not working!"

"Well, don't look at me! It's not like I sanitized the thing. Maybe you're not *supposed* to see anything about him."

"It doesn't make any sense. Not after everything I've seen," I said. "Are you coming out to Sooke?"

"I guess. I'm not sure if I can help, but I'll come. I'll look through my purse on the way. I think I've got something else."

We marched back to the car and found the guys where I'd left them. I felt a sense of camaraderie for a moment. And then we got into the back seat.

"So, where to?" said Cole.

"Um, I haven't seen anything yet," I said sheepishly.

"Shit." Jonah gave me a long look. "Well, what do you want to do?"

"If you're still willing to go, I still want to try."

"It's not like we've got anything better to do." Cole shrugged.

We wove through inner city traffic, and then the arteries out through the suburbs while Cole cursed at other drivers and exchanged outrage with Jonah. I spent most of the drive staring out the window until Faith, who had been rummaging through her bag, tugged on my sleeve. She passed me a tiny silver medallion on a chain, a Saint Christopher's medal.

As soon as I closed my fist around the medallion, the car disappeared in a flash and I saw Ilya walking along a beach, talking with a tall blonde girl. The sun beamed on a field of spotless blue. The late afternoon sky faded into a soft light gray as it met the sea on the horizon. Large waves curled onto the shore beside them. Ilya and the girl walked past several tents and clusters of campers around fires, like a campground, but located directly on a beach. It was the stretch of coastline from one of my first visions. They were on British Columbia's West Coast, but beyond that, I had no idea.

As they reached the natural end of the beach, they came up against a wall of bedrock that rose up out of the sand to meet the forest behind, forming a steep cliff low enough to dive off. I watched as they walked right through the rock wall. My vision blurred as though I walked through a room filled with thick smoke and the air suddenly cleared to reveal a new beach. Ilya waved at someone in the distance while his companion rubbed her hands as though trying to return circulation to them.

After a few moments of rubbing, it looked like small orbs radiated around her fingertips. She shook her hands again flicking something into the sand. I concentrated on her hands and my gaze moved closer. I saw that she shot tiny droplets of hot liquid to the ground before she wrenched her hands together again, continuing to make her fingers limber. She turned to look at one of the people who had come to greet them, and through her eyes, I came face to face with a woman baring large insect-like mandibles instead of teeth.

I suddenly dropped the chain. "What the hell was that?"

Faith scooped her chain back into her purse. Both guys looked at us.

"Did you get something finally?" said Jonah.

"What did you see?" said Cole.

"They walked right into a wall. Ilya and some blonde girl with glowing fingertips. And this horrible woman with an insect mouth," I said with a shudder.

"She must be talking about Camille," Jonah said to Cole.

"And Suzanne. Those mandibles are pretty unique," said Cole.

"I thought she was still down in the catacombs," said Jonah.

"Wouldn't you want something more remote, if you were her?" said Cole.

"Never mind that. I saw Ilya and the beach. Is he powerful enough to create an optical illusion to protect wherever he's hiding out?"

"Oh, totally," said Faith. "And now we know he wasn't kidnapped or anything like that. Were there more variants? In your vision?"

"I don't know. It was a beach, but people were camped out there like it was a campground. The place was full of tents and fires and clusters of people."

"That sounds like Sombrio Beach," said Cole.

"Is it near Sooke?" I asked.

"Yeah, it's just past Sooke," said Faith.

"It's pretty easy to find," said Jonah.

"I'm going to throttle this kid if he's been living hippie this whole time while his old man has people out looking for him," said Cole.

We started traveling faster, or it seemed faster to me as Cole zigged and zagged down the green corridor of the highway, hugging the curves of the narrow winding road. I watched the sky-scraping forest alongside the road thinking of how different things looked back in Prince George. In my hometown, trees were thinner, and the terrain was plainer and much more flat overall. From some viewpoints, the rolling hills by my home made the sky seem taller somehow, making the world seem bigger. But here on Vancouver Island, the landscape loomed close; ready to collapse as if made of rotting wood. Of course, my world was collapsing. I was being chased from every direction.

I looked out the window at the cedars, pines, and firs zipping past me. The tree line turned black as the sunlight faded. The whole landscape became a dark navy blue as the light disappeared from the sky. Nobody spoke as the searing guitar and guttural vocals of Cole's taste in metal music wound our nerves tighter inside his small car.

Chapter 20

Cole's headlights illuminated a wood sign that marked the turn-off to Sombrio Beach. The gravel path looked like any other provincial park, including the bright yellow metal barricade locked shut for the night.

"Damn it!" Cole shouted as he slammed on the brakes inches before hitting the gate.

"No worries," Jonah said. "We'll park here and walk. You do NOT need to bust up that gate. It's not like your car isn't safe here. Nobody wants to steal a rundown old Civic."

"Shut up, these are great little cars," said Cole.

"And we're already leaving." Faith followed my lead as I marched off past the gate and down the gravel path.

"Wait for us!" Cole said as he and Jonah jogged to catch up to me.

"There's something I haven't mentioned yet. The guys already know," I said to Faith. "I saw an incident between Rubin and my parents. I think he killed them. No, I know he did. He even admitted it. He tried to wipe their memories and something went wrong."

"Jesus, honey, that's horrible. I'm so sorry," said Faith. "What can Ilya do to help though?"

I didn't know what I'd do once I finally found Ilya. All I could do was tell him my story and ask him to help. Would he or could he help? That would depend on why he'd left home in the first place – and what he was doing with all these variants out on the ocean.

"Irina thinks Ilya can help uncover something bad at Innoviro," said Jonah. "All we know, for sure, is that Ivan is worried about his son and wants him to come home. What happened to Irina's parents was a horrible accident. Nobody is denying that."

Jonah and Cole were both disappointed with me, or with the situation. Either way, it didn't feel like they were on my side. I shifted my thoughts back to finally finding Ilya. If I found him at the end of the trail and he confirmed what I suspected about Innoviro – everyone would have to get on board.

Nobody spoke as we walked down the dark dirt path. We were unprepared for the inky blackness of the forest with only the soft blue aura of cell phones to light the path ahead. Except for the white noise of air in the trees, the crunch of gravel, and the snaps of twigs, we walked in silence, slowly descending through the brush. As those dark giants swayed back and forth overhead, my breath slowed and the cool air felt fresh and clean. I knew the trees on the Coast were old, but the sheer size disarmed me. I looked up to the black spires above, moving calmly, barely visible against the night sky. It was exactly the type of forest that could spawn and house monsters.

I brought my attention back down to the path and fear returned to its regular seat in my conscious mind. I stared at the black gap in the trees above the path ahead, I kept expecting a snarling, growling variant to burst out of the woods, baring drool-coated canine fangs below the fierce red eyes of my nightmares. The thought of Rubin and Hugo pouncing on us crossed my mind as well. I visualized bullets and electric bolts zipping through the trees. A pack of thugs could come after us. I waited, but nothing happened and no one came. Eventually, the sound of waves crashing in the distance brought a rush of relief.

"This is it," said Jonah as our path opened out onto an expansive beach that stretched into blackness in either direction.

"We're never going to find this rock wall at night," said Cole.

My phone's time read eleven twenty-five. Only a few campfires burned on the beach and not even a sliver of the moon could be seen.

"I need the necklace back," I said to Faith. She reeled around as though I'd revealed a secret, but I couldn't have cared less. "Seriously, right now!" I said, shoving my open hand into the air between us. Faith produced the medal and handed it to me by the chain, looking sheepishly at Jonah, who was oblivious. I rolled my eyes.

I accepted the chain, charm first. The medal grazed my palm and I clamped my hand shut. The beach shifted under me and I saw it from a new angle under a wash of late afternoon sun. I watched Ilya and the blonde girl walking along the beach ahead of me, replaying the conversation I'd seen earlier. My viewpoint was closer, although I still couldn't hear them over the crashing of ocean waves. Fortunately, our surroundings were sharper and more detailed.

Ilya and Camille walked past a group of roughly a half dozen teenage boys, each had a surfboard embedded in the sand near his seat. After the surfers, they passed a large fancy green tent with two twenty-something couples sitting by a copper fire pit. One of the women reminded me of Bridget and my heart sank as I thought of her, blissfully backpacking around Europe. The scene in front of me got hazy as though a fog had rolled in, almost like a smoky room.

I brought my concentration back to the vision and the picture sharpened again. As the two variants kept walking they passed another group of teen campers. My gaze continued to float far enough behind them to drown out their speech. After the last tent, the ground became uneven littered with driftwood, stones, and washed-up seaweed.

When they reached the rock wall I noticed a pair of glum beatniks layered with wool garments. They played a game of cards using a petrified tree stump as their table and driftwood logs for seats. Ilya nodded at them and they returned the gesture. The card players looked out towards the rest of the beach, seeming to make eye contact with me. And now all I had to do was follow Ilya's path, so I let go of the silver medal again and returned to the beach at night. "We need to go left from here."

"Are you sure?" said Cole.

"Even if she's not, what are we going to try instead?" said Jonah, chuckling.

"It's not like this is an exact science. And Irina's new to this stuff." Faith turned to me. She smiled and put her hand on my arm. "I'm impressed that you've done as much as you have. All for a guy you've never even met. Ilya's my ex and I hadn't tried to find him."

"I know you guys think I'm being stupid, but I can't sit here and do nothing for my parents. I believe Ilya is my only shot at justice. Even if Rubin hadn't taken my parents from me, Innoviro is doing something wrong, trust me."

I started walking briskly, staring straight ahead as I concentrated on the shoreline in the distance. I begged the night to reveal the stone wall from inside the endless blanket of dark. Each step in the sand slowed me down as I sunk into the damp loose grains. The beach stretched out somehow bigger now that I trudged along it. I veered over to the packed wet sand where the tide had gone, eager to take my chances with the icy ocean soaking my shoes in exchange for more stable ground.

Within a few minutes, I saw the ring of surfboards at the boys' campsite and the green tent shortly after; both were empty except for two surfers sipping the last of their beers. Finally, I saw the wall in the distance and turned to find Faith, Jonah, and Cole a few paces behind me. The card players were gone and two much larger men sat in their place. I froze for a moment, but my companions kept walking.

"Mike! How's it going? Brent, nice to see you," said Cole as he and Jonah shook hands with each of the wall's guards.

"Have you been out here all spring?" Jonah asked.

I looked at the guards, and back at Cole and Jonah. A pang of frustration swelled in my throat and I felt a frown deepen on my brow. Had Ilya been goofing off all this time? With my coworkers' friends? My bullshit meter flicked into the red zone. I'd had enough. I walked around the group, towards the wall of bedrock. As a shout of protest erupted behind me, I plunged headfirst into the rock face.

Adrenaline surged through me as the rock turned to thick fog and I emerged face-first on the other side. It was like walking through the dense air of a sauna, only cold like a walk-in fridge. I'd never felt anything like it. What lay ahead on the other side took my breath away.

Calling this settlement a 'camp' sounded completely inappropriate. The scene looked like a music festival wedged between a wall of forest and the open ocean. The torch-lit community started with open awning-style tents. The first was filled with bins of laundry and several racks of clothes hanging on lines, the second suggested a take-what-you-need clothing exchange, then another a station of dry goods shelving. The next tent looked even more bizarre; a sort of massage parlor and, from the items shelved there, possibly basic medical treatment.

I walked past each of these like an adolescent wandering through a bush party uninvited. Dozens upon dozens of people, I assumed all of them were variants, milled around and socialized. Voices chattered, mumbled, and laughed. At the far end of the beach where the light faded into dark I saw a jumble of small dome and A-frame tents stretching from the edge of the common area and into the blackness.

The largest tent in the centre housed a dozen or so picnic tables providing ample seating, although probably not for everyone on the beach. This tent had food service on the far side with a bar at the back, but only the latter was staffed. Dinner had been a buffet and it was almost depleted. Activity died down with only a few clusters of people still snacking, drinking, and talking.

A band serenaded it all from the far side of the tent, opposite the buffet. The band consisted of bongo and steel drums, a flute, and several acoustic guitars. The sound evoked a relaxed tropical ambiance making me forget for a moment that I was on British Columbia's southern West Coast. But the scents of sandalwood and amber mingled with salmon and burnt cedar brought me back. I understood why they wanted to hide this place.

I veered into the center tent, walking in the gap between the buffet and the picnic tables, until I reached the bar along the innermost edge. I looked back towards the start of the camp and I saw Cole, Jonah, and Faith making their way towards me, accompanied by two new strangers. Mike and Brent must have stayed at their post.

I ordered a screwdriver from the bar and I wasn't surprised that they weren't exchanging money. When I asked how much the drink cost, the middle-aged shirtless bartender simply smiled through his stubble and pushed the glass across the counter.

I took the drink and walked back towards the entrance where I sat facing the ocean to wait for my friends.

Chapter 21

I sipped my screwdriver and savored the sweet-sour zing of the orange juice with the warmth of the vodka. As my friends approached with the two strangers, the torchlight of the tent highlighted their features and I recognized both new faces. The tall tanned blonde girl was the masseuse I'd seen in my vision. The guy was the elusive Ilya. I'd know him anywhere.

"Check it out, the search is over," said Cole.

Jonah grinned. Faith's brow furrowed and she looked like she wanted to be elsewhere despite the utopian surroundings.

"Well, we meet at last." I extended my hand and resurrected the plastic smile I used for people like Innoviro's Melissa or customers at my old car dealership job. "I began to think you were a figment of my imagination."

"I did plant a few suggestions, so technically, I was." Ilya smiled warmly and shook my hand. "Took you long enough to find me."

Something in me softened. His presence made me comfortable, like coming home after a long vacation.

"So it looks like you guys have a lot to talk about. We'll grab some drinks and go mingle on the beach." Jonah led Cole, Faith, and the blonde girl back to the bar.

I looked at Ilya, taking in his features and body language now that I finally had the real thing in front of me. "I do have quite a few questions for you. Why *did* you plant visions in my mind? Was it to get me out here? And are there many other people like you that can mess with minds? Other than Rubin, for example?"

"I took a chance when I reached out. Before I left Innoviro, I heard my father talking about a new variant he wanted Rubin to recruit. He sometimes does that. If he finds someone he badly wants to study, he'll invest substantial resources in bringing that person into the Innoviro family."

"So I guess I have you both to thank for my little introduction to the screwed-up world of variants."

"My father would have found you even if I hadn't reached out. You were already a variant, so you would have had to deal with this sooner or later. I'm surprised you hadn't discovered that long before now. Most people notice it around puberty unless their variation isn't artificially induced later on. So what exactly did spark your psychic abilities? You must have had some trigger to wake it up after all this time."

I froze. I pictured my deck of Tarot cards. At that moment, I started to question whether or not it was a coincidence that I felt 'drawn' to them at the farmer's market. My rune security pendant and my herbal tea already suggested there was more than pure science involved – no science I understood, at any rate. Maybe my cards were more than Rubin made out as well. I sat there in silence, looking down at my hands.

"You have the look of someone whose life has been tampered with for someone else's gain. I felt the same way after I started spending time with the variants living in the sewer. One day, I overheard him thinking about 'disposing' of the people he was supposed to care for. He had his guard down and I saw a glimpse of his plan for our future. It's pretty bad. Once I realized his experiments weren't solely intended to benefit variants, I dug around in his mind a bit. I didn't get very far. Of course, the ever-vigilant Rubin noticed and reported me. My father was furious and started making Aunt Tatiana give me an injection that dulled my senses - all of them. When I couldn't take it anymore I left."

"That sounds pretty damn familiar. Ivan wanted me to take an experimental drug, which I did, but I also stumbled onto some sketchy stuff in one of the research labs. And that's only one lab."

"True. There *is* more going on at Innoviro than any of us knows. Before I had Aunt Tatiana's shot forced on me, I'd probed more than my father's mind, particularly when I couldn't get anything from him. I peeked into other staff members' heads, hoping to vindicate my father somehow. No such luck. I never found anything concrete, but I thought I'd gotten close with one of our techs named Brad."

"I know who you mean. I didn't know him well. I didn't get anywhere near as close to staff or the labs." I plunged my face into both palms. This whole plan was vague and hopeless. I sat back up and gulped down the rest of my screwdriver. "I'm going to need another one of these."

After I returned from the bar, Ilya continued educating me about his powers and his suspicions about the real mission behind Innoviro's research. "What you need to understand about me is how I'm different from you."

"You've lost me already."

"My gift is all about perception. Whether I listen to someone's thoughts or plant an image in their mind, I'm either interpreting what they think or giving them a new version of reality. Neither of which is necessarily fact-based. Most people's thoughts are never an accurate portrayal of reality."

I nodded, agreeing and comprehending.

Keeping his gaze focused on me, he continued, "You, on the other hand, have a window into true events of the past or present, as well as the possible events of the future. At least as far as I understand psychic ability versus telepathy in general."

I regretted drinking any alcohol, let alone having a second drink. I swirled the remaining orange liquid in my glass. It did make sense, on some level, that Ilya read minds, while I read reality as it had unfolded or would likely come to pass. The biochemical mechanics of both were an utter mystery and I fought the urge to try to understand how either was possible. I assured myself that the immediate problem was figuring out Ivan's plans rather than deciphering the specific cellular activity in my gray matter.

"I get that what we both do is pretty different. Everyone else's variation seems more obvious I suppose. What about that other girl? In my vision of you walking through the wall, you were with the same blonde girl, but her fingers glowed. What does she 'do' as her variation?"

"Camille is a healer. Some variations delve more into magic than science in my opinion, and I think hers qualifies. When Camille touches you, she can see if anything is biologically wrong. If you're physically or mentally unwell, she can often heal the damage. Not always, but she's usually very effective."

"Wow. That's just … wow. What about everyone else? You've all built quite the little commune out here. Are you planning to stay indefinitely?" I said, half joking.

"For now, I'm trying to gather as many benign or neutral-tempered variants as possible and offer them safety and community. I guess I'm endeavoring to do what my father only pretends to accomplish. But it's been difficult, reaching people that Rubin may be monitoring. And I have to be careful not to misunderstand a person's nature. We can't have the wrong sort of people joining us out here – or someone will tip off Innoviro. We'll either be threatened or taken by force."

"Shouldn't we put a stop to what Ivan's doing? If we shut him down, he won't be able to take advantage of anyone else and you won't need to hide out here."

"That's easier said than done. I'm not a hero and I'm not willing to start a war with my father. I'm hoping to understand why he's doing the things he is so I can help him change his ways, to get back on the path to making life easier for variants. He *is* my father and I have to believe he doesn't truly want to ruin lives. And we're all quite happy out here. Most variants have to live discreetly to some degree anyway."

"I agree that something awful is happening at Innoviro, but I think you've only scratched the surface. What will you do if my gut is right and Ivan is doing something unforgivable?"

"I've considered that of course, but I'll cross that bridge when I come to it. For now, no matter what you think, don't underestimate my father. Innoviro has offices in London, San Francisco, and Shanghai, with more research facilities. They have money and access to who-knows-what pharmaceuticals, weapons, and security personnel. I know you've met Hugo. There are others like him."

"I can't help but wonder about the end game for this company. What are Ivan and Tatiana trying to achieve? What, exactly, did you see in his mind? Jonah's expertise is in genetics, so his being there already makes sense. But Cole is a geologist. And I know other biologists on staff who work with animals. I've seen animals carried down in cages, but none ever return. If Ivan is willing to experiment on people directly, what does he need with live animals? And I arranged for him to attend a fossil fuel conference in Calgary. What's that got to do with anything?" I said.

"I couldn't say for sure, but it's probably not good. What I saw was … like Armageddon. He can't possibly intend that."

"What if he does? Let's go back and finish what you started. Let's find evidence. We'll call the police. There must be some documentation to outline what's going on, in all departments. He wanted us off social media; let's broadcast on every platform!"

"My father is a meticulous planner, so there probably is evidence. But he is certainly using security that we don't even know about. If we go public too soon, we'll tip our hand and make ourselves vulnerable, more than we already are."

"Why don't we call a meeting for everyone here who's worked at Innoviro? If we all put our heads together, something is bound to get clearer."

"Okay, but I don't want you frightening anyone. I've worked hard to keep these people calm so they feel safe here."

Chapter 22

I knew nobody at this camp was safe, not while Ivan had a grand scheme to accomplish something my intuition told me was horrible - that Ilya described as Armageddon. The more I thought about Ivan and pondered the red-eyed monstrous reflection I'd seen in my mind's eye, the more I became convinced that his plan was malicious.

Ilya led me down to the beach where our group huddled around a fire pit. Jonah, Cole, and Faith all knew most of this crowd. Both guys talked to an older man with a long tangled ponytail and a denim button-up shirt. He looked like a seasoned laborer, but his variation wasn't obvious until he spat on the sand near his feet. The ground smoked from whatever corrosive liquid he expelled.

Faith playfully juggled a tiny flame, alternately flicking it into and drawing it back out of the fire pit. She talked with striking platinum-blonde twins, women with matching pairs of bare leathery wings folded behind their backs. Their pale skin had a bluish hue. I saw what Ilya meant about some variants needing to conceal themselves from society.

I also recognized the winged women – at least one of them – as one of the variants I saw in my vision of the catacombs while standing under the shoe tree at Cymbals. Had I seen her for a reason? Or had my mind's eye merely grasped at an echo imprinted onto a tangible object? I had to believe that my visions were more than mental debris. As I considered the former, I puzzled over whom or what dictated what I saw, if indeed each image gleaned through my gift was information I needed. It was far too large a concept to ponder without getting lost in the possibilities.

My eyes wandered back to Faith, watching the natural ease with which she manipulated the flame and I became jealous that she'd had years to practice her gift. I'd only known about mine for a measly handful of weeks. For all I knew, everyone here had known about their variation their whole life.

Ilya put two fingers from each hand in his mouth and whistled a loud sharp tone that got almost everyone's attention. He announced that he wanted a meeting after breakfast tomorrow morning. He didn't give a time and probably nobody here checked, or owned watches. He then walked away with Camille and the denim-clad spitter. Their departure left me with Faith and the winged twins. I followed the trio back to where Jonah and Cole stood nursing their bottles of beer. They both nodded at my approach, but a vibe of irritation and discomfort radiated from both of them.

At this point, I hoped that Jonah had unloaded a guilty conscience on Cole about kissing and literally burning me. None of which was *my* fault and I was ready to say as much to both of them. Only the embarrassing prospect of being wrong about the tension between us kept me from calling out the elephant in the room.

I stood silently as they discussed reviews they'd read of a soon-to-be-released video game. I had no input, but as I warmed my hands over the fire, I looked up at each of their faces. Jonah's black hair shone with flickering yellowish-orange highlights reflected from the fire. His vibrant blue eyes stood out, glowing almost as brightly as they had the night we kissed. Then, I'd thought his eyes glowed because of his emotional state, but now I considered that proximity to the ocean energized him.

My heart sank. There was very little chance we would get back on the path to a closer relationship, but his perfect complexion, sculpted features, and lean body hadn't lost their charm. He was tall, but not tall enough to be awkward next to me. I remembered the dance floor at The Looking Glass; Jonah's chin rested perfectly on my head.

Cole had a distinctly different look, yet it matched his character. As I examined him by firelight, I had to concede that he was also handsome, however much he might make me nervous. He wore his sandy-colored hair in a mess of floppy spikes. Cole was more thickly muscular than most men, true to his variation. He usually wore skateboard clothes, including the Atari T-shirt and baggy board shorts he had on. Most days his face had a light layer of stubble and in the dim light, it looked darker than usual. I smiled at the memory of being afraid of him. Cole then crushed his empty glass beer bottle the way most guys crushed aluminum cans. He let the shards fall to the ground from his uncut hand. Jonah rolled his eyes.

"So I guess we shouldn't walk around here barefoot, eh?" said Camille, returning from the darkness.

"Oh, sorry, I, uh, wasn't thinking. I guess I forgot people

were living out here."

"You ass!" Faith stretched out her arm over the shards and the tiny flame she'd been playing with shot into a powerful stream, melting the shards into a glowing puddle. Jonah drew an orb of water from the ocean and doused the molten mass.

"Ilya found a couple of vacant tents for you," Camille said. "If you're ready to call it a night, I'll show you where they are."

"Sure, that would be great," Jonah said.

"I don't know, man," Cole said. "I don't want my car getting towed. I left it parked up in front of the locked gate."

"You'll have until eight tomorrow morning to go back and move it," Camille said. "If you go a few minutes early, you can circle back to the highway and roll in after the attendant unlocks the gate."

"Great, so I get dawn patrol. I assume I'll miss out on hot food too?"

"You can eat before you go. We start breakfast around six and keep it hot for a couple of hours because we have to eat in shifts. The sun and the tide coming in will probably wake you up long before either breakfast is over or the park attendant gets here. You might even feel like you're camping," she smirked.

Cole opened his mouth to protest but thought better of it.

Camille turned to show us to our tents and everyone followed. Walking behind her, I noticed how graceful she was. The white linen top and knee-length cotton skirt didn't look warm enough, but she moved comfortably. Her hair was piled into a messy bun on top of her head. Woven hemp bracelets around her wrists complemented a wood pendant hanging from a leather cord around her neck. As a masseuse and a healer, she seemed like the sort of person who experienced an emotional connection to nature and the planet itself. Then again, I had just watched my friends exercise their command over the elements. I was probably one of the few people on the beach that didn't have a physical tie to the natural world.

The night passed peacefully, at least for me. Mine and Faith's tent wasn't exactly hotel caliber, but the foam mattress was large enough for both of us to sleep comfortably and the sheets had been to the camp's laundry, such as it was. We both had our purses, so between the two of us, we had the basics to freshen up. I hadn't camped since my last year of high school, but I remembered how much the simplicity appealed to me.

Camille had predicted correctly; the sun and the ocean woke us. My phone read 6:35 AM when I finished tying my ponytail after slipping my jeans back on. We stopped at the camp's outhouse, which was in exactly the state you'd expect it to be. We used generous amounts of Faith's hand sanitizer before making our way to breakfast.

The basic scrambled egg, sausage, flatbread, and berry juice fare tasted amazing. I ate ravenously, frantically grateful for the food. As the last few camp residents finished their meals, they responded to an unspoken command to clean. Before I could offer to help, they were done and Ilya stood at the entrance end of the tent, waiting for everyone to gather. He didn't quite wait for the entire group before starting.

"Most of you have probably noticed that four guests joined us last night. Many of you are already acquainted, so I'll get straight to the point. You know why we're out here and that something sketchy is underway in the city at Innoviro Industries. Some of you worked there, but probably all of you were 'volunteers' for testing. I've asked you to meet this morning because it's time to pool our resources and collective knowledge. We have reason to believe that my father's work is even more dangerous than I'd originally suspected. I left Innoviro thinking that he was being morally and environmentally reckless, for personal and financial growth. Unfortunately, the situation may be even worse, but we don't know exactly how. To help us figure this out, I'm asking all of you to think long and hard, now and over the next few days, to revisit in your mind anything you worked on or anything you know of that could shed some light on what my father is doing. If you don't feel you can talk about it in front of the group, come find me later." Ilya paused to let the speech sink in and, I assumed, hoping for someone to speak in response. Heads swiveled back and forth as each resident assessed the group.

"I have something to share," said the older man with the tangled ponytail. "I did maintenance and janitorial work. When Tatiana hired me, she said Innoviro's research was too sensitive to let outside trades onto the property. Tatiana and Ivan wanted one person to be responsible for all of it. One of *us*. So, I know they have trust issues when it comes to non-variants."

"Thank you for sharing that Vincent," Ilya said. To the crowd, he continued, "In the interest of transparency, *I* should share that Tatiana is my aunt, Ivan's sister. She has a senior and extremely guarded position with the company. Maybe not all of you met her, but she traveled to several of our offices regularly." A sudden lurch of unease gripped me. I'd forgotten that Innoviro had other offices. Ivan made his own travel arrangements for inter-office trips and I never questioned why. Now I had no addresses or phone numbers for the other Innoviro offices. I hoped someone here knew.

Camille's hand shot into the air. "I have an idea," she said. "Let's tap Irina. She worked as his assistant. She was right there with him all the time. She must have seen or heard useful stuff."

"Um, I've told Ilya everything I know," I said defensively. "I'm not hiding anything. Of all people, why would *I* hold out?" I looked across the crowd searching for Camille's pile of honey-colored hair.

"I'm not saying you're holding out. I'm talking about your subconscious," said Camille.

"Why don't you search her mind? She could have seen something crucial, but didn't realize at the time," Faith said to Ilya.

Faith turned to me and gave me an encouraging look.

I resumed looking at the faces around me. In the daylight, I saw that most of these people could go out in public. And yet, there were eye-catching people in the crowd.

A young boy, maybe not past his mid-teens, blinked at me with solid golden-yellow eyes. His pupils were thin black ellipses, but more startling, his olive skin had a sheen to it that looked almost like scales. Past him, I saw an older woman with soft gray chin-length hair. She also had white serrated mandibles extending from the corners of her mouth. Another familiar face from my Cymbals vision. I tried not to stare as I wondered what else her closed mouth contained. I found Camille and saw an expression of concern directed at Ilya.

"I could try probing Irina, but let's not put anyone on the spot right now. We can talk about it later," Ilya said.

More variants continued volunteering bits of minutia, but it became apparent that Ivan had expertly isolated each project or experiment, restricting valuable data to a select few senior staff, none of whom were on the beach. I hadn't realized how many variants he'd tested pills and injections on, but most of the people under that tent had been test subjects rather than trusted employees. If Ivan wasn't sloppy enough to let his mid- to low-level staff know his secrets, he certainly wouldn't let a random test subject see behind the scenes. For the same reason I'd said yes to Ivan's injections, I felt myself warming to the idea of Ilya digging around in my head. So after the conversation dwindled and Ilya wrapped up the meeting, I made my way over to him.

"That didn't sound as productive as I'd hoped for," I said with a smile.

"No, I suppose not, but I didn't have high expectations," Ilya said. "I knew my father was careful."

"Then I guess I need to let you poke around in my brain." I shrugged my shoulders and sighed.

"It shouldn't be uncomfortable. I can put you into a state of deep relaxation and help you remember more details. It's not like watching surveillance footage. We're looking at memories reshaped by your perception." Ilya's expression was intense.

"Okay, I see what you mean. I don't have high hopes for this anyway."

"Don't worry; I'm a master of managing my expectations. Let's go back to my tent and get started."

Ilya's gentle tone and practical disposition set me at ease. I hoped he could sense my confidence in his abilities.

Chapter 23

Ilya's tent was an army-green canvas structure with plastic windows and roll-up curtains. He swept his arm towards his cot, prompting me to lay back and relax. He sat in a folding camping chair next to the milk crate nightstand. Ilya didn't give me the spiel I was expecting. He put his hand on my forehead and told me to loosen my muscles and think of my desk and daily routine at Innoviro. Like one of my visions, the tent melted away and I stood in front of the main door outside the office.

I heard Ilya's voice. "You're back at your office first thing in the morning. You're hesitating outside because you know it's going to be a busy day today. Ivan told you he needed your help planning a trip."

I looked down at my outfit and the coffee in my hand. The scene did feel familiar. I thought of the day I arranged Ivan's trip to California earlier that spring.

"Go inside the office. Tell me what you see," Ilya said.

"The office is empty. Melissa must be running late. I'm glad and I hope she gets in trouble," I said, replying to his voice as though he stood next to me. I felt a lack of control and I was compelled to answer him honestly whether I wanted to or not, like I'd had too much to drink or woken from a deep sleep.

"What is your top priority today? Where is the first place you go?"

"I'm going to my desk to put my coffee, coat, and purse away, and to start my computer. I need to be efficient today, so I want my computer booting while I find the papers I need to leave on Ivan's desk. I've found the folder I wanted. Now I'm putting his coffee on the coaster by his landline. We're planning a trip to San Francisco, so these pages are what I printed yesterday for each of the downtown hotels. Once he picks his favorite, I'll need to finish booking the room, renting his car, and downloading menus for nearby restaurants that look good." I reported to Ilya obediently.

"Since you're with *me* today, we're going to freeze time. Now, that you're in Ivan's office, time is standing still for everyone but us. You won't get caught. Take a look around his desk. Examine everything. Do you see his black leather day planner? Are any of his desk drawers locked?" Ilya's voice soothed me. I could feel him with me in Ivan's office.

"His desk is tidy. He doesn't keep many personal items here. I see that desk toy with the swinging steel balls and his stone coffee coaster. His black book isn't here. He always takes it wherever he goes."

"Is there anything on his computer screen?" said Ilya.

"No, it's still off. Wait, if I touch the keyboard it might trigger a vision and I'll see what he types." I reached out to touch the plastic keys. "It's not working. Maybe if I stay longer ..."

"Remember, you're only exploring your memory; you're not actually touching the keyboard. Take one more look around Ivan's office. Does anything else grab your attention?" Ilya's tone was encouraging. His voice helped me to concentrate.

"His snake, Chester, is awake this morning. I don't like that Ivan makes me feed his snake. Sometimes I think he enjoys making me uncomfortable. He must know I hate the snake." My own voice sounded robotic, but I couldn't help it.

"Is the snake doing anything at the moment?" Ilya's voice was tense.

"No, it's just staring at me. Wait, his eyes are different. They're red. They're like the eyes that were chasing me! Those horrible, evil eyes! They're going to tear me to shreds! That face wants to turn me inside out! I can feel it!" I relived the terror of my dream from the old room at the Capital City Motel.

"Irina, come back to me here at the beach. Now!" Ilya said urgently.

I sat bolt upright, screaming, on the bed, back in Ilya's tent. I'd only ever woken like that once before; the first time I spent the night at my boyfriend Adam's house and his alarm blared at five-o-clock in the morning. It was an instinctual cry. The sound coming from my mouth in Ilya's tent was a shrill scream of utter terror. I cut it off with a deep breath and sat panting. Confusion muddled my mind. How could Ivan's snake evoke my nightmare at the motel? Why had I seen the same eyes in Ivan's reflection, housed in a horrible silhouette?

"Are you all right?" Concern furrowed Ilya's face.

"Yes, it's fine. I'm fine. I saw something from a nightmare. It must have crept into the vision somehow." I massaged my face while stress pulsed through me.

"That walk took us through a dream? I was trying to probe a memory. That's unusual for one to seep into the other. Truthfully, I've never seen anything like it. Then again, psychics are extremely rare and I've never been into one's head."

"Great, well, you learn something new every day, right?" I laughed nervously.

"We did learn something, but poking around on the surface at Innoviro isn't going to be enough. I suspected we wouldn't learn much, but I wanted to be sure. Stealing my father's black book and hacking into Innoviro's network come next. Also, his snake is more dangerous than your average python. I had only suspected. Now I know." Ilya sighed loudly and paced inside the tent.

"There's something else. I saw Ivan in his apartment, at night. And I saw his reflection, but it wasn't him. The way the overhead light and the streetlights outside came together, I only saw the outline. But his reflection had red eyes, in the body of something like a serpent. I'd already had a vision of being stalked. And those fierce red eyes. Not just glowing. The iris looked human except it had the texture of an ember. It was frightening." I watched Ilya pace and my body's rhythm stabilized.

"I was there with you when your mind retrieved that image. I saw it too." Ilya paused mid-stride. "At least we know we're right about my father, even if we don't have all the details - yet. I think something or someone has a hold on him."

"You mean possessed?" I heard the fear in my voice.

"More like a kind of parasite. It's difficult to speculate without getting philosophy involved." Ilya's gaze drifted outside the tent.

"Maybe this is ignorant of me to ask, but what is stopping you from reading Ivan's mind?" I asked quietly.

"That's a fair question. I wish I had a better answer. The few occasions I've tried reading my father's mind are part of why I think something has a hold on him. His mind isn't like anyone else's. His brain is almost feral. His thoughts are a tangle of colors and shapes. At first, I didn't dare to ask him why; I'd have to admit to trying to read his mind. But, one day I plucked up the nerve and he said it was part of his variation. And then he looked at me for a long moment and told me never to go digging in his head ever again. It's one of the rare times I ever feared him." Ilya pulled his mind back into the tent with me.

"So tell me, how early does that bar open?" I laughed nervously. I had no intention of spoiling the day by drinking my fears into oblivion, but it was funny to contemplate. Ilya laughed and told me the bar had self-serve coffee in the mornings, although he'd get me the key to the liquor trunk if I wanted it.

I took my coffee in a chipped ceramic mug down to the beach, back to the fire pit we'd all been standing around the previous night. Watching the wild waves of the open ocean reach up and crash down in front of me drove the questions and worries from my mind. Each swell of water ascended, crested, and then fell in a delightful mess of foam.

The surf in front of me changed with every wave, uneven edges finding a slightly different purchase on the sand with each blow. Each curl of bubbling white and slate gray sucked back on the sand like a mouth drawing a breath, then launched forward exhaling froth onto the slick caramel sand. I looked farther down the beach to where the dry sand mingled with old seaweed and driftwood. The wind caressed the reeds and grasses sprouting here and there. The sky overhead was a cloudless pale blue, cold like the air around me.

"Hi," said a red-headed girl who appeared next to me. I'd noticed her standing inside the tent at this morning's meeting. She had a tired, sad air to her.

"Hi," I said back.

"So you're a psychic."

"Yep. And I'm a newbie. My name's Irina," I said.

"I'm Valerie. I'm a contortionist." Valerie stretched her arms with fingers interlocked, effortlessly dislocating her shoulders to roll her arms behind her back. I'd seen that trick from a distance at the circus, but before I could say so, she swiveled her head around too, lifting one leg and threading it through her clasped hands, remaining gracefully balanced on her other leg. She rotated her head back around to look me in the eye again and gave me a tiny shy smile.

I stared back at her wide-eyed and took a moment to compose myself.

"Impressive! That was something else, for sure. So I saw you at the meeting this morning. Did you used to work at Innoviro? Or go through some of their tests?" I strained to sound casual.

"I used to be in an underground freak show down in the States," she said bluntly.

I spray-spat my mouthful of coffee onto the sand. "Naturally. So have you got any insights into the problem with Innoviro?"

"I think your father is a bad man, but he's working with someone worse."

"No, Ivan is Ilya's father, not mine. But I think you're right, he probably isn't at the top of the ladder in this little tangle."

"I have to go now." Valerie instantly turned on her heel and cartwheeled off down the beach. I watched her twirling form spiral smaller and smaller as she picked up speed on the open sandy stretch ahead.

"Penny for your thoughts?" said a familiar voice behind me as I jumped.

"Cole! You shouldn't sneak up on people! Not around here." I said, shaken.

"Sorry, I didn't mean to startle you," he said sheepishly.

"So now you're being nice again?" I snapped. "All of yesterday you and Jonah acted like first-class assholes."

"I know, I'm sorry. It's… you know I like you right?" he said.

"Sure, I like you too," I said uncomfortably.

"No, you know what I mean. I've got a thing for you." He stared at the ground.

I could tell this was difficult for him.

"Yeah, okay, I had noticed."

"Jonah told me how he marked up your back. He knew I liked you and he knew he couldn't get with a girl. But he did it anyway. And then he confessed to me, rambling about how he was sorry. He's a dick, but he's my friend. I can't let myself get mad at him." Cole wrung his powerful hands as he stared at the sand.

"I pretty much figured out all of that too." I let out a breath. "But how is this my fault?" I thought of Jonah and anger swirled in my chest.

"It's not. But I wish you'd picked me. Or at least that you were still open to the idea. You should know that *I* can control my variation. *I* would never hurt you." Cole finally looked me in the eye.

The need to look away drove me to my feet, but I stayed. I

steadied my nerves and sat back down.

"I don't know what I'm open to anymore. I know you'd never harm me. I can tell you that whether it's you or Jonah, now is the exact wrong time for all of this."

I looked at the hopeful expression on his face and I felt my resolve weakening. My eyes must have betrayed me. Sensing his chance, Cole leaned in and kissed me. His arms closed around me and his lips brushed mine with tenderness. His grip was passionate, but not painful. I kissed him back instinctively, but then I pulled away.

"I'm sorry, but I meant what I said. It's not just about Jonah." I tried to push away, but his arms were rigid. Panic hit me and he saw the look on my face.

"No, I get it. I'm sorry too. I don't want to scare you."

"You don't scare me," I said, with a smile. He beamed in return. The aroma of Mexican food wafted past us on the wind.

"Smells like lunch is ready. We should get back," he said.

I took a deep breath, hoping Cole didn't realize I'd lied to him.

Chapter 24

Hanging out on the eastern side of Vancouver Island, in the spring, was like hovering on the edge of Eden. The air was full of chlorophyll and salt water. The rhythmic crash of ocean waves soothed me while the muted sun gently balanced out my energy level.

By dinnertime that night, I had almost entirely detached from any reality in which I or my friends faced danger of any kind.

I was completely at peace when we meandered into the dining tent. Several people chopped vegetables and filled skillets. I recognized Vincent's salt-and-pepper ponytail behind an armload of headless fish, still wearing their scaly skin over the distinctive peach-pink of salmon flesh. Hot trays of food and clean plates materialized on buffet tables. In a few more minutes, all seats in the tent were taken.

The work put into daily meals dominated many of the waking hours at this camp. Except for residents doing laundry and security shifts, most people were helping with food.

Dinner wasn't served quickly, but the simple vegetable stir fry, fluffy rice, and oil-grilled fresh salmon tasted like gourmet cuisine.

I'd eaten my dinner sharing a table with Faith, Jonah, and Cole. We had all come a long way since the first time we shared a meal at that artsy seaside diner, although for me, the journey had included two decades of knowledge to catch up on. We each had a glass of red wine to warm us. The artificial heat kept cold at bay while the wind stayed calm. As the sun set, the light reflecting off the golden ocean made the camp feel nearly tropical.

After the mumble of dinner conversation and the clatter of plates and cutlery died down, the camp band started playing again. Two acoustic guitars, a set of bongos, and a bamboo flute all serenaded the beach with lively, heartfelt music.

I looked around at the animated conversations and the many cheerful people, wishing I'd found this place under different circumstances. I felt guilty for having brought my problems to them. I knew 'my' trouble was everyone's trouble, but I felt as though bringing it to light was a trespass on this community. Vengeance for my parents' deaths wouldn't bring them back, but it could easily ruin, or even cost lives around me.

Alternatively, if I had never come to Victoria, would the people at this camp stay here another season? Another year? I contemplated whether or not Ilya's illusion could hold Rubin and Ivan off indefinitely, and then I heard a squeal in the distance.

My intuition told me the sound came from raw fear. Shouts escalated as I saw a wave of dark figures coming up from the beach. I saw Camille shoot glowing balls of I had no idea what into the first wave of attacking bodies. The light from one orb flew past a girl I recognized - the bus depot panhandler with lifelike tattoos. An instant later an illustration of a large spider rippled on her bicep, pushed its way up to a third dimension, and sprang off her arm at one of the winged platinum girls. Across the beach, her twin's wings flexed in pain and she whirled around to find her sister.

Beside me, Faith and Jonah had started shooting bursts of fire and pressurized streams of water with as much precision as their skills allowed. It was clumsy, but they knocked out a few black-clad assailants.

Cole lifted a stone seat plank from the picnic table next to us and ran to the beach to use it as a bat. Variants ran in every direction, some racing into combat while others fled into the woods.

I stood there paralyzed by fear and indecision. I had nothing to offer the fight, but I refused to leave my friends and flee. Vincent had been sitting at the table next to us. I looked over and we locked eyes. He stayed frozen too, despite his ability to spit something that could do some damage. Suddenly a dart flew into his chest, dropping him to the ground after a few seconds of swaying. Searching for the source of the dart, I saw a greasy, scruffy head I'd hoped never to lay eyes on again.

The moment I realized that Rubin led the assault, I felt a choking sensation while being lifted into the air. Hugo! He had me by the hood of my sweatshirt, pulling me up off the ground. Hugo yanked, hoisted me onto his shoulder, and plodded back towards the beach. I bounced seemingly in mid-air as we marched into the darkness. Their boat came into focus in the abyss of the night ahead.

The vessel had a flat open deck with high walls on either side. It reminded me of the military boats designed to ferry soldiers to beachfront battles. A small pile of unconscious camp residents lay on the deck, some already tied off to railings. Casey, the multi-armed bouncer from The Looking Glass handcuffed and tethered two people at the same time, working twice as fast with his extra limbs unfolded.

A whomping thud hit the mass behind me and the impact traveled through Hugo's arm as he dropped me like a rag doll. The icy late spring ocean hit my chest with a gigantic punch, knocking the air from my lungs. On all fours in the water, I fought against the cold and the weight of my wet clothes as I lurched up and waded back towards the shore.

Hugo's body became visible, in a heap several meters down the shore. Cole stood on the sand holding the concrete bench seat in one hand. The anger on his face sent a rush of adrenaline through me.

"Jonah and Faith are already in the woods. We're going for my car!" Cole shouted.

I paused, gasping for air, looking around for other escapees.

"NOW!" Cole dropped the seat and reached for my hand to yank me forward, but thought better in a blink, jerking his hand back as he saw fear on my face.

I knew we couldn't save them all. We'd be lucky to save ourselves. Right and wrong would have to come out in the wash later.

"I'm coming. I'm right behind you." I ran, but Cole scooped me into his arms like a baby. Cradling me, he raced into the woods. I felt like an idiot, but I tucked my head into his bulky arms. His body felt like dense pillars of hard muscle.

Cole didn't break stride as the hill got steeper. He ran directly through the brush in a straight line, far from the original path. I felt the terrain level out again and moments later we burst out of the trees onto the road. Headlights washed over us and got brighter as a car sped forward.

"It's me! Get in!" shouted Jonah.

Cole set me down and stepped onto the road as his car stopped between us. Jonah gripped the wheel with Ilya beside him. We each grabbed a handle on either back passenger door. Cole and I sandwiched Faith in the back seat. Jonah hit the gas again before we had the doors closed and the car shot off down the dark winding road back to Victoria.

Chapter 25

"What the fuck was that!" Cole screamed at everyone in the car.

"How the hell would *we* know?" Jonah shouted back.

Faith wept, wedged between Cole and me in the back seat.

"Ivan sent them. Cole, Rubin saw the beach in your mind last night when you went to move your car. He was focused on all of you waiting for some sign. When you left the protection of the shield I had around the beach, he found you in minutes. I heard his thoughts back there. He was revoltingly pleased with himself," said Ilya from the front passenger seat.

"I'm glad you decided to come with us," I said to Ilya, and then to everyone else, "So, I take it Ivan and Rubin are super pissed that there's a group of variants who isn't into voluntary testing anymore?"

"No, it's more than that. Ivan did want the camp broken up, but he wanted as many taken prisoner as possible. He plans to resume testing; there's even a priority list. Irina, you were at the top. Rubin is furious that Hugo lost you because Ivan is going to rip a strip off him for coming back without you. Psychics are that rare and he invested in you," Ilya said.

"We have to get somewhere safe." Cole cradled Faith with one arm. "Our aunt and uncle live over by University Hospital. Jonah, do you remember how to find Aunt Liz and Uncle Bert's place?"

"Yeah, I think so," said Jonah.

"It's not great, but it'll have to do," said Ilya.

"Have you got something better, telepath?" Cole glared daggers into the back of Ilya's headrest.

"I did until you broke our cover!" said Ilya.

"Did you think that hippie camp was gonna last? What were you planning to do when the weather turned? More plastic tarps? How long were you going to live like that? Were you waiting for Ivan to forget about you, his son? I seriously doubt you were ever going to make a move on your old man."

"Look, arguing is pointless now. We all had a sweet deal with Innoviro and it was Ivan who ruined that by treating people like guinea pigs. Do I have to remind anyone here that I just lost my parents to this psycho? It's Ivan's fault they're dead as much as Rubin's for botching their memory wipe."

Even as I choked back tears, my gut churned with fear of the threat still hovering over us. Whatever made Ivan's eyes glow like coals wanted to cause as much pain and suffering as possible.

The rest of the car ride back to the city was taut with anger and frustration, but everyone kept silent. All we had was each other. If any other variants escaped, they probably weren't in a position to help us. Having spent time with those people, I sensed how being visibly 'different' left you living in the shadows, ready to bolt if someone flicked on the light. We were not a group inclined to band together and mobilize for more than a meal or a party.

Jonah slowed to the speed limit once we came off the highway. I was glad that getting a speeding ticket wouldn't be added to our list of problems. I'd found my bus depot locker key, so we took a brief detour to pick up my bag and more importantly, my laptop. Then we backtracked down Douglas Street, past the turn towards my place, and veered right onto a sloping hill heading east.

We drove in the direction of the University of Victoria. I'd been meaning to go up there and tour the campus at some point. I had daydreamed (until recently) that in a few years, I could save up my wages from Innoviro and study psychology part-time on that evergreen-lined campus. If the actual school lived up to the promises made by the photos on their website, I wanted to convince my friend Bridget to relocate too. I even imagined transforming my role at Innoviro into a research position, qualified enough to call my coworkers peers. Now the idea of my going back to school was so utterly ridiculous I nearly laughed out loud.

We turned off the hill and continued south until I saw the lights of what must have been University Hospital in the distance. Jonah turned sharply and pulled the car into a gravel driveway the size of a parking spot. We were outside the picket fence of a charming little, not-quite-heritage home with wood siding. I couldn't tell what color in the dark.

"Okay, my aunt and uncle are probably asleep. They're an older couple and we will freak them out if we show up together. They don't know about our variations. They think we're troubled kids," said Cole.

"I'll go knock on the door and ask for the key to the shed. They still haven't converted it back," Faith said. "I used to live here for a while when I had a bad patch with our parents," She approached the house while we all waited in the car, sitting on our proverbial hands.

"I feel bad coming over here suddenly. We ought to visit more often than we do," said Cole. "Since our parents moved back to Toronto, Aunt Liz and Uncle Bert are more like a mom and dad. No, they're more like grandparents. They're in their late sixties and they're not exactly night owls."

A light came on and Faith disappeared inside the back door. Cole told us that she'd have to sit through a cup of tea and make up a story before their aunt would let Faith come out to go to bed.

The shed had to be the small building at the far end of the property, adjacent to where we sat in the driveway. It wouldn't have been much in the winter, although better than a tent. It was about the right size for one bedroom, but not a safe house for five people.

Faith emerged from her aunt's back door after about ten minutes. She trotted directly to the shed and beckoned at us to come over. The chilly wind and my level of shock left me shivering as I hefted my backpack onto my shoulder.

Inside, the shed held a bit more warmth. Cole fiddled with an oil space heater while Faith fired up my laptop. I sat on the bed with Ilya and Jonah, feeling utterly useless.

"I may be a low-level tech, but I know several network passwords from Innoviro. It was my responsibility to transfer data to other offices via their FTP server. Irina, I'm counting on your laptop having access to the network. I don't think anyone will get around to changing passwords until Monday morning. Not if they're detaining test subjects somewhere, knowing we're on the run." Faith's eyes didn't leave the screen as she clicked away on my laptop.

I had given my home computer to the IT department for access to the network after a conversation with Ivan about my working from home some days, in case of illness. I hadn't been excited about it at the time. If I made the decision I couldn't come into work, I wouldn't be in a fit state to do anything at all. Now, it was a concession that might just save our collective asses.

"What are you looking for? Irina's already got codes for several high-security doors," Ilya said. "All she had to do was touch them and I'm sure she could do it again."

"I'm looking for anything I can find. Details on the other Innoviro office locations, records of experiment results, and anything contextual. I know it's a long shot, but it's worth looking while we still have access."

"True, but shouldn't we try in person, before they ramp up security? Like you said, they're going to change passwords. And the codes Irina saw Tatiana enter will be useless," said Ilya.

"Won't Rubin be listening in on all of this?" Jonah glanced around the room, eying each of us. "I mean, if he was ready to pounce on Cole, won't he be tracking our minds like a hawk now?"

"No, I've kept a shield up around all of us since we left camp. The only drawback is that I can't look into Rubin's mind while I'm keeping him out. It's hard to explain, but if I make a connection, it'll go both ways between two telepaths," said Ilya.

"Fair enough," said Cole. "So if we go back, he won't know

we're there."

"Not from reading our minds, but the thought will cross his mind anyway, won't it?" asked Jonah.

"Probably. He's not Ivan's head of security for nothing," said Ilya.

"Is it worth the risk? Maybe we should give this up anyway. Maybe we should run," I said.

"You're not backing out now!" Cole glared at me.

"Irina, I believe you're onto something. The images I just saw in Rubin's mind, about what he's planning with Ivan, are dark and aggressive. The people he captured – plus the ones brainwashed into staying willingly – are all in for yet more experiments that aren't in their best interests. All so that Innoviro can do something big and awful." Ilya looked squarely at Jonah.

"Well, when you put it that way," said Jonah.

"I'll go," said Cole.

"I think I have to go too," I said reluctantly.

"Okay, the three of us," said Jonah. "What about you, Ilya?"

"If I go with you, I can't keep a mental shield around Faith," said Ilya. "I'll stay here and keep her concealed from Rubin while she hacks the network."

"Still looking out for my sister? That's sweet," said Cole.

Faith shot a look at her brother, then Ilya, and refocused on the laptop. The white glow of the screen illuminated the blush on her cheeks. Ilya had a look of tight-lipped frustration.

"No, he's got a point," I said quickly. "Besides, I think we can defend ourselves. You two watch the door while I get our medical files and whatever other documents we can find."

I begged the universe to get on our side and give me a viable path forward.

Chapter 26

Jonah tossed the car keys over to Cole and we followed him back to the driveway. I'd stopped shivering, but I was chilled to the bone, and worse, petrified of what we were about to do. I'd broken into Innoviro's secure lab once before, but I wasn't confident I'd get away a second time. Not when they knew we were coming.

I wanted Ilya's protection, but it made sense for him to keep his shield around Faith. At the brick-and-mortar office, Rubin would expect us whether he could read our minds or not. He'd be more likely to miss off-site network activity. He hated computers, even his phone.

After the short drive downtown, we parked near the entrance to the Market Square, in front of a cafe and a boutique as though we were going to a nearby club for a night out. We passed a few pedestrians, some dawdling from late dinners and others sauntering eagerly toward just-opened bars and pubs. I wished so badly that we planned to walk the few blocks to The Looking Glass instead of the insane course of going back down to Innoviro's underground bowels.

Once we reached the gate back into the Market, we were alone on the street. The shops and offices in the interior courtyard below Innoviro had closed long ago. I prayed no one would witness this break-in. My heartbeat thumped between my ears. I imagined finding Rubin on the other side of Innoviro's main door, perhaps waiting patiently at the front desk where Melissa usually sat. I pictured his smug smile at having anticipated our arrival, listening to each of our fears amplify with every step we took. For all we knew, Hugo stood at the entrance, waiting to tackle us. It was such a stupid idea to come here. We faced too much risk for such a small chance of discovering anything of value.

My rapid breath left my mouth dry as we crept up the inner stairs to the second level of the courtyard. Imagine our collective surprise when Cole turned the doorknob and it slid open like it was business as usual. Dread gripped my chest. An easy break-in would have been suspicious. But unlocked?

Cole flicked on the light and the front room looked normal. Then I noticed Melissa's desk. Her computer and the files on her desk were gone. I ran down the hall to the alcove where I sat. My desk remained, stripped of all paper and my computer.

Ivan's office was the same, gutted of the essentials including Chester's cage. Each room still had furniture, fixtures, and artwork; anything replaceable had been left. They'd taken every computer and scrap of paper. Nothing with any useful information survived the clear-out.

"It's gone. They took everything," I shouted from Ivan's office towards the front room. I wanted to keep venting, but I considered that as far as other tenants or passersby, we were potential criminals. I walked back to the reception area.

"Do you think it's even worth going downstairs?" I asked the guys in a hushed voice.

"No, probably not, but we risked coming here, shouldn't we at least look?" said Jonah.

We all nodded, so I called the elevator and Cole punched in the code that took us down to the main lower level of research labs. It sank in at that moment – all three of us were officially unemployed, without references. Having Ivan and Innoviro look after us had been an extremely spoiled existence.

It struck me that I had nowhere to go. No parents to go home to, no real home for that matter. Even if I had made my way through a certificate or diploma, Rubin might have wiped that out too. Would anyone from the car dealership remember me? Maybe Ilya could reverse Rubin's memory wipes, starting with my sister Gemma. I would have so much to sort out when the dust finally settled.

The elevator bell rang and the door opened to an eerily silent lower level. Cole and Jonah headed towards their workspaces in the large lab down the hall. I touched the door to the specimen and drug lab. A vision of a snapping, growling dog greeted me instantly. I recoiled from the shock and then looked around in embarrassment. The guys had disappeared already. I put my hand back on the door and held on as I saw the dog again, more clearly, chained in a muddy backyard. Someone outside my field of vision threw some unrecognizable meat at it and the dog snapped it into its jaws with ravenous zeal. As the dog ate, I noticed there was something wrong with him. His hindquarters were covered in some kind of armor – an exoskeleton! – and his tail got larger as it curved upward. A rat skittered past, but before it cleared the dog's reach, his bulbous tail struck.

I let go of the door handle and punched in the code, bewildered at why I saw that dog. I paused before turning the handle. There must be some biological specimen from the dog stored somewhere in this little lab of horrors. In a sense, I'd guessed correctly.

I opened the door and stepped into the dark room. The heavy steel door thudded shut on its spring-loaded hinges. I cursed realizing that I'd forgotten the step of setting the door gently ajar on its latch. My eyes adjusted to the room. A minuscule amount of bluish-white light lit the room from the handful of small LCD screens on the frozen storage tanks opposite the refrigerated specimen cabinets. I discerned empty racks behind the glass fridge doors. I scanned the surface of the bare counter.

My gaze came to rest on the filing cabinet along the wall closest to me. Half of the room stayed dark. My eyes couldn't distinguish more in the dim light. I felt around on the wall next to the door hoping to find a light switch. I knew it was hopeless to expect that cabinet to still contain files, but I couldn't leave without looking.

A menacing snarl erupted from the darkest corner of the room. And out of the pitch black, a four-legged figure kept getting taller and closer. I screamed at the half-dog, half-scorpion monstrosity in front of me.

I took a step backward. An ear-shattering SCREEEEEE and a deafening CRACK went off behind me. Light spilled in from the hall past the wreckage of the door Cole had ripped from its hinges. In a flash, he had the steel door in both hands and brought the end down with earth-shaking force, severing the dog at his mid-section before the tail could strike. The force of Cole's blow rammed the door into the concrete below the floor and the dog's blood seeped into the crack from both sides quickly drowning the dust.

Sound faded from my perception as Jonah pulled me back from the impact. Instinctively, I fought him. And then I thought of the files. I tried to form words with my mouth still gaping from shock. My senses returned to normal as I stood in the hall, looking at Jonah's terrified face with curiosity as the words he yelled took shape.

"Were you going to let that thing eat you alive? You could have been killed!"

"Sorry about the door, but I didn't want to use my bare hands. That thing probably had venom." Cole stayed calm as he joined us in the hallway. "Can we get a move on now?"

"Let's go through the sewer," I said shakily.

"You've got a bloody death wish," said Jonah.

"No, she's right," Cole said. "We could have drawn some attention from anyone upstairs in this section of the building or even on the street."

I led the way to the door at the end of the hall, up the stairwell, and into the cavernous main room. As I'd suspected, not one variant remained. "This is the fastest way out. And if this place is any indication, everyone squatting in that sewer catacomb is long gone by now."

Chapter 27

Cole drove back to his aunt and uncle's house carefully maintaining the speed limit the whole way. I squirmed in my seat for the entire ride. I wanted to lock myself in that shed and never come out. It was time to go home to Prince George and stay forever. Tears rolled down my cheeks as I remembered, yet again, that I no longer had a home there.

The light was on in the shed when we pulled into the tiny gravel driveway. I checked my phone. We had only been gone two hours. It was almost two in the morning. As the relief of being relatively safe wore off, exhaustion took hold. We went into the shed to find Ilya skimming through an old magazine and Faith, reading intently on my laptop. For a one-time couple, they seemed at ease in the tiny room. I caught myself puzzling over which of them had ended the relationship and why. A split second later I cringed inside and mentally apologized to Ilya, although he gave no sign he'd heard either thought.

Faith looked up at me and grinned. "Get some sleep guys. We've got lots to do tomorrow."

"What did you find?" said Jonah.

"Only the addresses of all other Innoviro offices in a memo from Ivan to Tatiana. It's over a year old, but it's a place to start. I mean, there are a few pop-up-type field stations and research labs, but this is a sweet score." Faith looked extremely proud that her digital detective work had yielded results.

"The deeper we get into this thing, the worse I feel about it," I said, hoping I didn't sound wiped by fatigue and defeat. "I'm still sure Innoviro is dangerous – and I want justice for my parents. But I shouldn't be rallying everyone to go to war. We have no idea what we're getting into, do we?"

"Yeah, I'm not so sure about this either," said Cole. "Last thing I remember, I had a good job, with a good salary. What happened to that? We weren't even fired!"

"We're past that point, now aren't we? The fact that we turned up to an abandoned, yet booby-trapped office reinforces Irina's angle," Jonah said. "We got more than a brush with death from that trip downtown. I'll miss my job too, but I won't question whether or not it had to happen."

"Where's the nearest office?" I asked.

"Thankfully, Vancouver," said Faith.

"What time do you want to leave in the morning?" I eyed her wearily.

"There was something else worth looking at on the network," said Faith. "Innoviro received a bill from a property management group for a house in the Highlands. Melissa forwarded the invoice to Ivan asking him to approve the housing expense for Hugo Greenwald. I peeked into the web-based version of Melissa's email." Faith smirked. "Jonah, here's a fun fact. Your name was her password."

Jonah sat with his face in his palms while Cole laughed. "Nice! That bitchy uptight secretary turned out to be good for something. I wish I could see the look on her face when she tries to go to work tomorrow!"

"So you want us to turn up at this house and knock on the door?" said Jonah.

"I looked it up on Google Earth," said Faith. "The property is pretty isolated, like half the houses in that area. We could sneak up to the back door if Ilya keeps his shield thingy around us. And we can fight if necessary. We need to take a stab at finding someone who can tell us where those people who got captured are being held. They could be at this house. Wouldn't you want someone to come after you if the tables were turned? If we go to Vancouver and leave them behind, who knows what'll happen to them?" Faith's face was full of passionate conviction.

"You're right. Let's get some sleep so we can deal with that in the morning." I curled into the fetal position on the cold musty bed.

I woke the next morning with Jonah spooning behind me, only without the hug part. Wisps of my breath curled into the air in front of me. Someone had covered us with a blanket, but the shed had become unpleasantly cold. The chill of the night had overtaken our body heat and the small radiant space heater kicking in and out didn't do much to warm the place.

Faith and Cole were gone, inside their aunt and uncle's house I assumed. Ilya clicked away on my laptop. I sat up and rubbed my eyes.

"They're bringing some breakfast back soon." Ilya noticed I was awake and closed my computer. "We have to wait for their aunt and uncle to leave for work before we can go too."

"Why is it again that these people are so freaked out about guests back here?" I said.

"They think Faith and Cole might be into drugs or crime. They're also religious," Ilya said quietly.

I looked over at Jonah still asleep. The silence with Ilya made my limbs stiffen awkwardly. I'd foolishly been hoping to be alone with Jonah.

"He likes you too, you know." Ilya smiled with sympathy.

"I keep forgetting you're like Rubin. It took me weeks to get in the habit of watching my thoughts around him. I guess I'll have to do it all over again."

"Rubin and I are similar, but I'm better at tuning people out. Maybe he doesn't try. Still, if there's anything private you don't want me to know, bury it. I can stay out of your head, but sometimes things 'pop out' of some people," Ilya said through a thin smile.

"Great. Thanks for the tip."

Jonah stirred and stretched. The door to the shed opened and Faith came in with a plate of muffins. We each grabbed one and I forced down bite after bite of stale store-bought bran. Dehydration left me parched, fighting with each starchy morsel.

Faith and Cole gave the shed a cursory search for anything useful for our trip to the Highlands, or in general, while the rest of us finished getting ready. We took turns in the add-on closet-sized bathroom with nowhere near enough soundproofing. Less than half an hour later we left the locked shed behind and were on the road, heading back out of the city to a remote suburb.

The Highlands were about a half-hour drive from the part

of town where we spent the night. We skirted downtown and took a highway northwest. The forest became denser and Cole turned off the highway. Each house we passed looked more rustic than the last. The combination of gigantic cedars and pines mingling with cabin-style buildings formed a neighborhood that resembled how I'd always pictured the American Ozarks. I craned around looking for vehicles, people, animals, or other signs of normality. It was exactly the sort of place I'd pick to hide in if I wanted to conceal something strange.

"I think this is it." Cole consulted the map on his phone.

We slowed past an inconspicuous gray wood house. The small building clung to a steep slope, one story in the front and two in the back. Rubin's little hatchback was in the driveway alongside an old pickup truck.

My heart started beating faster. "Now that we're here, I don't know if I can go through with this."

"Too late, this is happening," said Jonah.

"Don't worry," Ilya said. "I can hear thoughts in there. Rubin and my father are the only people who can block me. Nobody has any idea we're coming and if Rubin knew, he would have briefed at least a few others. Hugo thinks it's pointless to hold up out here. He thinks we're headed for the mainland already. Rubin insisted they stay on the Island. Hugo is losing patience. Some of the other variants are here too. I don't think it's everyone that got captured, but the twins, Vincent, Camille, and a few more."

"You're listening? Doesn't that mean that he can hear you in return?" I asked Ilya who ignored me.

"I'll find somewhere down the road to park," said Cole.

He pulled over after the next corner and I stuffed my

backpack on the floor. Faith handed a grainy black-and-white satellite map to Jonah. Climbing out of the car, we followed him down the embankment.

There was no trail to follow so we slid and stumbled down the loose earth on the hillside. A long spring had helped the growth of grass and shrubs, which slowed our progress but kept us concealed as we closed in on Hugo's house.

The backyard was picturesque. Trees hemmed in the lawn like a miniature meadow. A gazebo and garden resembled a fairy tale illustration. As we neared the edge of the tree line, we heard a rustling and saw Hugo's massive form emerge from around the side of the building. He had someone slung over his shoulder, dripping wet and splattered with blood.

I had never seen torture in real life. Where would I? But it looked to me like the limp body Hugo carried had experienced exactly that. I shuddered as I watched him open the sliding glass door to the basement while holding his victim.

"That's a man named Ronald," whispered Ilya. "He's conscious, but in a lot of pain. He believes he's going to die."

We all stood there, speechless, each waiting for someone else to say something.

"Tatiana was here last night," Ilya said. "She's got a few lackeys helping her. Now that this has degraded into a captive situation, they're not being gentle with their experiments. Tatiana told Hugo that none of these subjects will live."

"Hey, are you sure you can read the minds in there without Rubin listening back?" No sooner than the words left my lips, a whizzing thud hit Cole in the back. He dropped like a stone. Darts hit Faith and Jonah next, and then Ilya as he cried out.

I whirled around looking for the sniper. I saw nothing, frantically whipping my head back and forth before something bit me. And then the world went black.

Chapter 28

The room was dimly lit and full of thick, musty air. My head throbbed. I felt my hands bound behind the back of a hard chair. Cracks of sunlight gleaming through gaps in the curtains helped my eyesight adjust. The threadbare shag carpet had bits of debris ground into its filthy fibers. I saw other seated captives. Faith, Jonah, Ilya, the twins with their wings looking painfully crunched, plus a few others I didn't know. Cole was strapped to the only bed in the room with an IV in his arm. All were unconscious.

I badly wanted to free my hands and crush my skull to dull the burning pain that escalated with my level of awareness. A sudden wave of nausea launched me forward and I threw up what was left of my muffin with swirls of yellow bile. I spat several times unable to wipe my mouth. I tried to speak, but the residue of stomach acid on my dry throat stifled me.

All I needed to do was rouse Cole and he could free us all. But I suspected the fluid being fed into him was designed to keep him incapacitated. Could Faith or Jonah burn or freeze our bonds loose? Probably not a good idea. I'd seen their lack of precision and I valued my fingers.

Footsteps echoed in the hall ahead. Faith groaned from her chair across the room. Her spot in the corner was farthest from me. I'd have to speak up to get her attention, so I concentrated on the person walking down the hall towards us. The footsteps got louder and closer as I squinted at the doorway in the dim light.

I recognized the man immediately. Brad, the lab tech from Innoviro, brandished a shiny cylinder. He met my gaze and smiled as he walked over to Cole's IV and injected the contents of the syringe. He grabbed the back of one of the twins' chairs and dragged her back out the door. The platinum girl left behind remained lifeless for a few minutes, but a jolt to her body startled us both. From what I'd seen on the beach, the twins seemed to share sensations. The twin in front of me moaned. Then she cried out, once and then again. The twin's suffering ended, but the other girl wasn't brought back.

Faith and Jonah stirred but didn't wake. Instead, I heard footsteps again and Brad reappeared.

"We're finally ready for you." He grabbed the back of my chair and tilted it onto its back legs, dragging me behind him. I tried to speak again, but only a croak came out.

"I'm glad we can dispense with all that fluff and pretense now. I've always thought it's easier to treat lab rats like lab rats, not coddle them with jobs and apartments and stupid corporate picnics." He dragged me down a sunlit hallway and through the main room in the house's basement. We reached another hallway and he turned into the first doorway.

The plain square room had a bare concrete floor, a stainless steel counter, and a few cabinets. Brad picked up a syringe of the familiar lavender liquid Tatiana had injected into me. I grunted again, still feeling more wakefulness returning. As Brad approached, I wriggled in my seat to fight him.

"If you don't sit still, I'm going to break this needle in your arm. And I'll keep sticking you with needles until I get five milliliters into you and I don't care how much it hurts. Totally up to you."

I let my arms go limp, defeated and exhausted. I felt Brad's needle in my arm and the pressure of liquid being forced into my flesh. Nothing happened for a moment, but then Brad's grip melted away and I watched him walking along an urban road at night. He was a much younger man. He approached a woman wearing slick black pants, long over-the-knee black boots, and a fitted black biker jacket. Her perfectly ironed blonde hair gleamed down her back. Brad said something and she responded with a smile on her bright red lips. Her eyes were fringed with thick black makeup but still had a playful sparkle.

Brad caught her by surprise as he yanked her jacket down off one shoulder and put a needle in her bicep, much like he'd just stabbed me. The woman struggled to free herself from his grip but quickly fell limp. Brad heaved her onto his shoulder and started back the way he'd come. As he passed under a streetlight, I saw her features more clearly. Camille's unconscious face bounced above Brad's back with each step. Under all that black armor, she looked very young herself.

In a flash I slipped back to that concrete room, watching Brad dispose of the needle and tidy his work area. Thirst and exhaustion tapped my energy and my eyelids got heavier and heavier. The room grew hazy and faded as Brad walked past me out the door.

A crash out in the hall woke me. I put my feet on the ground and twisted my chair. A cry of rage slapped my ears. A body flashed past the open door. All I made out was a white coat, but I hoped it was Brad. Cole burst into the room and I'd never been so delighted to see him.

"We're gettin' outta here." He gently lifted me off the chair, leaving only my hands bound behind my back. "Idiot bound us with zip ties. Faith melted hers and she's pulling off everyone else's right now."

"Hugo … here. Rubin's car. Watch yourself," I said groggily.

"Yeah, Jonah's all over that. We all saw those vehicles on the way in, remember?" Cole said.

My memory seeped back through the fog of whatever had knocked me out. Suddenly I wondered what Jonah could do to Hugo with a spray of water. And then I remembered my burns. He'd have to lay hands on Hugo to harm him. I followed Cole out into the center of the basement where everyone had gathered, including Camille, the twins, and Vincent.

"Wait, where is Faith?" I asked.

"She went after Jonah. He thought he saw Hugo and she didn't want him going alone," said Ilya.

"Sonofabitch!" said Cole.

"What about Rubin? His car is here and he's probably reading our minds right now. He'll be long gone …" I grabbed my head as the intense ache returned.

My mind's eye took over again and I saw Rubin, bloody and unconscious behind the wheel of his car. He was in a ditch somewhere nearby. I couldn't tell if he was dead or alive, or whether or not the accident had even happened yet.

"Cole, go after him now. He's in his car, out on the road if he hasn't crashed already. Leave us here. Go!"

He paused and then ran up the stairs.

"Faith and Jonah found Hugo." Ilya bolted towards the open sliding glass door and ran into the backyard. Jonah screamed. I ran after Ilya, racing toward the sound.

A huge flash of flame flared next to the gazebo at the very end of the long narrow yard. Jonah lay on the ground and Faith had a stream of fire aimed at thin air behind his body. A shout of rage turned into screams of agony as the flames revealed a massive charred figure.

Hugo dropped to the ground on his knees and keeled over, lighting the leaves and grass around him on fire. Faith shrieked as she darted to Jonah's limp figure. I ran to them.

"No!" I yelled. "This isn't happening!"

"Irina, don't!" Ilya shouted.

Jonah's form was intact, but warped. His arms hung limp, draped over his head like a puppet dropped to the ground. One of his legs leaked blood onto his thighs. I heard the pounding of someone running behind me and I turned expecting to see Ilya. Instead, Camille barreled towards us.

"He's dislocated his shoulders. He has a spiral fracture of his left femur. Let me hold him." She dropped down beside Jonah's twisted body. "Go inside, this will take a while."

Chapter 29

We returned to the basement to find Vincent securing zip ties around Brad's hands as he sat lifeless in a chair, bleeding from a head wound. One of the twins wrapped a strip of cloth around and around his mouth.

"At this point, I don't think it'll matter if he screams," I said.

"Yes, I'm afraid it does." She tied off the restraint and stood back with her hands on her hips, smiling at me as she surveyed the scene. I couldn't help but stare at her wings. "Brad here can suck your brain out through your ear. I'm Sage. My sister is Rose. I don't think we were ever introduced." The girl extended her hand and I shook it.

"They'd look nicer with feathers, wouldn't they?" Rose had come into the room behind me.

"I'm sorry, I didn't mean to stare," I said sheepishly.

"Don't worry, everybody stares," said Sage.

"Dare I even ask what enables Brad's brain-sucking?"

"This man's got what you might call a silver tongue," said

Vincent.

"His variation is kind of like a symbiosis," Ilya said in a tone of clarification.

"Every time I learn something new about variations, I get a bit more freaked out." "Honey, you've hit the tip of the iceberg. Wait until you've been living this life for a few more years," said Rose.

"I realize that every day."

I stared back and forth between Rose and Sage's wings as they discussed the pros and cons of our group remaining in the house. I took in the details from the bone and cartilage frames to the thick smooth wing skin. If they shifted towards a light source, I saw a network of veins. The closest form in the natural world was a bat's wing.

I watched the way the twins stood and the tiny nuances of their body language. They moved with grace and strength. It was a shame they had to conceal themselves from most of the world. I knew Cole had been dealing with his variation since adolescence, and maybe Faith too. But wings? Unless they were 'made' like Jonah, the twins would have been obvious from birth. Were they born in hiding? Wouldn't hospital staff have seen them? Or an ultrasound technician? Those variables depended on their age – and mother's access to care. Regardless, these weren't questions I could ask, not anytime soon.

No matter how they had stayed hidden, these girls must have lived a whole lifetime of never being able to function in the world doing the little things everyone else took for granted. Going to school, shopping, getting a job, going on vacation … anything. Ilya's beach would have been a sanctuary for them. It made my heart ache to picture them returning to somewhere like the catacombs.

"We don't have to decide right now. Let's go upstairs and see if we can find some food, or at least somewhere comfortable to rest," said Sage. Rose and the other three variants who introduced themselves as Thea, Chloe, and Gilbert made their way up the stairs.

I turned to Ilya. "Is there any way we can interrogate this guy without his tongue attacking us?"

"I'm working on it."

"I could always spit on him. It'd be sort of ironic if he died that way, wouldn't it?" said Vincent.

"Died?" I said with alarm. "That's a bit drastic, don't you think? I'm not cool with being on the hook for that. I won't take part in a murder."

"What do you think happened to Hugo?" said Ilya.

"Chances are pretty good that Cole crushed that psychopath, Rubin," said Faith. "And I know I torched that giant properly. Besides, we need *this* asshole," Faith gave Brad's chair a violent kick, "to talk about Innoviro, not live into old age."

"Ilya, why don't you read his mind?" I asked.

"His thoughts are as tangled as Rubin's. I can try again, but it could take time, if I can ever get in there properly," Ilya answered.

"Until he comes around, there's nothing to debate. Seems a waste to have Camille heal him. I'd like to put a few more dents in him if I can't melt his face," said Vincent.

"Hey, isn't Josh telekinetic? How about getting him to 'hold' Brad's tongue back? That way he could talk, but he couldn't attack," Faith suggested.

"Will he be able to talk if someone is holding his tongue? Wait, who is Josh?" I asked.

"Josh worked security at Innoviro because he's got a sub-dermal exoskeleton stronger than steel," said Ilya.

"Steel-man could come in handy. Where is he?" said Faith.

"Josh got a job with a military contractor. Same work he did before Innoviro. He travels around, so he's rarely in town," said Ilya as Vincent coughed violently into a nylon rag. The rag smoked from Vincent's spittle.

"Are you all right?" I asked.

Vincent nodded as he recovered.

"Looking back now, I'm surprised my father let Josh take that job. I think he wanted to keep a low profile more than he wanted everyone under his thumb. And it was important to him that people see Innoviro as a benevolent force," said Ilya. "Besides, Josh still comes back to Victoria regularly."

"Damn, Ilya, why didn't you ever give us a heads up about your old man?" said Faith.

"I wasn't sure. I've never been able to read him. He was careful about what he said and documented – at least as far as I know," said Ilya.

"Enough of that talk. I don't give a shit what Ivan's reasons are. If I see him, I'm going to spit in his face," said Vincent.

"Can we deal with Rubin first?" I asked. "He might still cause problems if Cole didn't catch him."

Footsteps thumped down the wood stairwell behind me. "He's nothing to worry about now," Cole said with a flat darkness in his eyes. "I caught him pulling out of the driveway. So I ran after his car and threw it in a ditch."

"Remind me never to get on your bad side," said Ilya.

"Did you leave him in his car?" I asked.

"He's dead. I'm sure about that. Nobody survived that impact unless Rubin's variation is more complicated than we thought," said Cole.

"I believe you. I had a vision of Rubin in his car, in a ditch. I must have seen a few minutes into his future. I thought of Rubin and I had a vision almost instantly. The injection Brad gave me must have ratcheted me up another notch." I put my hand on Brad's forehead. Nothing happened.

"I'm not getting anything." I sighed and moved my hand to his chest. "What the hell? Goddammit!" I moved my hand again, frustrated, trying to restart my mind's eye.

"Let's just chill while we wait for Camille to heal Jonah." Faith's voice was shaky.

"What happened to Jonah?" asked Cole.

"He tried to kill Hugo," I said.

"What do you mean 'tried' to kill him?" said Cole.

"He tried to drain him dry, but Hugo didn't weaken quickly enough," said Faith.

"So Hugo got away?" said Cole.

"No, I killed him." Faith's shock had turned to anger.

Cole looked at her with a subtle furrow of concern on his brow.

Camille entered the basement through the sliding glass door and we all turned our heads at once.

"Jonah is sleeping now," she said.

"Is he going to be all right?" asked Faith.

"I healed his arms and legs. He also had a few broken ribs, but there's something deeper that I can't heal, something fundamentally wrong right down to the cells," said Camille.

"His experiments," I whispered.

Cole walked briskly past us all and out into the backyard. A minute later he came back in with Jonah in his arms and carried him back to the bed where he'd been strapped down himself less than an hour earlier.

We all agreed to lick our wounds for a while in the Highlands. The benefit of being hidden outweighed the risk that Ivan would try to check in with Hugo, Rubin, or Brad. The twins cooked us pasta, chicken, and vegetables, having found the kitchen surprisingly well-stocked.

Faith, Cole, and I took turns sitting with Jonah while Ilya, Vincent, and Camille rotated a watch over our captive. As day turned to night, the twins made plans to take the others back to town in Hugo's extended cab pickup truck. I almost asked why they didn't up and fly people home, and then I pictured them being spotted dropping off one or more of their friends like a pale harpy landing in suburban Victoria. The truck made sense.

We still had Cole's car. Everyone knew the safest course of action was for all of us to disappear for a while, ideally, each on our own, making us a multitude of targets instead of one variant jackpot. Ilya wanted to confront Ivan and reason with him, to talk him out of whatever plan he had for all this intense testing.

We agreed that with Rubin in a nearby ditch, we had to leave at dawn before his body was discovered. Even though his death appeared accidental, we didn't want to answer questions if the police started canvassing the neighborhood, such as it was. If Brad hadn't yielded any information by morning, we would split up and move on—after removing him to somewhere he'd need time and effort to escape. Cole had already buried Hugo's body in the woods.

It was my turn to sit with Jonah at around eight o'clock when he woke. I grinned at him and he smiled back weakly.

I'd spent most of the afternoon and evening replaying what Ilya had told me about Jonah's feelings for me, contemplating whether or not I wanted to talk to him about it.

"Am I back in the basement of Hugo's house?"

"Yes, but Hugo is dead. So is Rubin."

"I feel like roadkill," said Jonah.

"Well, you were practically in pieces, so that sounds about right. What were you thinking attacking Hugo like that?"

"I wasn't thinking, of course. I panicked when I saw him. I couldn't let him hurt anyone else."

"So you tried to grab him? How long would you have to hold on to do damage to a guy that size?"

"I know, I know. Faith got him then?"

"Yeah, there wasn't much left, but Cole got rid of him anyway."

"And Camille must have worked her magic on me," Jonah said.

"Thank God she was here and in one piece. If she'd been knocked out, or heaven forbid, worse-" My words caught in my throat and I took hold of his nearest hand.

I leaned over and kissed him lightly on the lips. In his weakened state, I hadn't expected any reaction, emotional or physical. As I pulled away, he lifted his head and grabbed the back of my neck, kissing me with intensity. His lips were firm and his tongue earnest. He pulled me down on top of him. I wrapped my arms around his lower back, finding his muscular butt with my hands. He rolled me beneath his body, straddling me as he kept kissing deeper and deeper.

The familiar burning sensation started again. I felt light-headed. A moment of gratitude swept through me that he'd been weak enough to last that long before hurting me. The instant my gratitude turned to guilt, a gasp at the door broke us apart.

She disappeared again before I focused clearly on the doorway, but I knew it was Faith. I disentangled myself from Jonah to go after her, but he grabbed my arm.

"Let her go," he said.

I sat back down on the bed and sighed. Both brother and sister would probably hate me before the night ended.

<h1 style="text-align:center">Chapter 30</h1>

A few minutes after Faith ran out, Camille came to tend to Jonah. The sympathetic look on her face told me everything. Whether Faith confided in her or Ilya translated our thoughts, she knew. I squeezed Jonah's hand and left him with the healer.

I walked down the hall and out into the large central room of the basement. I heard voices upstairs through the stairwell. Vincent and Ilya debated the finer points of Vancouver's nightlife, anticipating the trip. Vincent favored a pub near a bus depot and Ilya wanted to hit an underground bar on Granville Street. I couldn't stop thinking about Faith, picturing her sulking, and cursing my name. So I opened the sliding glass door to the backyard and walked out into the dark.

Even though I believed that Rubin and Hugo were gone, I dreaded the oppressive black wall around me. Light from the house dimly illuminated the yard transforming it from a picturesque meadow to a creepy cave. The gazebo at the end of the lawn wasn't as inviting as it had been when we first approached. As I evaluated whether or not to stay outside, I felt a hand on my shoulder and my whole body flinched.

"Wow, you were lost in thought," said Cole.

I felt warmth in my cheeks. I looked down at the ground for a moment.

"I've got a lot on my mind. My life has taken a few sharp turns since I left home. And now I can't go back. If Rubin told the truth – and I think he did – there's nobody left from my hometown who even knows me, let alone would help. It's like my life outside Innoviro doesn't exist anymore. It's hard to believe. I know I should call my sister, but if I do and she doesn't remember me, I think I'll lose it completely."

"I knew Rubin could wipe memories, but I've never heard of him doing it to an employee before, let alone erasing someone's past. Techs from Innoviro would have to be complicit. Hard copies would be out there, like photographs or any mention of you in a newspaper."

"Doesn't it seem impossible? How can you erase a whole life?"

"Haven't you checked it out?"

"Not really. You mean Google myself?"

"For a start." Cole pulled his phone from his pocket and started tapping. "Where would you expect to find your name online?"

I wracked my brain. I had never played sports or won an academic prize. I thought briefly about the sticky end of Nechako Motors. I was too far down the ladder to matter to anyone. To comply with Ivan's policy of no social media, I deleted every profile I had.

"I can't find you so far, but when we get time at a computer, we'll sort this out," Cole said. "This is going to sound selfish now, but I figured you were out here thinking about your love life."

I let out a loud breath. "Are you asking if we can talk about it?"

"I think we have unfinished business." Cole looked at me expectantly.

"I'm sorry if I left things ambiguous after you kissed me on the beach." Remorse surged in my belly. "I didn't want to hurt your feelings."

"So it's Jonah then?" Cole demanded.

"It's nobody. I'm torn up over this. I never wanted to lead you on." I wrang my hands.

"You didn't. I knew you liked him. I stupidly hoped you'd end up liking me too."

"I do like you, Cole, but I fell for Jonah. I think he feels the same way."

"He does, at least from what I can tell. You know, you can't *be* with him though, not in the long run. And I'm not talking about his capacity to suck the life out of you. He's sick. His variation is unnatural and it's getting more unstable. I think he was so quick to defend Ivan because he was counting on the cure they were working on. Jonah either needs to stabilize his genetic changes or reverse them altogether."

"He hinted at that. When Camille found something wrong with his cells, I knew she meant his variation. All the same, I can't help the way I feel." Heat flooded my face again.

"And you know Faith has a thing for him too?"

"I got that impression, but I wasn't sure until about half an hour ago," I said.

"They dated for a little while after Ilya broke up with her.

Faith's variation is the right match for Jonah's. He doesn't hurt her. They made sense, but he must not have been into it. He was already my best friend, but as the second guy to dump my sister in a year, he was on my shit list for a while," Cole said with a joyless quiet tone.

"I never knew." I didn't want to be the nail in their friendship's coffin. I felt awful, so low that I practically had to scrape myself off the ground to turn around and go back. But I did, and Cole followed me.

By morning Brad was awake and alert. Ilya and Vincent wanted the tie left around his mouth and nobody argued. Ilya tried repeatedly to read Brad's mind but made no progress.

I offered to take a turn and see if I could spark a vision. I tried concentrating like I had the day before when I saw Rubin's car crash, but I couldn't replicate the intensity. Vincent assured me Brad's bonds were secure, so I placed my palm on his forehead. I was transported to a rundown building in a light industrial park, standing in front of an open bay door.

To my left, more structures obscured the skyline of downtown Vancouver. The royal blue sky of early night glowed with hundreds of orange and white twinkling lights peeking out from behind the dark black buildings nearby. To my right, I saw the water and a large pile of something yellow, maybe sulfur. The patina-green Lion's Gate Bridge stretched ahead into the forest. The downtown core was across the water somewhere to the south. Floodlights revealed the industrial coastline of the North Shore. I tried to walk into the building in front of me, but my feet felt heavy. I forced myself to move and as I walked in through the bay door, blackness enveloped me. It was complete nothingness.

I withdrew my hand from Brad's forehead. My eyes came to rest level with his. The glare of hatred unnerved me. He mumbled what I took for a verbal version of the cursing in his mind.

"I saw a crappy building in an industrial park somewhere in Vancouver. It had a partial view of downtown from the North Shore, near a giant sulfur pile. But I couldn't see. It was dark, and when I went to walk inside, the world disappeared, like everything, everywhere was gone."

Ilya considered the situation and said, "Rubin must have erased his memory of that place. I think he did it to me a few times; I'd try to remember somewhere I'd been and it was like falling into a pit. I never had the guts to talk to my father about it."

"There's something worth looking at in this building then," said Vincent.

"Great. Let's leave for Vancouver right now." Irritation radiated from Faith, permeating her gestures and movements.

"Camille and I will stay behind. We've talked and we just can't get involved any further. It's too dangerous," said Vincent.

"What! You're going to leave it to the five of us?" said Faith.

"No worries man, I know you've got a family. Besides, we don't have room for everyone in my car anyway," said Cole.

"I think we should hold off until we've got more than this to go on," said Ilya.

"Yeah, we need a better plan than walking around the North Shore until the setting looks right. Even if we did find the place, there's no telling what messed up scene could be waiting for us," said Cole.

"I've already tried to heal Brad's mind. That gap isn't from a traumatic experience. I agree that the memory was – taken. There's nothing more I can do. I'm sorry I can't help, but I don't have it in me to go to war right now," said Camille.

"We understand. I'll spend more time with Brad. Eventually, he'll let a thought slip out or Irina will have a new vision," said Ilya.

At the prospect of being probed further, Brad wrestled against the bonds around his wrists and ankles. He twisted his neck and jaw, frantic to release the tie around his mouth. Vincent kicked one of his legs.

Cole stomped on the ground and the basement shook. His foot left a crack in the concrete and the room went silent. "Sorry about that, but we need to get out of here. Remember the car I threw in the ditch? Unless something's changed, eventually the cops will turn up here. Sooner or later they'll find what remains of Hugo too. Does anyone have any ideas other than going straight to Vancouver?"

"Why don't you try one of those old buildings in Chinatown? There are a few with signs in front about a development coming," Vincent said. "I think they're empty, but I don't know if they're condemned or hazardous. They probably have squatters already, but you could blend in. Camille and I will stay here and when the cops come, we'll give them the runaround."

"Works for me. Let's go squat downtown for a while and see what shakes loose from our friend here. I'll wake up Jonah," said Ilya.

"I'll grab my car. You guys get ready," said Cole.

I'd left my bag in Cole's car, so while Faith, Camille, and Vincent went upstairs, I splashed water on my face in the basement's grimy bathroom. As I stared in the mirror, I thought back to the bathroom in my parents' home. I thought about my sister and my parents and how simple things were in Prince George.

I thought of Bridget, still backpacking through Europe where Rubin hadn't been able to reach her and a glimmer of hope emerged. She would remember me. Now that Rubin was dead, she always would remember me. If I returned to Prince George one day, Bridget would know me. Even if Rubin had wiped the minds of everyone else who knew me, in my best friend, there was proof I existed.

I splashed water on my face again to refocus. In light of what I'd lost, being at odds with Faith didn't seem so bad anymore.

Chapter 31

We found the soon-to-be-demolished buildings Vincent described in Chinatown. We chose one and slipped in after Cole pried open a section of thick steel fencing. The security measures on such a run-down property were surprising to us, but we were also shocked by the number of people experiencing homelessness in Victoria.

Ilya explained that the volume and relative visibility of the downtown street population were part of Ivan's logic while choosing the Innoviro office location. It would be easy for his sewer-dwelling variants to blend in when they emerged.

Ilya easily shielded our cumbersome entry onto the property from the few pedestrians we passed. Either his illusion was flawless or the people on the street were completely apathetic, but Cole was able to carry Brad – aggravated and restrained – down the street and through the construction zone without drawing any attention.

Of the building's five floors, we chose the second for the best compromise between safety and ease of access. We were too far up from eye level for anyone on the sidewalk to see us, but we could get out quickly. The space had a main reception room with four smaller offices, a boardroom, and a basic kitchen. Two bathrooms greeted us at the end of the hall and I made a note to check the taps to confirm if the floor still had running water.

The office must have been an old law or marketing firm. Lettering on one of the walls had been scraped off long ago leaving only partial outlines. Under a layer of dust I could still make out a pattern on the dark carpet. Small tan fleur-de-lis and flourish swirls formed borders around open squares of negative space, like woven golden grout. I saw crumpled bits of paper, unused staples, paper clips, and flakes of old leaves all mingled with the dust.

The domed light fixtures overhead were embellished with scrollwork around the edges. A brass handrail ran the length of the dividing wall between the reception area and the hallway down to the offices. The wallpaper was a creamy color, textured with ridges. Varnished crown molding ran along the edges of the ceiling and the floor. The lack of furniture contrasted with the mess triggered memories of Nechako Motors and how it had been emptied with haste. What had happened here, before the space was abandoned in this state?

While Faith and Cole rounded up crates to sit on and brought blankets in from the car, Ilya wasted no time trying to get back into our captive's head. Although Brad had worn down somewhat, his willpower and rage were still powerful enough to derail any attempt at getting to his underlying thoughts.

While Ilya struggled with Brad, I took the opportunity to pull my cards out of my backpack and try for an update on

Bridget. I slipped into an empty office and closed the door behind me. I sat down cross-legged on the dirty carpet and shuffled my cards while picturing Bridget's face. I closed my eyes and remembered her giddy smile the last time I'd visited her. While I sat on her bed and watched, Bridget packed her new hiking backpack with her European wardrobe.

In a flash, a new image of Bridget snapped to mind shoving out the memory. Bridget sat on a wide bank of stone steps leading up to a Roman-style building, a courthouse or a gallery. She and another girl I didn't recognize ate sandwiches, alternating between bites and excited outbursts. A familiar greasy-haired figure approached them. NO! Not Bridget too! When had this happened?

I watched helplessly as Rubin introduced himself to Bridget and the other girl, shaking their hands. Bridget's smile dropped away leaving confusion behind. The other girl abruptly stood and left with a blank expression below empty glassy eyes. Rubin sat next to Bridget and put his arm around her. Bridget's confused expression melted into a completely blank look. I knew her memories of me were gone.

I pulled myself off the stone steps, away from my one-time best friend and my recently deceased adversary. I was back in the dark condemned office, already on my feet. I bent down to pick up my cards and threw them at the wall. Why Bridget too? Couldn't that sonofabitch have left me a single shred of my old life? I couldn't even ask him. I felt a rush of satisfaction that Rubin had died a violent and painful death.

My cards sat in a scattered pile on the floor where they had bounced off the wall in an explosion of paper rectangles. I didn't feel like sharing my news about Bridget. I'd cried enough in the last week. I gathered my cards back together, slipped them into their box, and tucked them in my back pocket.

I needed a distraction. I returned to Ilya and offered to take over Brad's interrogation. Ilya was happy to pass the task. Instead of palming Brad's forehead again, I decided to grab his hand. For all I knew about my gift, touching a different body part could access different information. Or maybe the passage of time would suffice. To be safe, I shuffled my plastic milk crate around to the back of Brad's chair where his legs wouldn't reach.

When I took his hand, he crunched my fingers together with a devastating grip. I yelped and Ilya kicked one of Brad's shins. He cried out but the fabric in his mouth muffled the sound. I shook my hand, waiting for the circulation to come back and for the throbbing to subside. Then I grabbed his forearm, well above his wrist. My strategy finally paid off as the room melted away to my former boss' office. Ivan sat at his desk with Brad in the guest chair.

"… I have a new recruit on her way, so I want your schedule flexible for testing on-demand. I'm not sure how quickly things will progress, so I want your undivided attention when the need arises," said Ivan.

"Absolutely, sir. I can assure you the new subject will be my priority in the lab, and I'll keep you apprised of all results as soon as I have them. When do you anticipate obtaining the first specimen?" said Brad.

"I believe we'll see her within the week, but we'll know more once Rubin makes contact …" Tatiana's entrance interrupted Ivan.

"I have that correspondence transcription you requested. It confirms what we discussed," she said.

"That's fine, leave the file with me," said Ivan as he reached for the folder. "Oh, and please take this document back to our associate. It's an 'eyes only' file regarding the Compendium." He passed her a white envelope with Innoviro's logo in the center.

As the paper made contact with Tatiana's hand, the office dissolved and I stood at an intersection on a stretch of highway I'd never seen. To my left, traffic flowed down to a small suburban mall. I looked to my right and saw a concrete cube building with a large ventilation tube. It had to be where the envelope went. I concentrated on the inside of the building and my viewpoint jumped forward. In a moment, my gaze left the ground and my mind's eye focused on a desk inside one of the windows on the top floor. I concentrated harder, looking for some identifiable marker in the office. Out the door and across the hall the door read "402".

I let go of Brad's arm as he wrestled harder and harder. Vertigo hit me hard and I fell off my crate and thudded to the floor clumsily. Ilya knelt beside me with an empathetic look. I returned to rubbing my sore hand.

"What did you see?" he said frantically.

"Some envelope that was important to Ivan and Tatiana went out to a Federal building on the highway somewhere. I've never been there, but I think it's here in Victoria. Near a mall."

"Good, good. Can you describe it in detail?"

"Yes, but I feel gross. I need to lie down first."

"Here, take this," said Ilya as he handed me a notebook and a pen. "Go take a nap. We brought a few sleeping bags and blankets from Hugo's. Write down everything you remember before you pass out."

I took the notepad and did as he suggested. I grabbed a sleeping bag and took it into one of the offices facing the street. The carpet had the same dirt and debris as the rest of the floor, but surprisingly this room was a bit warmer than the rest. I looked down at sun-bleached patches of carpet and took the hint. I unrolled the bag over by a window. A pocket of warm air welcomed me as I sat down in the padded nylon cocoon. I looked out the window at the people walking below, young and old, marching and meandering. Then I wrote. And wrote.

My narrative covered Ivan's office, the documents, the highway, the intersection and mall, the building, and room 402 across from the envelope's final destination. Then I closed the notebook and pulled it to my chest inside the sleeping bag. Shifting and twisting, I tried lying on my side, on my back, curled up, but comfort and sleep eluded me. My eyelids responded slowly over dry eyes. My forehead throbbed and my stomach grumbled. And then tears came, pooling in my eyes. I didn't know why I was crying, but it felt completely justified. Out of nowhere, Jonah's hand touched my shoulder.

"You got room for one more in there?" he said with a playful smirk.

I stared up at him, at a loss for words. I rubbed my eyes to hide the tears.

His smile disappeared as he read the expression on my face. "Have you changed your mind about me?" Jonah's voice was quiet with concern.

"No, but… last night, it happened again. That draining thing," I said avoiding those bright blue eyes. He touched my cheek to comfort me. I flinched and he retracted his hand.

"It will get better when I finally nail down the research I was doing with Ivan. It's self-serving, I know, but I'm hoping that if we get access to Innoviro's databases, we'll find everything he had squirreled away about me. If Ivan's been doing some shady stuff, maybe he's made progress on my case that he hasn't shared yet, to keep me working there longer. The funny thing is, I felt so indebted to him, and I may have stayed loyal even if I had seen something dodgy."

"You didn't know. Every test you had was one you gave informed consent to, and maybe the others consented properly too, not knowing that Ivan was working on something bigger than them. You shouldn't have to give up on getting better. When this is sorted out, we'll find a way to get your work back on track."

"I don't think you realize how rare Ivan's company and research is. Do you think there are other people out there researching genetic variations that most people think are pure science fiction? To even try to stabilize my condition, I need a lab and supplies, which costs money. And over the long run, I'll need a job to start paying rent and bills again. I haven't been stashing money in anticipation of Ivan being a sociopath. I knew I wouldn't have it that good forever, but I still thought life after Innoviro was years away."

I looked squarely at Jonah and realized I knew exactly how he felt. Maybe we had a lot in common after all. As I studied his features in the soft white overcast light from the window, I saw how ill he looked. The skin around his eyes had a mildly bruised sunken look and his complexion was too pale. Camille hadn't said exactly how serious his problem was and neither had Cole.

"Be honest with me. How sick are you? Are we talking about finding a way for us to be together? Or is this about keeping you … healthy?" I almost said 'alive' but I couldn't finish the sentence.

"I'm not sure. Ivan had me on a weekly injection, but that's over now. And my situation is complicated. Most variants are born different or modified with advanced expertise, before birth or as a child. I was pretty much an adult and what I did to myself was all thumbs compared to Ivan's staff. I was studying under a man working on a cure for cystic fibrosis. He had a theory that he could use a combination of viruses to both manage symptoms and change a person's genetic makeup. One of his projects was a genetically altered cold virus. One of its effects was to reduce sinus fluid production."

"Were you trying to prove him right and volunteer yourself for testing?"

"If it had been like that, I would have told you. It wasn't heroic. I was sick one semester - regular colds and allergies. I wanted my sinuses to stop going overboard. I got drunk one night and I broke into the lab thinking that I'd never get sick again if my sinuses stopped producing too much fluid. The virus had a completely different effect on me. I blame the fact that I'd been drinking absinthe when I injected the virus. I was drunk enough to think the idea could work and lucid enough to know that I would lose my courage when I sobered up," said Jonah, looking at the ground. "It was by far the stupidest move of my entire life. I've got only myself to blame for the trouble I'm in now."

"So it's getting worse, but is it going to get bad, like you're going to turn into a fish or something?" I said, laughing nervously.

"If I turned into a fish, I could dive into the nearest lake or ocean, depending, and forget about everything else," he said with a forced smile. "No, this is going to kill me. The moisture my body craves now will overload me sooner or later. We're made of a lot of water, but there is such a thing as too much."

"We'll find a way to reverse it. If Ivan can inject me with a psychic-enhancing serum, there's someone somewhere who can help."

"Genetics is a complex science. Even if we derailed the proverbial train I'm on right now, there's no way to know we'd find a cure for what's wrong with me. We have to remember all the other people who've had their lives damaged. We still don't know what Ivan wanted to do with Innoviro."

"This all started because I wanted revenge, on Rubin and Ivan. Revenge and my gut feelings," I said, frustrated and frowning. "Such shitty reasons to tear everyone's lives apart."

"Nothing will bring your parents back, but after talking with Ilya and seeing how many others wanted to hide from Ivan, I think it's worth listening to your gut."

"Thank you, I needed to hear that. I meant what I said about getting your treatment back on track though."

Jonah smiled and cuddled up to me. He stayed on the outside of the sleeping bag and I let him. Would each kiss hurt him now as much as me? Or would he get worse at the same rate regardless?

Chapter 32

The abandoned building was cold at night. I tossed and turned in my sleeping bag, listening to the intermittent sounds of traffic and the occasional intoxicated rant from the street.

I looked over at Jonah, who lay on his side reading, his head propped up with one arm. I'd created a makeshift floor lamp by propping up one of the utility flashlights we swiped from Hugo's. A sudden cry of rage drew both our attention to the door. Jonah sat up, we looked at each other and Ilya yelled again.

"Arrrrrgh! Useless… hopeless… sleazy… " screamed Ilya. "Asshole!" he shouted as his voice got closer. He stormed into the room. "Brad is gone! That shifty bastard escaped!"

"How? I mean, you had him strapped down six ways from Sunday. Where did he go?" I said.

"How should I know where he went, Irina? Does it matter now?"

"No, but what's the point of freaking out if we're not going after him?" said Jonah, rubbing his eyes.

"We've got enough to go on without him. I think I can find the office and the envelope I saw in my last vision," I said.

"We needed more than that!" said Ilya.

"No, we *wanted* more. But let's worry about what we've got, not what we lost," said Jonah. Ilya's heavy breathing slowed and stabilized as he considered Jonah's perspective.

"What the hell is going on in here? I go get one lousy cup of coffee and the sky freakin' falls," said Faith.

"Brad escaped." My eyes met hers.

"Great. Now we can get on the ferry to Vancouver," she said flatly.

"No, Irina had a new vision. There's something important here in Victoria. A document," said Ilya.

"Fine. Let's go get it then." Faith's bitter tone made me cringe.

"I'm not sure exactly where this place is. I *think* it's here," I held up the notebook and handed it to Ilya. He flipped it open to my dog-eared page and skimmed my writing.

"That sounds like Arbutus Mall. Yeah, that's here. And I think I know the building you mean. It's a federal environmental research building. We've got two options. I could get us in with an illusion tomorrow morning when it's open, or we could sneak in tonight," said Ilya.

"I feel like crap," said Jonah.

"I think I'd only need one other person. I know exactly what to look for and where. Well, almost exactly. I'll find the envelope once I'm in the office. I'm sure," I said.

Faith glared at me but didn't say anything.

"Someone should stay behind. I'll maintain the illusion that the side door is boarded up," said Ilya.

"I'll stay too. If Ivan's people find us here, I want a crack at them," said Cole.

"So it's just me and Irina?" said Faith.

"I'll try it alone. I'm not scared," I said.

"That's not the issue. It's a bad idea to do something like this alone," said Ilya. "You guys go together and we'll stay here with Jonah."

"Faith, you can probably short out the building's alarm. It's a government office, not a high-tech military base. You'll be in and out as soon as Irina finds this file," said Cole.

"Why don't *you* take Princess Premonition and *I'll* stay with Jonah," said Faith.

"A short circuit is better than a broken door. Stop being such a brat and go with Irina," said Cole.

Ilya and I looked at each other sharing the sensation of awkwardness. I knew that Ilya knew about me and Jonah. And about Cole and Faith's feelings.

"Fine. Give me your keys," she said to Cole, and to me, "Are you ready right now?"

"Yup, you bet. Let's go," I said nervously.

Cole handed his car keys to Faith. I followed as she stormed out.

We went down the stairwell and around the block to Cole's car. As we walked up the hill towards Government Street, I mulled over possible conversation starters, some of which included "I didn't realize you still had feelings for him" and "Why didn't you tell me how you felt?" and "Does this mean we can't stay friends?" when an RCMP officer rounded the corner at the intersection and locked eyes with Faith. She froze and so did I. A hand grabbed my wrist and yanked it behind my back as another hand twisted my free arm backward.

"Irina Proffer, you are under arrest for breaking and entering, and theft over five thousand dollars. Do you understand?"

The man didn't wait for me to answer, he kept speaking and I stood in shock as I watched the officer behind Faith do the same thing to her.

"You have the right to retain and instruct counsel without delay. We will provide you with a toll-free telephone lawyer referral service if you do not have your own lawyer. Anything you say can be used in court as evidence. Do you understand? Do you want to speak to a lawyer?" he said briskly.

"No, I don't understand! Where did I break and … oh," I said.

"Remember now, do you?" said the cop.

"This is a mistake. I didn't steal anything; I work there. Well, I used to work there. The place is shut down now," I said as the cop forced me along the sidewalk. We back-tracked towards a police sedan Faith and I had passed half a block back. I heard Faith shouting behind us.

"There's no mistake. The owner wishes to press charges. We'll arrange for a lawyer in the morning," said the cop.

I wracked my brain for what I took that could be worth five thousand dollars. My personal medical file? Could you place a dollar value on that? I couldn't think of anything else I took. Considering the outrageously worse things Ivan was guilty of, I couldn't believe I was the one being arrested. Faith was shoved into the other passenger seat in the back of the cop car. Her rage overflowed.

"Hey, losers! Do you seriously think we have stolen property? Do you know what our boss is guilty of? You can't arrest us on the word of a guy who's been experimenting on people, illegally. And half of them were kidnapped! He's probably breaking the law right now. Stealing *and* kidnapping! And fucking god knows what else!" shouted Faith.

"Young lady, you need to watch your language, or better yet, follow your friend's lead and keep quiet," said the cop who had cuffed me.

While Faith's cop stood outside speaking to someone on the sidewalk, my cop sat in the front passenger seat making notes. He stared intently at his writing, surveyed the street, and checked his pockets; he looked everywhere but at us. I wanted to see the look on his face to see if he would give something away. How had they known where to find us, on the street like that? Could Rubin still be alive, listening to us again? Were they fake cops, working for Ivan? I flexed and pulled against the cuffs on my wrists. They felt real. In another moment, the lead cop got in the car and we pulled away from the curb.

A short drive carried us from Chinatown to the police station. Things kept getting real from there as the cops led us out of the car and through the central office space on the main floor of the building. Faith and I were fingerprinted and moved along to a large room of wall-to-wall concrete. Our cell had a single long wood bench along the inside wall. The sickly pale lime green floor sloped inward on all sides, creating a large funnel towards a grate in the middle of the room. It smelled of urine, body odor, and more than anything, stale vomit. The combined smells nearly made me sick. I felt my gag reflex tug at the back of my throat several times before I became numb to the stink.

"You'll stay in custody overnight until you see a judge sometime tomorrow. We'll have lawyers come in to meet you in the morning," said my cop. Faith's arresting officer had disappeared after commenting about paperwork. He locked the iron bar door behind him leaving Faith and I alone. She sat down on the bench and I followed her lead.

"This place is foul! I had no idea jail was so awful," I said. I felt momentary relief that we had something much more important to talk about than Jonah.

"Regular jail isn't that bad. We're in the drunk tank," Faith said with firm certainty.

"How much time have you spent in jail cells?" I asked.

"Enough. It's not the first time I've seen a drunk tank," she said.

"Have you been in real jail?" I said.

"You mean a juvenile detention center? That's what it is when you're a kid. Well, a teenager. I don't think they send little kids to jail," said Faith.

"So that's a yes." I felt a stab of shock, but I believed her immediately.

"I used to get in fights. Often. Now I've got roller derby. Sorry, I *had* roller derby," she said. I could still feel some hostility in her voice. "We should get some sleep." Faith promptly turned her back on me and curled up on her end of the bench.

I wanted to ask more questions. What was going to happen to us? Jail until a trial? Would there be a trial? What would happen if we were found guilty? I looked over and saw that she had already closed her eyes. I surveyed the rest of the room, still trying to blot out the stench of countless other intoxicated visitors to that cell. I wracked my brain for some way to spark a vision, hoping I'd see a future in which all of this worked out alright. But the prospect of placing even a knuckle or a fingernail on the walls or floors produced a fresh wave of nausea. So I copied Faith, again, and curled up on my side of the bench, closed my eyes, and waited for sleep.

It was no good. I got up and paced. Our bags and phones had been taken, leaving us with nothing to do. I stood and thought – about Ivan and what he wanted from his testing on variants, about Jonah and my feelings for him, and then about his health. I thought about going to Vancouver and what we would do when we found another Innoviro office or lab.

I stared across the hall at the frosted glass window and the mottled orange light of the streetlight behind the glass. I heard a click-creak from down the hall.

Chapter 33

Minutes passed between the sound of the door closing and the clicking footsteps that followed. It wasn't the click of high heels, but the deeper sound of men's dress shoes. Since I was sure no lawyer would come to see us in the middle of the night, I braced myself for something unpleasant.

The clacking footsteps came closer. A slight and freckle-faced officer approached us leading a large barrel-shaped woman. The officer stood slightly shorter, yet much narrower than the woman. The new prisoner seemed familiar. Her hair was shaved into the combination of a pixie and a crew cut. Her dingy hooded sweatshirt stretched tight across her solid chest. As I stared at her arms, I noticed the lines where muscles bulged off each bicep. I wanted Faith to wake up immediately to bring her roller derby personality into the situation.

"Faith, wake your lazy ass up," said the stocky woman.

The officer unlocked the cell door and slid it sideways along the wall of bars.

"Irina, it's us. Wake Faith so we can get the hell out of here," said the police officer.

"What now? Us who?" I said with a confused frown. Television drama scenes of prison violence played out in my mind. I sized up the officer's build. He was no match for the woman whose arm he held, let alone the combination of three healthy girls.

"Dude, she can't see through it. That's probably a good thing, right?" said the stocky woman. Her voice sounded distinctly male the second time.

"Cole? Is that you? Ilya?" I asked.

"There you go!" said officer Ilya. As I concentrated and focused on his face, the image flickered, shimmering like waves of heat over pavement on a hot summer day. Ilya was underneath, but as soon as I looked away and back again, the officer was restored. Cole had woken Faith and had her standing up, taking in the scene.

"I have to say, you make a really ugly chick." Faith grinned at her brother's expense.

"Do you want out of here, or what?" said Cole.

Faith smiled again and walked past us out into the corridor.

"We don't have much time. I can't maintain this disguise longer than a few more minutes. I'm not sure I got this officer's features right. People are a lot harder to change than scenery. And the real guy could stroll back in here anytime," said Ilya as he marched ahead. "Visuals aside, being someone else is extra tricky. You can't duplicate their memories, knowledge, personality … it doesn't last long or end well," Ilya whispered as we got to the end of the hall and went up a short flight of stairs. We emerged into the office space we'd passed through hours earlier. "Now everybody shut up!" he hissed back down the stairs.

Ilya walked purposefully, but slowly through the office. We all kept pace close behind him. I ventured a glance around the partially lit floor. Where bodies and voices had formed a hub of activity earlier, rows of empty chairs and piles of perfectly still papers remained. A few people sat at their desks. Doors on either side of the room were all closed. None of the people at their desks even looked up, let alone challenged our exit.

Fortunately, Ilya's mental strength held out and we glided past the desks and out the front door. We were halfway down the block before anyone spoke.

"Remind me to keep you in the loop anytime I'm doing something I might get arrested for," said Faith.

Ilya and Cole stayed ahead and rounded the first corner. I saw Cole's car parked another half block away.

"You're lucky I can hear Irina from that far away," said Ilya.

"I was wondering how you knew where to find us," I said. "Wait, so you were listening to every thought I had?"

"Just while you were here. When you and Faith didn't come back, I reached out for you. I couldn't hear Faith, but you were thinking about how boring and horrifically awful-smelling the drunk tank was. I didn't have to listen for much longer to figure out what happened," said Ilya. We arrived at Cole's car where he promptly crawled over the driver's seat to unlock every other door.

"Good thing I had my second set of car keys handy," said Cole.

"Hey, at least we got picked up before we made it to your car. Saves the hassle of trying to pluck the car out of an impound lot," Faith said proudly.

"Can we get back on track and go get this goddamn envelope now?" said Ilya.

"I'll feel better once we're off the island," I said.

"I'm one step ahead of you," said Cole. "Jonah is packing up back at the building. He'll have all our stuff at the downstairs door, ready to go when we get back from this government place. After that, we're on the next ferry out of here."

"Hopefully the first boat of the morning," I said.

"Where are we staying in Vancouver?" asked Faith.

"No idea," said Ilya.

Cole sped up as we left the downtown core on the Island highway that stretched ahead like a streak of wet charcoal paint. Streetlights blinked in and out of view as we accelerated down four lanes of fresh pavement.

"You know, it's not like I had an illustrious career ahead of me, but it's starting to sink in how much this is going to suck, even best case scenario," I said.

"We *are* talking about living like fugitives. Is that necessary? I mean is Ivan seriously going to have some thugs chase us down?" said Faith.

"I don't know. But my father takes Innoviro more seriously than anything else in his life. I was practically a toddler when he started the company. Before that, I think he did more of the same kind of research. It's his life. I don't know exactly when it morphed from helping people into selling science, but I'm hoping we find something at this facility that points the finger at someone else. Or even just a good reason for what he's doing."

"Buddy, I used to think your old man was a pretty awesome guy, but from what I've seen in the last few days, I don't know if I can get behind him anymore," said Cole.

"If you think you might have a problem staying on the other side of the line from your dad, do you want to bow out and stay here in Victoria? You could try to rebuild what you had on the beach," I said to Ilya.

"No, I'm with you guys. Regardless of his reasons, I know he's doing something dangerous. I always figured I'd make peace with him though," said Ilya.

"We're probably a few flimsy locked doors away from finding out some bad shit here, something that could be worse than any of us thinks right now. Sure, it could clear your dad, but if it's something else ..." Faith drifted off not knowing how to finish her thought.

Cole slowed down for a red light at an intersection ahead and I suddenly recognized where we were. I knew there was a mall down the hill on the left. On our right, I saw the government building with its weird snaking ventilation looming ahead.

Chapter 34

At twenty minutes past midnight, a handful of cars trickled up and down the highway. A few vehicles turned up the hill toward the gray concrete cube from my vision, but they all passed the building without a glance.

The building itself was unremarkable other than the twist of exterior ventilation on the roof. Small rectangular windows dotted the solid, flat walls. A lush lawn surrounded the sides of the building that faced the highway, sloping down to tall weeds that ended in a ditch next to the road. On that lawn, the sign bore the Government of Canada logo with no other indication of what offices were housed there.

Cole followed the cars turning off the highway and parked on a residential side street near the government property. As he turned off the car, Ilya held up his hand in a gesture of pause.

"What now?" said Faith.

"Shhh, I'm listening. There are a lot of people still awake in these homes and I have to concentrate to filter the chatter," he said irritated and focused. A few moments later he said, "Okay, there's nobody in the building. I'll stay behind and maintain the illusion that the place is empty and locked. Turn on lights, make noise, do whatever you need to do and nobody will see or hear you."

"Sure, 'cause that worked so well back on the beach," Faith said with a derisive laugh.

"The beach incident was my fault, even I know that," said Cole. "So could you snap out of your little mood swing until this thing is done? Who knows, maybe if we score some intel from Ivan's inner sanctum, we'll find the cure for bitchiness." Cole stepped out of the car and slammed the door behind him.

I looked up at Ilya in the passenger seat. He stared out the front window and refused to look back at us. Faith glared at me and rammed her car door open.

"We won't be gone long, but if you see anyone coming towards the building, text me," I said nervously.

"I don't have a phone," Ilya said flatly.

I paused for a few seconds trying to come up with a solution. Faith followed Cole towards the building. I took a deep breath and sprinted to catch up to them. How bad would it be if a security guard walked in on us? I felt fairly certain I'd already seen the inside of Victoria's worst jail cell. And I trusted Ilya, for the most part.

To catch up I had to jog down the street and along a clean-cut brick path to the entrance where Cole and Faith argued.

"What do expect me to do, melt the handle apart? Do you know how much light that will give off? And I might not short the right circuit," said Faith.

"Fine, we'll do it my way. If an alarm sounds, it's on you." Cole reached out and gripped the aluminum doorknob. It popped off cleanly in his hand and the door eased open. We froze, waiting for a siren, bell, or flashing light. Nothing happened.

"Are we going to wait for an invitation?" Faith slipped inside. Cole and I followed.

"Irina, do you know where to go from here?" said Cole.

"I'm pretty sure it's on the fourth floor. The room across the hall is number 402. If we go up to the fourth floor and find 402, the office we're looking for is right across from that." My skills finally came in handy. I'd become an asset instead of a walking collection of nightmares.

We went up the nearest stairwell and found the door to room 402. Directly across the hall was room 410. I tried the handle and noticed the keypad next to the doorjamb. Faith reached out and I knew her next move was to try melting an electrical wire.

"NO!" I blurted, then whispered, "I can figure it out by touching it. I did it at Innoviro, remember?"

Chapter 35

The dark hallway was silent, but white noise rushed through my head. I stared at the keypad next to the door and took a deep breath, stalling as I imagined police officers thundering up the stairs before hollering in our faces. I took another breath. I softly touched one of the numbers, careful not to depress the button. I expected the hallway around me to fade, but nothing happened. I shifted to place my whole hand on the keypad gently.

The hallway dissolved, shifting slightly to a day-lit version. A man with short salt-and-pepper hair walked towards me. As he checked something on the stack of papers cradled in his arm, the hall disappeared and I was back in the dark. A sharp shove in my back jolted me forward and my hand, still touching the keypad, pressed every button.

An electronic buzzer sounded two quick beeps that the code was incorrect. Then a melodious female voice chimed, "Your code entry contained an error; please try again."

I stood in shock and then whirled to glare at my friends.

Faith and Cole stopped wrestling. I gave them a look of incredulity. The woman repeated herself. "Your code entry contained an error; please try again." She repeated the command, the third time adding, "Failure to input your code will trigger an armed response. Please enter the correct code now."

"Holy shit!" I said.

"What's the code already?" said Cole.

"I don't know! One of you pushed me into the keypad and snapped me out of it before I saw anything!"

"What kind of armed response comes to a government building? Probably the cops. Try touching the keypad again," said Cole as the recorded voice repeated its threat.

"Who cares! Rip the door off!" Faith shouted as a siren wailed overhead.

"Goddamnit!" Cole groaned as he reached out and jerked open the door.

Instead of removing a flimsy doorknob as he'd done downstairs, he strained as the entire doorjamb popped away from the wall. He pulled back and the steel frame slid off several giant bolts inside the solid core door. I felt a moment of exhilarating vindication knowing that something valuable sat inside this room if that door was justified.

I rushed into the office and scanned all surfaces frantically. The room appeared messier than I'd seen in my vision. I must have seen the envelope where it originally landed when it finished its journey. What if someone had beaten me to it? Had Rubin and Hugo come here before going to the Highlands?

I searched the bookcase beside me, the hutch next to the window, and each drawer of the large L-shaped desk. Only one was locked.

"Cole! I need this drawer!" I called over my shoulder. He stepped in and pulled the drawer out as though it had never been locked.

Inside, like a shining medal, the Innoviro logo on pure white paper rewarded me with its presence. I snatched, gesturing at Cole and Faith to follow me.

We bounded down all four flights of stairs until we burst into a side hallway of the main floor. Blue and red lights flashed on the opposite wall reflecting the activity in front of the building.

"How do we get out?" I shouted over the wailing alarm.

"This is your stupid plan!" yelled Faith. "You're supposed to know that already!"

"Ilya said he'd conceal us. I think we have to trust him. We don't have any other choice unless either of you has a surprise up your sleeve. Stay behind me." Cole stepped out into the hallway before I could stop him, not that I stood a chance of holding him back.

I held my breath and followed Cole closely, sensing Faith behind me. I peeked around Cole's shoulder and saw a blur of lights ahead. I couldn't make out cars or bodies, but I assumed several officers in uniform had guns pointed at the entrance.

"I don't think they can see us." Cole sounded less than confident. "Now we've got to find a way to get out the door."

"Maybe they won't see that either," I said softly, putting one foot in front of the other.

"Why don't you give it a try?" Faith glared at me.

After we got out of this, I'd have to find a way to make things right with her.

"Any occupants of this building, identify yourself and come

forward!" shouted an aggressive male voice outside the entrance. A few moments passed. None of us said anything. A group of male voices muttered outside.

"We are entering the building! Identify yourselves and approach slowly with your hands up!" shouted one of the men. I heard the stomping of shoes running up the driveway. I peeked around Cole and glimpsed two officers inspecting the damage done to the front door. One gestured that he was going to enter. He slowly wedged the door open with his foot.

After the first officer scanned the lobby, gun pointed and ready, he beckoned for the others to follow him. The last man to enter kicked the hinged doorstop down on the damaged door, propping it open.

Cole looked back at Faith and me with an earnest expression and nodded towards the open door. He walked carefully and quietly towards the door. We copied his movements, creeping out the door, down the walkway, and past the empty cars with lights still flashing parked on the street.

I had to resist the urge to run as we marched back to Cole's car. Each of us eased open our doors and slipped into the car. Cole started the engine and casually drove back out to the main road as we held our breath.

"Well, what happened? Did the police see you?" said Ilya as Cole turned back onto the highway towards downtown.

Faith expelled the gasp she'd held since we left the building. "That was intense!"

"No, they didn't see us. That was close! We almost botched the entire thing. Could you hear that alarm from the street?" said Cole.

"I think you could have heard that alarm from across the city," said Ilya. "But it's a good thing I had that horrendous sound to warn me how much I'd have to concentrate on you before those cop cars arrived."

"*You* had to concentrate? Try being on the inside!" said Faith.

Cole glared ahead at the highway. I looked down at my hands and the precious envelope.

I opened it right there in the car and pulled out a single sheet of thick white Innoviro stationary lit by the undulating cool orange of streetlights. The memo read,

Attn: Dr. David Plume,

As per our recent negotiations, this letter is to offer you contract work with Innoviro Industries.

The scope of your work will include supervising aspects of Project Compendium Transmuto as outlined in the master document we discussed. Using your knowledge of global climatology, you will work with geologists, geneticists, biologists, and cryptozoologists.

Your contract with Innoviro Industries must be completed before the end of this calendar year, barring any redefinition of project parameters, initiated and approved exclusively by me, Ivan Krylov.

Should your participation in this project be terminated at any time, you remain bound by confidentiality not to discuss your work performed for Innoviro Industries with any other parties for any reason.

Please contact my office at your earliest convenience to arrange a time to meet with me and sign your contract.

Sincere Regards,

Ivan Krylov, BSC, MBA

CEO, Innoviro Industries

I flipped over the sheet of paper. Stark white blank paper mocked me. All this letter told me was that Ivan had hired a climatologist and that the real information remained hidden somewhere else in a master document.

"It's not here," I said weakly as Cole, Faith, and Ilya bickered.

"What?" said Cole. All voices stopped.

"It's a letter offering to hire a climate guy. It mentions a project and another document that has everything they're working on. I think," I said quietly.

"So all we have is another lead – maybe?" said Ilya.

I felt disappointment and frustration emanating from all three of them.

"Fuck it," said Faith. "Let's go to Vancouver anyway." The rush of our brush with the police still coursed through her veins.

"This doesn't change anything." Ilya twisted around to look me in the eye. "We knew this envelope might not contain anything useful. We didn't even know for sure we'd find it. But we'll have more than enough cash between the five of us. I know what Innoviro paid for wages. Unless one or more of you have a serious drug addiction or gambling problem eating all your cash, we should be able to afford to stay in Vancouver for several months."

"I think you're forgetting that Faith and I got arrested tonight. We're wanted, maybe even twice over now," I said.

Faith laughed out loud and the guys chuckled.

"I'm having serious second thoughts about being a fugitive," I said. "Even if we drain our accounts, what do we do afterward? What are we going to live off of? And where? Before, I was just on my own. Now, I've got cops after me."

"Weren't you listening to yourself reading that letter? Ivan's experimenting on more than people. This is about more than just our friends. You knew he was dangerous and convinced us. What happened to that conviction?" said Faith.

"But you're talking about living outside the system, maybe for years. Running from the law." I heard desperation in my voice. A deep sense of helplessness mingled with the hope that my life would change in the next ten minutes.

"When we pick up Jonah, we'll take an official vote. If he's still in, I say we hit the nearest bank machine and take everything we can. We can still board a ferry first thing in the morning. Once we've got somewhere safe to stay in Vancouver – probably the downtown East Side if we want to stay under the radar – we'll start looking for this mystery warehouse," said Ilya.

"I dunno man, this is getting intense. My little sister is an adrenaline junkie, but that doesn't mean this is a good idea. Irina's right. We're talking about crossing a line. I don't wanna go to jail." The steering wheel squeaked under Cole's grip.

"What did you think we were after tonight? Your friend may be dying. No, he probably *is* dying. And Faith is right. It's become more obvious to me every step of the way that my father has set something in motion that's bigger than unethical genetic experiments. If it were *your* father, wouldn't you try to find out why?"

"I feel you on the responsibility angle, Ilya," said Cole. To the car, he asked, "Let's think; is something this big down to us to handle?"

"I'm scared, but now that I'm thinking harder, who do we hand it over to? And I know it's not going to bring them back, but I still want justice for my parents," I said. "Rubin is gone, but Ivan still has to answer for it."

"Like I said, let's hop over to Vancouver." Danger had improved Faith's mood.

Cole parked on the street outside our abandoned Chinatown walk-up. As promised, Jonah had been watching and waiting. But he wasn't alone. He and Vincent emerged from the shadowed alley carrying several backpacks and tightly rolled sleeping bags.

"To what do we owe this visit?" Ilya sounded like he'd come home to find an unexpected friend over for coffee.

"I wish this was a social call. I had a run-in with Ivan. Or I should say a near miss," said Vincent. Ilya's face fell as the rest of us tensed with anticipation.

"He was waiting for me in my apartment. He had a new friend; a replacement for Rubin and Hugo combined. If I hadn't spit at the man on sight, I'd probably be dead right now."

"How can you know he was there to kill you?" said Ilya.

"Buddy, seriously?" Cole said to Ilya.

"I don't like it either, but we're all going to have to come to terms with the fact that this isn't going to end in a vindication for Ivan," said Jonah.

"Why don't you tell us exactly what happened, Vincent?" My immediate concern was to find out what our new opponent was packing for a variation. The idea of someone as powerful as Rubin and Hugo combined put my financial future into a less catastrophic light. Why would I need money if I wasn't going to live to spend it?

"We didn't exactly have a heart-to-heart conversation. I shouldn't have gone home, but I thought I had time to pack a bag. I walked into my apartment and sensed something was wrong. Like most of us, I live – sorry, lived – at an Innoviro building. The one out in Oak Bay. So there were no signs of a break-in. Instinct had me on edge when I walked into my living room. Ivan was sitting in my reclining armchair, next to the balcony. But when I rounded the corner, what I focused on was the beast that confronted me. This may sound stupid…"

Vincent paused and took a breath. "It looked like a caveman. He had wild hair, long and matted, not like dreadlocks, but like a stray dog with dirty tangled clumps of fur. His skin had a dark tanned hue –practically scorched or burned. He grinned at me with sharp brown teeth. His pale orange eyes were bloodshot. I don't even remember what he wore other than that it was filthy. I'd never seen him in my life. He would have stood out, even in the catacombs."

Vincent fell silent and we absorbed it all. The possibilities of Ivan's reach and the likely multitude of other variants in the world hit me like a pair of dumbbells.

"Well, what can he, you know, 'do'?" I said.

"Yeah, this guy sounds ugly, but if you spat on him, shouldn't he be out of commission now?" said Faith.

"He should, but my venom rolled off that skin of his. He probably needs new clothes now. Aside from his thick skin, I don't know what he can do. But Ivan's telekinesis is as strong as ever. My television hit the dividing wall next to where I'd been standing. If I hadn't turned to run, the blow would have turned me into jam."

"I'm sure he found a way to enhance his gift," said Ilya. "He always used to talk about maximizing variations, as well as making sure they were stable and under control. Every time he shared those philosophies, it was always general. His goals always sounded scientific, altruistic; like he was dedicated to the betterment of humanity."

"We all felt that way. You're not alone. But if he doesn't need that bodyguard, what's the real reason to have this new guy?"

said Jonah.

"Probably doesn't want to do the dirty work," said Cole.

"All the more reason we need to get a move on," I said.

"I figured you were on your way out of town, but I couldn't in good conscience miss a chance to warn you." Vincent extended his hand to Ilya. "Good luck in Vancouver. I wish I could be more help."

"Thanks, my friend. We're going to need it."

Chapter 36

Cole and Jonah took our combined possessions and quickly stuffed everything in the trunk of Cole's car. Jonah squeezed into the back seat on my side. I sat uncomfortably wedged between him and Faith as Cole started the car. Ilya consulted a Vancouver map he'd fished out of the glove compartment.

"So, what did we score at that government building? We need some good news. Did you find anything cool?" Jonah asked hopefully.

"Yes and no," said Ilya. "We've got another lead, but we still need to go to Vancouver if we want the truth about Innoviro."

"Right, of course. We knew it wouldn't end that easily," said Jonah.

I heard the disappointment in his voice. None of us had expected to find a cure for Jonah's genetic breakdown in a simple paper envelope, but we'd all hoped for a stronger lead.

"The only thing this envelope says is that they're working on a big project, across several branches of science." I looked down at the floor as I spoke. I felt responsible for not producing more information. We needed results, Jonah most of all. "It's bigger than genetics. But that's pretty much all the end of the update. I'm so sorry."

"Don't be. Even if I don't get better, we're obviously onto something. Who knows how much chaos Ivan has planned," said Jonah.

The car fell silent as Cole pulled over at a Royal Bank. Faith and I hopped out and took turns withdrawing as much money as the ATM would let us.

"Can anyone think of why Ivan went after Vincent? Is it possible Ivan knows about what happened in the Highlands?" I said as Cole turned back onto the dark, slick highway.

"My first thought is that Brad found my father and told him what happened when we escaped. That guy lived pretty high up on the Innoviro food chain. If he knew where to find my father, I'm sure he went straight to him the first chance he got. I wish I could listen to Brad, but he can shut me out. My father can too," said Ilya.

"Brad was actually in the first vision I had about this envelope. In my vision, Ivan talked with him about a new variant, which could have been me. Then Tatiana interrupted them and he gave her the envelope."

"I'm glad we were smart enough to hide in Chinatown instead of going home. One or more of us could have met Ivan's new beast thing," said Cole.

Faith continued glaring out the window as Cole drove, but Ilya listened to the air.

"I wish we knew what this new thug was capable of," I said.

"I'm not sure the mystery man is our biggest problem. If my father attacked Vincent himself, he would have won. He doesn't need that beast, not physically. Between the two of them, Vincent shouldn't have been able to escape so easily. Brad *was* there when we made plans to hide out in Chinatown. My father *must* have found where we were hiding. So why would they bother ..." Ilya continued listening to something distant. "I'm such an idiot!"

"What?" I said.

Faith paid attention again.

"Vincent didn't escape. He's setting us up. That beast thing has his daughter." Ilya concentrated behind closed eyes. "Why didn't I probe his mind back there when I stood right next to him?"

"Where are they now? If you can't track your father, follow Vincent to the beast," I said.

Ilya concentrated again. "Already done. I found them. Even from this far away, that beast's thoughts are a primal snarl. All rage and blood lust. I can't make out words or ideas. He's a walking hunger for violence." Ilya's voice shook.

"It doesn't matter now. We'll be off this island before breakfast and the whole mess will be in our rear-view before you know it," said Cole.

A few minutes after three o'clock in the morning Cole parked his car on the gravel shoulder before the entrance to BC Ferries' ticket booths.

"I'm glad we're getting the hell off this rock. I'm going to hit the little girl's room in the bushes." Faith slammed the door and in a few steps, she disappeared into the tree line.

"Not a bad idea." Jonah walked up the road and the blackness of the roadside forest enveloped him.

"I can't get over the feeling that something is still wrong. The beast is getting louder, which probably means closer," said

Ilya.

I heard the fear in his voice and wished I could do something to help.

"We're already at the end of the line. Where exactly do you want us to go from here? If Ivan knows we're going to Van, should we abort?" said Cole.

"I don't know," said Ilya, his paranoia contagious.

"Why aren't Faith and Jonah back?" I asked.

Chapter 37

A guttural GRRRRRRRRR ripped through the bushes behind me. The primal rumble was deeper and more sinister than the scorpion dog I dodged at the lab. It was Ivan's beast. My feet instantly froze to the ground.

Cole saw the look on my face and his gaze shifted to focus on the landscape behind me. His concerned expression shifted to rage. He bolted towards me. Survival swept me into action. I leaped off the ground and dove at Ilya. I felt the stab of my hip hitting the concrete and the sting of gravel opening tiny wounds in my hand and forearm.

I saw Cole tackle a large shape. They tumbled into the blackberry brambles lining the road. The crunch of footfalls on gravel and Ilya's wide frightened eyes confirmed a second presence. I turned to face Ivan.

"I can't tell you how much it pleases me that the two of you have been working so brilliantly together. I never expected you'd get on so well before being properly introduced." Ivan's wicked smile blossomed into an evil grin as he put his hands in his trouser pockets.

"Tell us right now that this is all a misunderstanding," Ilya pleaded with Ivan. "Tell me that when we go to the Vancouver office, we're going to find this *Compendium Transmuto* and that it's all going to make sense. Tell me why you needed to hurt variants."

"Right to the good stuff, hmmmm? Well, you won't find the Compendium in Vancouver. You won't find it, period. The Compendium is an eyes-only document, shared with need-to-know personnel. And you, my former son, do not need to know."

"Mr. Krylov, I know this is all a mistake too. We want to understand why you've been testing on people so aggressively. You're taking risks like this for a reason, right? Just tell us why."

"I'm not telling you squat about my work, love. But you're right, I have my reasons. Starting with bringing you back home, with your brother, where you belong."

"My *what?*" Instinctively, I looked over at Ilya.

"Your twin brother. Your combined mind-reading and premonition abilities should have produced that information already. Clearly, I still have work to do with you, Irina. I dosed your Tarot cards with my experimental serum, right before I had Rubin plant them in your town and compel you to buy them. I already knew the formula worked when I asked you to submit to an injection regimen. And I had a feeling that Ilya's anguish and isolation in his little sanctuary would cause him to project imagery. I love being right. That you couldn't recognize your own twin … well that's just hilarious." Ivan stepped forward.

Cole emerged from the brambles wrapped from shoulder to

hip in some kind of silk twine. The same sticky threads sealed a patch over his mouth. The creature we'd heard so much about ambled behind him, shoving him forward every few steps. His dirt-streaked skin, brown fang teeth, and matted hair showed faintly in the dark of our surroundings. But his vivid cat-like yellow eyes shone in the pale white moonlight. Cole fought helplessly against his restraints. What kind of thread could hold the strongest man in the world?

Ivan flicked his wrist at a stump nearby, telekinetically ripping it into the air. Dripping crumbs of dirt, the stump followed the arc of Ivan's arm and came to rest right in front of him. He stepped over it and sat carefully.

"Let me introduce you to Mr. Thorn. He is a special friend, and he's agreed to join us at Innoviro. When the four of you return to work, he'll take over Rubin's post as head of security. Ilya, you'll need to resume your studies as well."

"We aren't going to forget all of this and go back to the way things were," snapped Ilya. "Mind games like pretending that Irina is related to us won't distract me."

"I can't go back to work like nothing ever happened," I looked at Ilya, certain that Ivan was telling the truth about him being my brother. "None of us are going back," I added defiantly.

Ivan nodded at Mr. Thorn, who then shoved Cole to the ground and walked off in the direction Faith and Jonah had gone. The crack-snap of twigs and brush under his feet faded and I refocused on Ivan.

"This is not a request. Your choices are to cooperate willingly or to be my captive. Any of you cause trouble of this scale again, and I'll have Mr. Thorn use his claws instead of his webbing."

Ilya took a step forward and then paused. He was at a loss for words and ideas. I stood up and walked toward Ivan myself.

"If Ilya's my brother, then that makes *you* my father." I looked him squarely in the eye. "Take my hand and prove it."

Ivan eyed me up from head to toe, assessing me, and deciding. After a moment, he extended his hand and I grabbed it. The road faded away and I stood in a bright fluorescent medical room. I turned around and I saw my mom lying on her side on a hospital bed. A woman in green scrubs held her hand, helping Mom brace against a contraction. A young Ivan stood on the other side of the bed. His expression wasn't the empathetic concern of a husband. He had an intent expression, willing my mom to give birth.

Mom screamed again and a second woman in blue scrubs appeared. The two women helped my mom change positions and she pushed hard. The woman in blue obscured my view, but a primal infant wail rang out over Mom's deep grunting. The woman in the green scrubs took the child off to a table a few feet away while the blue woman continued to coach Mom through another big push.

The woman in green scrubs returned with a swaddled infant and handed it to Ivan. He let go of Mom's other hand and accepted the child. Both women kept talking at my mom, all their attention on her movements. Ivan slipped away with the child while Mom gave birth again. Another man entered the room after Ivan left – Rubin! He wore green scrubs too. His hair was brushed into a relatively tidy ponytail, but I'd recognize that asshole anywhere.

I let go of Ivan's hand and slid immediately back onto the wet island road under the moonlight. "It's true. He kidnapped you a few minutes after you were born. And Rubin was there to wipe everyone's memories of you," I said to Ilya, turning my back on our father.

"So now that we've dispensed with the formalities, let's get off this road before I have to send Mr. Thorn after some unfortunate civilian witness," said Ivan.

Ilya shot me a meaningful look and I turned back to Ivan. I saw Vincent's denim shirt creeping along the bottom of the ditch beside us, below the overgrown brambles. I saw Thorn approaching with Faith bound in his silky thread.

"Do you want me to go back for the water-boy?" Thorn asked in a horrible raspy voice.

"I'm afraid so, Mr. Thorn. He's not going to be of much use, but I can't have him running around telling stories and causing trouble."

Thorn pushed the back of Faith's calf with one of his feet and she fell to the ground in a clumsy collapse. Vincent stayed hidden a few paces away in the ditch. I had an idea.

"Okay. We'll come back to you, back to Innoviro," I said to Ivan. "But, if you want our full commitment, we need the big picture. Remember what I said in the alley after you showed me the catacombs? I still believe this work has to be done, for us, variants, but there's more going on here. Trust us. Tell us what you're working on."

"Dad, I know you wouldn't do this if you didn't have a good reason. Irina's right, you can trust us," said Ilya.

"Speak for yourselves, you soulless sheep! Fuck you, Ivan!" snarled Faith.

"Don't listen to her, Ivan. We want to help," I said.

"Bitch!" Faith yelled at me.

I looked over at her face and saw eyes brimming with venomous hate. "Shut your mouth," I said callously.

"All right, you deserve a small taste of what's coming," said Ivan.

I took a few steps forward, obscuring Ivan's view of Cole and Faith.

"I'm gathering variants, here and around the world. Big changes are coming for this planet. Can't you feel it? Humanity treats this world like a giant waste bin. We deserve to take it, re-make it in our image, tailor the very ground we walk on and the air we breathe solely to our mutations, and start over without them. Any one of you is worth sacrificing for that," Ivan said, looking from me over to Ilya and back.

"Even if you *can* control our genes, you can't control the earth. You can't change geography. You can't solve climate change yourself!" I said.

"Who wants to solve anything? Climate change is part of the plan. Humans did that themselves. All I need to do is help it along and add a little terraforming. You'd be surprised what a few ocean currents and earthquakes can accomplish, once enough ecosystems have been ruined. There's enough greed and stupidity on this planet to make it look legit. Until it's too late."

"You can't possibly be serious, Dad. The science doesn't exist, not even for Innoviro," said Ilya, disbelief in his voice and an expression of disgust on his face.

"How soon?" I quickly added, "How soon can you make it happen?" I tried to sound eager. Ivan's eyes narrowed and he assessed me for a moment. His gaze shifted quickly to my side. Out of the corner of my eye, I saw Cole sprinting forward.

One swoop of Ivan's arm cracked the pavement underneath Cole and curled it off the ground, wrapping around Cole like a blanket. The asphalt roll detached and soared up over the roadside brambles in an arc that reached the marina in the distance. Still encased in the peeled-off pavement, Cole crashed through the roof of a floating wood boat garage.

I turned around as Vincent dribbled on the back of Faith's bonds. The sticky silk ropes dissolved with a hiss. Ivan's outstretched arm came to rest facing Faith and Vincent.

"I can't move! What is this? What are you DOING to us?" screamed Faith.

"I'm done with lectures for the evening." Ivan called out, "Mr. Thorn! Leave the boy. It's time to go!"

He turned to say something to Ilya and me. The air went cold and a surge of sea water knocked Ivan to the ground. Like the stream of a fire hose, the water sent him tumbling. The stream came all the way from the shore and underneath it stood Jonah. His face bore the pained look of a man fiercely concentrating, using every ounce of his strength.

"Look out!" shouted Ilya.

Thorn raced down the road back towards us, shooting silken darts in our direction from the back of his mouth. With each breath, his mouth opened unnaturally wide and a muscular ripple in his throat released each repulsive bolt. They missed us, flying high and wide as Thorn ran.

A glint in Faith's eye was all it took. She held a fireball in her hands. She pitched it at Thorn, pushing a continuous stream of rage-fueled fire behind it. The molten orb hit him with an explosive flash. He screamed, instantly meeting the same fate as Hugo. I shuddered as his blackened form fell sideways onto the concrete.

The water dousing Ivan receded. Jonah collapsed out of exhaustion. Faith ran to his side. I looked over at Vincent. He wasn't moving. I heard Cole's thunderous footfalls crashing through the brush.

Ilya walked to Ivan as I ran to Vincent. I immediately saw one of Thorn's threaded darts lodged in Vincent's neck as he struggled to breathe.

"AAAARRRGH!" Cole yelled as something crashed into him. Out of the corner of my eye, I saw Cole deflect a large boulder and charge Ivan. I kept my attention on Vincent.

"Are you okay? No, stupid question, of course you're not!" Camille was long gone as far as I knew and I struggled to think of some other solution. I stood uselessly wringing my hands and then reached out to touch him. If nothing else, I could stay with him.

"Do you want me to pull it out?" I asked.

Vincent tried to answer. He convulsed and I saw that the bolt went straight through the back of his neck. I could do nothing but comfort him.

"I'm right here," I said shakily. I grabbed his hand, holding it firmly. As I looked into his eyes to reassure him, his life faded. I held on for a moment, filled with remorse and panic. Then I sensed Ilya at my back.

"They wouldn't return his daughter until he reported back on our plans. Without Rubin, Ivan became frantic and kidnapped the girl. It wasn't Ivan and Thorn waiting for Vincent in his apartment; it was his ex-wife with Ivan's ultimatum. Vincent never wanted to give us up to my father. He thought that right at me before he charged to our rescue," Ilya said.

"He had a family. What are we going to say to them?" I said.

"We'll have to figure that out later. As it is, they'll have some idea." Cole had Ivan's limp body in his arms. Ivan looked so pitiful like that, crumpled and unconscious.

Disgust and agony twisted Ilya's face. He reached out and took his father's hand. Ivan remained motionless. *I'm so sorry Ilya. I wish this had ended differently*, I thought.

"Are you going to kill him?" I asked Cole.

Cole looked at me, then Ilya, then down at Ivan again. "He's as good as dead already. I'm going to leave him on the side of the road like garbage. He doesn't deserve any better."

Ilya released Ivan's hand, giving Cole a nod and turning his back on all of us. Cole flung Ivan's body into the ditch like an apple core.

Jonah and Faith walked forward, the former leaning heavily on the latter.

"So, are we still going to Vancouver?" Jonah had regained some energy.

"I say we finish what we started. We know he had partners. And from the sounds of his insane little rant there, he has a lot worse than human testing on his social calendar," said Faith.

"We're still definitely unemployed." Ilya laughed awkwardly and looked back towards the ditch where Ivan lay.

I glanced around at the scene. Miraculously, Cole's car remained parked on the side of the road, untouched except for the spray of ocean water that left droplets as though it had just rained.

"Should we bury Vincent? He has a right to whatever dignity we can give him. But his family needs to know he's not coming home and that won't happen unless someone finds his body," I said.

"I'll find somewhere to lay him to rest where he'll still be found quickly," said Cole.

"After that, we should get some food," I said. Hunger gnawed at my stomach more aggressively than my guilt. "There should be a convenience store around here."

Cole tossed his car keys to Ilya. Faith helped Jonah into the back seat and I opened the front passenger door. I looked over as Cole scooped Vincent into his arms and jogged down the road.

"Do you think Ivan is dead?" I said to Ilya, over the roof of the car.

"I do. His mind went dark," said Ilya.

"I'm so sorry. I know you hoped he had his reasons. I don't think anyone wanted to see it end this way," I said.

"He's not my father anymore. I still don't understand what steered him down that path." Ilya sat down behind the wheel and turned the key in the ignition.

"Look at it this way - you lost a father, but you gained a sister," I said. The information hadn't sunk in for him until that moment. Ilya looked back at me. I saw myself in his eyes.

We picked up Cole, bought gas station groceries, and headed to the ferry. The glow of sunrise warmed the horizon when we pulled into one of the ticket gates. We paid the fare and Ilya drove into one of a dozen lanes of parked traffic. "Ready to get the hell out of Dodge?" Ilya said to the rest of us.

"You bet your ass," said Faith.

Jonah nodded and I smiled.

"Right then!" said Ilya as he pulled into an empty spot. "The only thing we have to do now is 'hurry up and wait' for the boat." He turned off the car.

I closed my eyes and saw my Mom's face, followed by Gemma and Bridget. I thought about all the other families I'd known and the many billion more at stake. I pretended to sleep until Ilya restarted the car and we rolled onto a giant boat.

– *Epilogue* –

Sometimes, I look at the world and it seems perfect – like a toy playset or a vibrant watercolor painting. Other times, I examine the streets while I wander, dwelling on all the ragged edges, scraps of trash, dingy surfaces, cracks, holes, and dents. When the world looks like it's falling apart, every house, office, and storefront appears more like the crappy cardboard and homemade plastic props I used to make for my secondhand Barbie dolls.

As a kid, I'd sometimes preferred that worn and faded view of the world because it helped me to relax and stop pining for stuff and things. On the days when I felt neglected and forgotten, the raw side of things only made me despondent that my life would never get better and that no amount of patience or hard work would lead me anywhere clean and good.

Here, in the Bella Maria Hotel - a dingy single-room occupancy dive in Vancouver - I did not choose between shiny and dull, treasure and trash. I looked out the window and saw a street full of suffering with glitz and privilege along the skyline. Ivan had been right. This fragile imbalance has reached its tipping point.

I needed time to myself, so I took my laptop to a nearby business cafe with complimentary wifi access. I searched for my name. I searched for Gemma and had no trouble finding her achievements – the most recent being a win with the UBC girls' volleyball team. And then I clicked on an obituary for Tabitha and Darryl Proffer. It confirmed the worst. They were survived by their only daughter, Gemma Proffer.

As if reading an obituary for my parents wasn't bad enough, I decided that I needed a hard copy of the article's photograph. They used an old one of my parents standing in front of our PG house. I thought it would make me feel better. I printed the photo right there at the cafe and took it 'home' with me.

What happened when I touched the photo destroyed me all over again. I held it in my hands and my room disappeared. I stood in Ivan's office. Rubin leaned against the door while Ivan sat at his desk.

"Start with the parents. Wipe them both and incapacitate the mother. She's got latent variant DNA that I might want to play with one day. Kill the stepdad; he doesn't matter," said Ivan.

"I'll let you know when it's time for Brad to step in on the tech side. Make sure he's got all his research done before tomorrow. It won't be my fault if he leaves any loose ends," said Rubin.

I dropped the newsprint and snapped back to my dingy room in the Bella Maria. On my bed, shaking, I felt a surge of rage in my guts. I balled up my fists. I punched the wall ahead and yelled. I took a few deep breaths and picked up the photograph using a take-out sushi menu to avoid touching the image directly. I couldn't risk seeing more of my parents. I needed my anger to stay fresh and not slip back into depression.

So now, my bleak world is made of grime-streaked glass that balances on a house of cards. I'm desperate to unravel Ivan's plan to turn his proverbial leaf blower onto the whole world. Avenging my parents has to happen at some point. Yet, we have no idea how complex his work had become or how far Innoviro had gotten. We must assume that many of his destructive projects are still operational, like multiple motors inside a sophisticated machine.

It feels like Ivan's plot is a force of nature and my friends and I are waving our hands uselessly against a hurricane. But we have to do it. With Jonah, Cole, Ilya, and Faith, I have to keep putting one foot in front of the other, to find a cure for Jonah if possible while we track down every geological event, every fountain of pollution, and every scrap of mutated genetic material that Ivan planned to unleash.

I need to fight what's left of Innoviro, to ensure that the Compendium doesn't outlive its creator. Whatever it takes.

About the Author

Christine Hart is a metalsmith and mother who writes speculative fiction. Her backlist includes The Electric Girl (MG) and The Variant Conspiracy (NA) trilogy. Her debut Watching July (YA) won a gold medal from the Moonbeam Children's Book Awards.

She holds a BA in English and Professional Writing, as well as current membership with the Federation of BC Writers. When not writing, she creates wearable art from raw stones, vintage glass, and unique gems for her online shop, Hart Fabrications. She shares her eclectic home with her husband and two children.

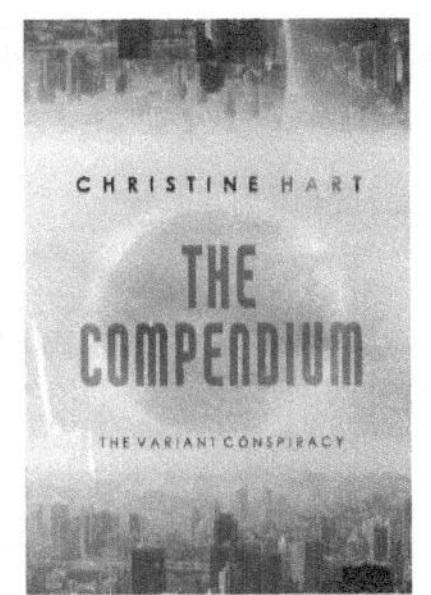

The Compendium (The Variant Conspiracy)

Irina and friends are scrambling to pick up the trail of Ivan and Innoviro. They race from Vancouver to Seattle and south to San Franciscio, hoping to recruit more variants - and stop an engineered earthquake. All while Irina fights to keep her lover's unstable genetic degradation in check.When the group reaches a secret facility in the Mojave Desert, they uncover a shocking new horror.

Terra Nova (The Variant Conspiracy)

The end of humanity and an unrecognizable future Earth are days away. After their first glimpse of the Terra Nova virus, Irina and her friends know that Ivan's scheme is almost complete. After surviving a catastrophic earthquake and destroying a secret viral testing facility, Irina's crew has traveled by a variant portal to London. On the other side of the world, they know stopping the Terra Nova virus is only the beginning.

The Electric Girl (Middle Grade Novel)
Polly is trying to forget that her mom has cancer. Until a freak electrical storm and a unicorn arrive. Sy'kai wakes on an orchard floor. She doesn't know where - or what - she is. Polly and her friends find Sy'kai and two questions hang over their heads. Can an alien deliver a miracle for a human mother? Can a group of teens defeat an interdimensional demon?

Watching July (Young Adult Novel)
16-year-old July has been through hell. Her mom was killed in a hit-and-run. Her other mom packed up and moved them to the middle of nowhere. And then July meets the boy down the road. Surprised to find herself falling in love and making friends, she starts to see the possibility of a new life. But when it is revealed that her mom's death was not what it seemed, July finds herself in a world of danger.

www.ingramcontent.com/pod-product-compliance
Lightning Source LLC
Chambersburg PA
CBHW031938210726
48290CB00006BA/1854